SISTERS MAKING MISCHIEF

MADDIE PLEASE

Boldwood

First published in Great Britain in 2024 by Boldwood Books Ltd.

Copyright © Maddie Please, 2024

Cover Design by Head Design Ltd

Cover Images: Shutterstock

A CIP catalogue record for this book is available from the British Library.

Paperback ISBN 978-1-80483-739-9

Large Print ISBN 978-1-80483-738-2

Hardback ISBN 978-1-80483-740-5

Ebook ISBN 978-1-80483-736-8

Kindle ISBN 978-1-80483-737-5

Audio CD ISBN 978-1-80483-745-0

MP3 CD ISBN 978-1-80483-744-3

Digital audio download ISBN 978-1-80483-743-6

This book is printed on certified sustainable paper. Boldwood Books is dedicated to putting sustainability at the heart of our business. For more information please visit https://www.boldwoodbooks.com/about-us/sustainability/

Boldwood Books Ltd, 23 Bowerdean Street, London, SW6 3TN

www.boldwoodbooks.com

For David and Emma, wishing you every future happiness.

1

I'd spent weeks getting everything ready and I was very excited. I had spent the last three Christmases at other people's houses; this time my family were coming to me. I'd felt rather lost over the last few years after everything that had happened, things had not been as ordered or predictable as they used to be. This year it would be different.

I started buying presents in September and had wrapped and labelled them by October. I'd even found the packs of Christmas cards I'd bought in the January sales – for once I had not put them in a really safe place where I wouldn't find them until I had bought some replacements – and I spent some dark November evenings in front of the fire, writing and addressing them. I'd even, in a particularly festive moment, waited until the new Christmas stamps were out so that I could finish off the job properly with a nod to the joys of the Yuletide season.

For the first time in many years, I could see that it was possible to organise my life but now perhaps to my own satisfaction, and not just worry about what my ex-husband Stephen would say or think or want.

I'd been stockpiling all the food my granddaughters liked, woken up at the crack of dawn to bag a Christmas delivery slot with the supermarket, and ordered two cases of wine from the man Stephen had always used. Which was, in retrospect, a step too far. Stephen had always been able to have meaningful, rather pompous, chats about wine and south-facing slopes with Mr Truman, whereas I would just pick out the nicest label. Still, it gave me a certain satisfaction to see the wine rack filled for once. How long twenty-four bottles would last was anyone's guess. Knowing my lot, not long.

Going by the rather difficult atmosphere of their last visit, my daughter Sara would be looking for gin the moment she arrived while her husband Martin stood in the hall, wearing a Christmas sweater that was so subdued that it wouldn't really count. He would be jingling the car keys in his pocket as though he wanted to be off again, waiting for the moment when he could make some acerbic comment about consumerism.

I could almost hear him. *'Very nice, Mrs Chandler,'* (he never would call me Joy as I'd suggested), *'but don't you think your decorations are a bit over the top?'*

And of course, this year, they definitely were.

Their twins, Poppy and Mia, would probably be head-down on their electronic devices, looking up only briefly to take in the fact that the car had stopped, and they had arrived at Grandma's house, and then they would be off to the attic room to bag the best beds by the window before John and Vanessa arrived with their two daughters, Jasmine and Elizabeth, or Bunny as she was always known.

It had seemed a good idea to put their four beds in one room. When we were married, Stephen clung to the misty and completely false illusion that the four cousins would bond up there, enjoying some fun times together, that there would be laughter and the occasional midnight feast. Being more practical and having actually had a sister, I knew that it would just lead to shouting, thumping footsteps overhead at all hours, and a lot of plaintive cries of '*Mum, tell her...*' coming down the stairs. But, as always, Stephen would not be told.

During the bright days of summer, I liked to imagine the winter evenings as something warm and cosy, the curtains closed against the snowy landscape, the wood burner glowing, chestnuts roasting on an open fire, all that stuff. My daughter and son would be coming home again, bringing their families with them, all of us in good spirits, hugs and laughter, excited faces in the afternoon candlelight of the Christmas Day feast.

I don't know why because it had never really been like that.

There had always been some drama or other, Martin – or rather Marty as he now wished to be called because he thought it made him sound cooler – my son-in-law, having to arrive late and leave early allegedly because of work. Vanessa, John's wife worrying about some imagined ailment or danger to one of their daughters. And then Stephen stamping off to his study with a glass of whisky after lunch when our family had delighted him enough for one day, leaving me to sort out the carnage that was the rest of the house, before he saw it and blew a gasket.

That first Christmas after Stephen had left, Sara and her family had already booked to go skiing, and John had taken his lot to Centre Parcs. And to be honest it had been good to get away from their endless worrying about me.

Yes, I was apprehensive then about the future, about every-thing really. They had probably needed a break from me as well. Stephen had been such a dominating presence in all our lives and his departure had not been easy for any of us. I don't think anyone believed I would be able to cope without him. I don't think I had either, not at first. But there I was four years later, still standing, still managing.

I'd spent last Christmas with Sara and Marty in Cheltenham and the one before that with John and Vanessa in nearby Worcester. That first solo year I had escaped for a week from all the outrage and family fussing to my sister Isabel's place in Brittany where we had done a lot of loafing about on her sofa, eating chocolate, drinking Peartinis, thoroughly trashing Stephen and tearfully watching sentimental Christmas films. Plus, enjoying her annual Christmas party when all the neighbours and a lot of the customers from her husband's bookshop had been round. After eight months of ploughing through all the legalese and paperwork after Stephen left, it had been a welcome change to be somewhere different, to meet some new people, even though it was sometimes so chaotic and noisy in Isabel's house.

This year I was determined to do everything perfectly. To make it – dare I say it – magical.

'Don't go to any trouble,' Sara had said, 'just do as much as you feel comfortable with. And don't worry, we'll all muck in to help.'

My son had said much the same thing. 'Don't wear yourself out, Mum. We're all quite capable of helping. Did I mention I think Jasmine's going off meat? Well, everything except bacon sandwiches, she doesn't seem to have a problem with those. I'll let you know.'

It was the day before Christmas Eve, and I was ready for my guests to arrive. And I really was looking forward to it. The beds were all made up, I'd put flowers in the rooms and plenty of towels. I'd decorated the Christmas tree and in a spurt of unexpected enthusiasm got out all the other decorations, hoarded over the years, to cover every surface with little light-up houses, candles, and ornaments. Stephen hadn't approved of a lot of them, he said it made the place look tacky, and it probably did but I didn't have to worry about his opinion any longer.

I'd put a small Christmas tree in the attic bedroom for the girls and decorated the staircase, which looked marvellous with a swag of artificial greenery, some fairy lights, and festive ribbons and under the tree an exciting pile of presents all beautifully wrapped and decorated. Even Marty, who had once voiced the opinion that sticky tape was not needed on a properly wrapped gift, couldn't fail to be impressed.

I went to open the fridge door, to have a last look at all the things in there. A very pleasing collection of lidded boxes neatly stacked up. I had even bought a pineapple, some goat's cheese, and fresh figs, and I can't stand any of those things. Then I went on to the pantry to admire the stocks of emergency gin and Baileys, and the monstrous turkey that had been soaking in brine and spices for two days.

I took a deep breath. Everything was ready and, courtesy of the big bowl of potpourri on the hall table, the house smelled of Yuletide cheer. I felt a little bubble of happiness and hope well up inside me. I'd been through some dark times over the last few years, but now perhaps I had got a grip of my life again, and I was ready to show it to my family.

* * *

My mobile rang. It was my daughter.

'Sara! Merry Christmas Eve eve! I've just been looking around the house, and I think it looks great. Everything's ready for tomorrow, I've even got that whisky Marty drinks and the pigs-in-blanket crisps the girls like. I can't wait to see you all.'

There was a strange pause on the other end of the line. At last, my daughter spoke, her voice giving a funny little croak.

'Is it okay if we come early?'

'Yes, of course. I'm usually up by six anyway, so anytime really.'

'I meant now,' she said, rather brusque.

I was a bit startled for a moment. This was totally out of character. Sara and Marty were well known for their timetables and rigid adherence to them.

'Now, yes of course. Is there a problem? What time will you get here?'

There was another little pause. 'Actually, we're outside.'

'What? You daft thing... hang on a minute.'

I went to unlock the front door, wondering what on earth was happening and despite my festive frame of mind, feeling very uneasy.

Sara's car, a fairly new, gigantic four by four, which apparently was necessary to ferry her daughters to school, friend's houses and after school clubs, was parked at an untidy angle on the drive. Sara was sitting in the driving seat, her forehead on the steering wheel, and Poppy and Mia were peering out from the back. No one looked at all excited, happy, or Christmassy.

Sara got out, I could see she was in a bit of a state and had been crying.

'What on earth's the matter?' I asked. 'What's happened?'

'Can we just get the girls inside,' she muttered.

'Where's Marty?' I looked into the car rather foolishly, as though he might be hiding in the passenger footwell for some reason.

'Let's just...' Sara shook her head and shepherded her daughters into the house.

Not sure what to do next, I opened the boot of the car which was packed with many bags, backpacks, and cases. And then I shut it again and followed Sara into the hallway.

'Poppy, Mia, go up to your room and whatever...' Sara said.

She sounded as though she was on the verge of tears again and I reached out to put an arm around her shoulders.

The twins did as they were told without any sort of discussion. This in itself was different. At fourteen years old, they were already skilled at arguing and pushing their mother's buttons.

'Hey, come on. What's happened?' I asked again.

Sara shut the front door. I followed her into the kitchen where she pulled out a chair and sat down with an *ooof* noise. And then she looked at me.

'Marty's not coming,' she said at last.

I wiped away the ungracious thought of *good, all he ever does is snipe and complain,* and then realised we were talking about something serious.

'I know we were supposed to be coming tomorrow, but to be honest, I couldn't stay there a moment longer. I needed some space, some time away from it all, from the whole situation,' Sara said, 'and so did the girls.'

'Away from what? What situation?'

Sara took a deep breath. 'Oh God. I don't know if I can... okay... deep breath... Marty has been having an affair. With his secretary, such a cliché. I'm embarrassed to say it.'

I felt the air being sucked out of my lungs.

'Oh, Sara. Are you sure?'

Her lower lip wobbled, and she dabbed at her eyes with a tissue. 'He's gone to Zurich with her for Christmas. He took great pleasure in telling me they would be staying in some fancy hotel with a wonderful view of the mountains. So yes, pretty sure it's not a business meeting.'

I took a deep breath, taking in the information.

I'd never really got on with Marty in all the fifteen years they had been married, but no one knows what makes one marriage work and another fail. I'd assumed everything was fine between them. Despite his arrogance and self-importance. And the way he never bothered to conceal his boredom when the conversation wasn't centred around him. And the way he held his knife when he was eating.

One thing I did know, I certainly didn't want him to treat my daughter like this.

'Oh, sweetheart. I'm so sorry. Are the girls okay? Do they know?'

Sara waved her hands about in frustration.

'Of course they know! When their father stamps out of the house with both the big suitcases, shouting *"this is all your fault. You're a useless wife and a crap mother"*, it rather gives the game away.'

What should I do next? What did people do in these circumstances?

'I'll put the kettle on, shall I?'

Sara pulled out a new tissue and blew her nose.

'I'd rather have a stiff gin, actually,' she said.

I looked at the clock. It was eleven thirty in the morning, perhaps a bit early? Never mind. Sara didn't look as though she was in the mood for a cup of Yorkshire's finest and a mince pie, and it was Christmas after all, when many nutritional rules go out of the window.

We sat there for a few minutes in silence, Sara slugging back the (very weak) gin and tonic I had made for her, me wiping the worktops down yet again while I waited for the kettle to boil. I suppose subliminally I was trying to wipe away these problems, too, and that was completely unrealistic.

'So tell me about it,' I said at last.

I knew I should be coming up with all sorts of good, motherly advice, saying the right things and giving some comfort, but just then all I could think about was how this was going to affect her and my granddaughters.

My mind was darting around to what might lie ahead. Custody battles. Legal fees. Court appearances. Which one of them would move out of their huge house. Sara had been a stay-at-home mother since the girls were born, how would she manage for money? Where would Marty live. What about the girls' schooling. And how long did this sort of thing take anyway?

'Things haven't been great for a while,' Sara said at last, having got the basic information out, she now wanted to talk. 'I knew something was going on, but I had no proof and Marty said I was paranoid.'

'Typical,' I said, 'trying to blame you.'

Even then I was aware I shouldn't voice the many negative thoughts I'd harboured about Marty. They might, despite everything, resolve their differences and carry on with their marriage, and then everyone would know what I'd said, and *I* would be the problem.

No, this was not the moment to say what a narcissistic twat Marty was, how he had never been good enough for her, that he was nowhere near as clever as he thought he was, and she would be better off without him. I wouldn't mention the way he had gradually got less attractive over the years as the habitual sneer on his face took over. How he had become expert on the casual put down, the snide comment, the impression that we as a family weren't really good enough for him.

'And that woman— that absolute— goes all out to get him. Blonde cow. Cosying up to me at the Christmas party, Marty telling me what a great support she was.'

'She must have known he was married,' I said.

'Her sort never care about that. I hope she's proud of herself, behaving like a tart. Latching on to someone else's husband.'

I thought about also allocating an equal share of the blame to Marty, but this didn't seem the right moment.

'How long has this being going on? And how did you find out?'

Sara finished her drink and put the glass down on the kitchen table with a thump.

'Years.'

'So more than one, less than ten?'

'About three if Marty is to be believed. Nothing would surprise me now. They went to that conference in Bracknell and one thing led to another. She led him on of course. He said she was a man eater, and he was weak...'

I fought down the mental image of some random blonde floozy taking bites out of Marty's leg and focused back on the conversation.

'Three years! And now he's trying to say it's her fault? And your fault! What about him?'

'Nothing is ever Marty's fault,' Sara said bitterly. Her eyes filled with tears again. 'And now it's bloody Christmas. Hooray.'

Hmm. Not the sort of festive cheer I had been hoping for. Ridiculous thoughts crossed my mind. If Marty wasn't coming I would have to rearrange the table, and I had too many crackers.

'And the twins. They must be devastated. Have they said anything?'

'Not much. Mia just shrugged and said all her friends' parents are divorced and Poppy asked if she would still be able to go on school trips. And then Mia asked where we would be living, and I said I didn't know. And that's when I lost it and got everything into the car.'

I went to hug her, my heart filled with sorrow and sympathy and anger in equal parts.

'I'm glad you did. I'll do everything I can to help. I do understand. You know that.'

She hugged me back and cried into my cardigan, while within me, my anger against Marty railed into a black swirl, almost choking me.

'Bastard,' I said, unable to keep quiet any longer, 'absolute bastard. How dare he. Just give me five minutes alone with him and this—' I picked up the nearest object, which unfortunately was a cheese grater, 'and I'll sort him out, good and proper.'

Sara gave a shaky laugh and blew her nose.

'I wouldn't give much for his chances,' she said.

'No, nor would I.'

From upstairs there was a distant shout and a scream and Sara sighed.

'I'd better go up to them. They were quiet as mice on the way over here, but we both know that won't last. Bloody hell, it's Christmas Eve tomorrow. Tidings of comfort and joy. Pour me another gin, would you?'

* * *

I had planned to walk round that afternoon to a neighbour's house for a pre-Christmas get together and drinks. Obviously, I didn't go. My house, while decorated to within an inch of its life and scented with cinnamon and oranges, was filled with tension. Sara was alternately crying and drinking gin, which didn't help, while the twins skulked upstairs on their electronic devices, occasionally coming downstairs for snacks or to voice complaints about each other. No change there then.

After cobbling together an unplanned and unsatisfactory dinner (I'd planned a solitary feast of a newly opened tub of Celebrations and some white wine) we watched some dull documentary on television about an endangered snail, then a decades-old re-run of a comedy show. Sara talked all the way through, by turns morose and slightly intoxicated and then furiously angry, hissing insults and threats against the more delicate parts of Marty's anatomy.

'You need some time to get over the shock,' I said soothingly, after first hiding her car keys in my handbag in case she was tempted to go back to her house and do something foolish.

I quickly realised that it would be better to keep my daughter calm and positive, rather than fire her up with my own anger and experiences and possibly send her back to the marital home to slash his expensive suits and ties in a blind rage.

'Oh, Mum, I don't know,' she said, running her hand through her hair, 'I'm sick at what he's done, and equally sick wondering what to do next. Do I go to a solicitor? Should I go home and get the locks changed before he gets back?'

'From what I know, I don't think that would be wise.'

'I don't think I could bear it anyway. To be in that house, surrounded by all our stuff, knowing that he has been there with that— that trollop.'

'He *didn't*?'

'Oh yes, he did. When the twins and I went for two weeks to Cornwall, and he was going to join us three days late because he had *so much work on*. And then he went back early too. When we got back, I found a pair of knickers under the bed that I didn't recognise. He fobbed me off with some nonsense about me having a bad memory, but yesterday he admitted she'd been there. Why did he need to tell me that? I think she did it on purpose, like some old dog marking its territory.' Her expression hardened, 'She's welcome to him. I knew they weren't mine; they were from John Lewis. When did I ever buy knickers from there? M&S is the limit of my extravagance. Do you know, not once in all the years we were married, did he put the loo seat down? Or empty the dishwasher. Or bring me breakfast in bed. Even when I was pregnant. God, I was a fool, putting up with it.'

'You need a good night's sleep,' I said in my best soothing voice, 'you need time to think calmly what's best for you and the girls.'

Sara's lower lip wobbled. 'All I wanted to do was get here, back to this house. I was always so happy here when I was growing up. Everything feels right here. It's like a sanctuary. So organised and tidy. Nothing ever went wrong here.'

For a moment I thought back, remembering the reality of her shouting matches with her brother, towering piles of dirty crockery and mildewing food under her bed, disagreements with her father about what constituted a suitable outfit, the sulking that sometimes went on for days.

I reached over and stroked her hair.

'Well, this was your home when you were little, we had a lot of happy times, didn't we? You can always come here,' I said.

She started to cry again. 'Thanks, Mum. You're the best mum ever, have I told you that?'

'No, not that I can remember.'

Actually, at that moment I could only remember Sara at fifteen shouting at me that I was useless and didn't understand what it was like to be young. Still, at least she had a different perspective now, which was reassuring.

She gave a shaky laugh. 'I ought to go to bed. It's nearly midnight. I should go up to the girls again, and see they are okay.'

She picked her phone up and scrolled through it for a moment.

'Don't text him,' I said, in my best retired schoolteacher's voice.

'I already have, several times. Telling him exactly what I think of him. He hasn't replied. I've got a good mind to—'

I held out my hand. 'Give it to me. Just until the morning.'

It was like being in charge of the fifth form again.

'Mobile phones in this box until the end of the lesson.'

She hesitated and then handed it over with a sulky expression.

'Oh, okay then. What time are John and the Stepford wife getting here tomorrow?'

'Lunchtime. And don't be nasty. Just because Vanessa is a bit fussy about things. He says he has an important announcement, he was very secretive, said that he had some news.'

'Knowing John, another promotion, a fatter salary, a bigger house, a faster car. Life's very unfair sometimes. How can my younger brother, who took three attempts to pass GCSE maths, be running a finance company?'

I didn't like to say that I'd thought the same thing over the years. John was intelligent and charming, but he had been known to count on his fingers until he left university and as far as I could see had no obvious ability with organising anything. It was a good job Vanessa was in charge of that household or he would have gone to work in his pyjamas.

'Look, go to bed, I'll clear up here. Try and get a good night's sleep.'

Sara hauled herself up and stood swaying for a moment as the gin, the warmth from the wood burner and the turmoil of the last twenty-four hours took effect.

'Thanks, Mum,' she said, 'I meant what I said, I do feel better when I'm here, I feel safer. I already feel more able to cope with things. Is that daft at my age?'

'Not at all,' I said, giving her a hug. 'Go to bed, and don't forget to brush your teeth.'

She gave a little laugh at that, and went off, her footsteps heavy on the stairs as she went back to what had once been her childhood room.

I turned off the lamps and then sat for a moment in the flickering light from the fire.

Poor Sara. I could see how devastated she was, and yet there was a part of me that remained unsurprised by her news.

Stephen, very early on in their relationship, had once voiced the opinion that Marty had it within him to be untrustworthy and at the time I had disagreed. But it seemed that he had been right. Well, in light of what had happened, he should know. It was a good job he wasn't around to nod wisely and tell us all he was spot-on yet again.

'You see, Joy? I told you. You wouldn't listen.'

I cleared away the glasses and the half empty bottle of gin. There were some paracetamol in the kitchen drawer, and I took them out and left them helpfully by the side of the kettle.

2

When I woke up, my first thought was one of excitement – it was, after all, Christmas Eve and John and his family would be arriving later. A split second later I remembered Sara and her daughters were already in the house, under a significant cloud.

I got out of bed, showered, and dressed faster than I usually did, in the hope that by the time they came downstairs, I would have had time to clear away any overlooked debris from the previous night, set the table for breakfast, and done some preparations for the day ahead. I wanted to make everything perfect for them. To show them that I was managing now, that I could cope.

They had seen me through the months after Stephen had gone when I had just sat looking bleakly into the future, crying, angry, and frightened. Vanessa no longer had to organise a rota so that someone came over every few days with a casserole or flowers as they used to, back when I had been torn between relief that I didn't have to spend another day alone and embarrassed that I was so pathetic.

Five years ago, Stephen had decided that we should move to a house with a smaller garden because ours was getting a bit big for me to handle and heaven forbid, he would ever help me. To get the ball rolling, Stephen had produced Gillian, an estate agent, to come around and value our place. She was a middle-aged, horse-faced woman who wore tweed and was a member of a local, titled family who had tenants in cottages, nannies and shooting parties. She had the unmistakeable air of landed gentry about her which was catnip to a snob like Stephen. Seven months later he had moved out to live with her in some Cotswold manor house with positively acres of garden and we had divorced. In our settlement, I kept the family home, Sara and John had warned their father it was non-negotiable and for once he had listened.

I read an article about such things in the paper only recently: 'Silver Splitters', we were called. Sixty-year-olds who, having weathered the decades of struggle with jobs, children, mortgages, health issues and looming infirmity, made one last break for the sunny uplands of freedom or romance. I hadn't seen Stephen for a long time after the divorce was finalised and Sara and John didn't enlighten me, but I could only assume he had found what he was looking for. Which essentially was a wife with money.

Anyway, that morning it seemed a hungover daughter and her two teenage girls were able to sleep far longer than I could.

Ten thirty came, and I had tidied up the discarded cardigans, handbags, lip glosses and teen magazines. The Christmas tree lights were on as well as all the battery-operated candles because Vanessa said burning real ones was eco-unfriendly and also detrimental to her children's health, and there was still no sign of anyone.

Never mind, Christmas is a time when there is always a lot to do, and I set to trimming and preparing all the sprouts, wrapping two million sausages in streaky bacon, peeling potatoes, scraping carrots and generally behaving like Mary Berry *getting ahead* for the following day. I began to feel on top of things again. I had an important role to play, and I was going to do it flawlessly. I wanted to show them and myself that I was moving forward with my life.

I had already constructed a lasagne for that evening's dinner, and I whipped up some garlic butter ready to plaster onto the French sticks I had bought the previous day. They were – as is the way of French bread – by now slightly stale. Why is that? I really should find out when an English loaf lasts for days. No wonder the French are always off to the boulangerie.

At eleven o'clock I wiped down the worktops again and went into the hall to listen for any sounds or signs of movement from upstairs. There were none. I polished the dining room table and dusted the sideboard although they didn't really need it.

Then I began to worry. John and Vanessa were due to arrive for (decaffeinated) coffee soon. Why do people drink it? I thought caffeine was the whole point of coffee. I'd already set out the tray and arranged the (ordinary plus gluten free) mince pies on a Christmas specific plate decorated with snowmen.

What if Sara was unwell, or perhaps had *done something silly?* What that would be I wasn't sure, an overdose of multivitamins? There was only a shower in her ensuite so she could hardly drown herself in the bath.

I hesitated, my foot on the bottom stair and then I heard a muffled thud and an annoyed scream, which I think must have come from the girls' room. So, she hadn't smothered her daughters in the night. Actually, at fourteen, Poppy and Mia were already as tall as Sara and having been to after school rugby and football clubs since they were seven, more than strong enough to compete against a gin-weakened mother.

'Breakfast anyone?' I shouted up the stairs and went back to the kitchen where my mobile phone was vibrating its way off the table.

'Joyeux Réveillon de Noël, ma soeur! Merry Christmas Eve! Joy to

the world!' Isabel shouted down the phone, repeating the usual Christmas pun. It was almost as though she was in the next room, and for a moment I wished that she was. 'You should have been here last night; we had an absolute blast. Is everything okay your side of the Channel?'

'Merry Christmas! I would have rung you, but by the time I got to bed it was nearly midnight. Things went a bit crazy here. Sara and the girls arrived a day early, without Marty,' I said.

'No surprise there then. As he told me last time I saw him, the city and money wait for no one,' Isabel said.

'Bit different this time. He's gone to Zurich with his secretary for Christmas. Sara found out they were having an affair. Everything has gone to rat poo, and the three of them still aren't up. Although I did hear the first scream of the morning from the girls, so perhaps they are on the move.'

Isabel gasped and then made a dismissive noise. 'Poor Sara, but I can't say I'm surprised. Marty never could speak to any woman without being a bit creepy. All that back rubbing and patting. So, what's she going to do?'

I pulled out a chair and sat down. 'Don't know. She self-medicated with gin last night and did a lot of crying and threatening. Perhaps this morning she'll be too hungover to do much. I've hidden her car keys.'

'Very sensible. We had such a great evening; I wish you'd been there. I made Felix shut the bookshop early and everyone came round here. Remember that Christmas when you came and stayed with me? It was like that, but more so. Pierre had found an accordion somewhere, it was awful. I was nearly sick laughing.'

I felt quite sentimental for a few minutes, thinking back to the Christmas when I had been with her in Brittany, the first one after Stephen left, in her chaotic, rambling farmhouse, with dogs asleep under the kitchen table, people everywhere, bottles of wine circulating the room and platters of charcuterie.

It all felt very different from the Christmas that was unfolding in my house. Certainly, much noisier. But then I was beginning to realise there's a difference between the noises of a lot of people laughing and enjoying themselves over a few glasses of wine, and the continuous racket of back chat, arguments and occasionally screaming that had been my soundtrack so far this Christmas.

'Sounds fun,' I said wistfully, 'still, John and Vanessa will be arriving later, perhaps that will cheer everyone up.'

'At least Sara's twins will have someone else to squabble with,' Isabel said, 'unless they have grown out of that? And perhaps they will try to be a bit more tactful, things being what they are?'

I sighed. 'I doubt it. Mia asked if she would now be getting two lots of Christmas and birthday presents like her friends do, and Poppy was nagging about a school trip to Barcelona. Not exactly tactful. Anyway, tell me what you are doing today, so I can think about something else.'

'I would come to you and give you some moral support, except Felix has promised to put the Christmas tree up today, then this evening there is the special Christmas Eve meal, *Le Réveillon*, so I'll have to do all the preparation for that. Pierre and Sylveste are coming round, plus their girlfriends, and Felix's mother will come up the lane from her cottage, and a few friends from the town will probably turn up. Then Midnight Mass if we can still walk in a straight line. I have to roast some beef and a goose, make the dauphinoise potatoes, slice the smoked salmon, make the *Bûche de Noël*, which is basically a glorified Swiss roll, prep the vegetables. It will be chaos. We are supposed to be eating at eight, the way things are going it will be closer to ten. Felix's mother Eugénie will be tutting and interfering, the boys' girlfriends will want to 'help' so you know what that means. So pretty much the same as you do tomorrow.'

'I don't think it will be the same at all,' I said, feeling rather wistful.

'Well, you are coming to me after they all leave, aren't you? That's what we agreed. Focus on that.'

'Yes, that sounds like just what I need. Hang on, I can hear a car. I think it must be John. He's early, too, I hope there are no disasters there.'

'There won't be. Have a fabulous time,' my sister said, 'don't let Sara's bombshell spoil things for you all. Being with her family might be just the lift she needs. And John will be around to help with things; he's always been so capable. I'd better go, too, Felix is back with the salmon knife; he's been sharpening it out in the workshop so it will be like a razor.'

It was true, I thought as I went to open the front door, John might not be much good at simple maths, but he had been an absolute rock. He had done so much to help when his father had left, he had worked methodically and patiently through all the paperwork and officialdom, I don't know how I would have coped without him. And despite their argumentative childhood, I liked to think he and Sara were getting closer as they aged.

'Mum! Merry Christmas!' he said as he came inside to hug me. 'You're looking great!'

I looked down at my work-stained apron and ran one hand through my hair to try and bring order to chaos. My hair used to be quite well-behaved, whereas at sixty-three it seemed to have taken on a new, less controlled personality.

'I think you're being kind,' I said.

John's wife, Vanessa, was shepherding their daughters up the drive and gave me a little wave and a smile. Even muffled up in a thick coat and scarf, she looked thinner than ever.

'Merry Christmas, Joy,' she said, sounding exhausted already although they had only had a twenty-five minute journey to get to my house. 'I see Sara's here already.'

'Tiny bit of a problem in that department. Let's get you all settled and I'll explain,' I said.

* * *

The next hour was taken up with bringing bags and suitcases into the house, settling Bunny and Jasmine into the attic room with Mia and Poppy, and then ignoring their wary looks at each other as the boundary lines were drawn up and new hairstyles were scrutinised, we gathered in the kitchen.

'So, no Marty,' John said as he messed around with the coffee machine.

Sara lifted her chin. 'No Marty,' she said, 'not now, not ever.'

'So apart from anything else, no more of him trying to explain the Duckworth-Lewis-Stern method when he obviously doesn't know one end of a cricket bat from another. Good,' John replied, 'good riddance.'

Vanessa, sitting neatly at the kitchen table ducked her head and gave a little gasp.

'Well, I'm glad you can see something to be positive about,' Sara said, 'I'm devastated and so are the twins.'

'It'll be fine,' John said, 'when you get used to the idea.'

Sara stifled a sob and ran out of the kitchen and into the living room where she could be heard noisily crying for a few seconds, until Vanessa went in to her with a box of tissues.

'Still taking the tactful tablets, John,' I said. 'Can't you see how unhappy she is? She's barely stopped crying since she got here. I was hoping you would be helpful.'

John sighed. 'Okay, I'll apologise, but I can't say I'm sorry about Marty when I'm not. He was always so pompous and such a show off.'

We sat and had coffee and then Vanessa and Sara returned, Sara looking particularly tragic and red-eyed.

'Sorry, Sara,' John said.

'I know you never liked him. I know he didn't really fit in,' Sara replied, 'I'm just so...'

She grabbed for another handful of tissues and gulped and sniffed for a bit while Vanessa rearranged the mince pies on the snowman plate so that the gluten free ones didn't touch the ordinary ones. Perhaps she thought that the gluten would leap across and contaminate the whole lot?

We spent the rest of the morning chatting while I prepared lunch, and tiptoeing around Sara as though she was an unexploded bomb. The four girls eventually came downstairs looking sulky because there wasn't a television in their room, and apparently Jasmine had some new Converse trainers that had been pronounced *lame* by Poppy and Mia. I wouldn't have said there was a proper, Yuletide spirit in the house, which was, at best, disappointing.

Dinner that night was the lasagne, garlic bread and a salad. Jasmine immediately declared that she was '*thinking about becoming a vegetarian*' and leaned away from the bubbling dish as though it was radioactive. This unfortunately started an ill-informed discussion about the evils of meat in general and factory farming, which caused the other three girls to stare at me as though I had proudly produced a vat of botulism and unimaginable suffering covered in cheese sauce.

I thought about the turkey resting peacefully in its bath in the pantry and wondered what sort of reaction that would produce. Perhaps I should increase the volume of vegetables I was planning to serve the following day?

At last, the four girls slunk off from their unsatisfactory meal and into the sitting room where they could watch some reality show Christmas special and eat Celebrations, and I got out the liqueur glasses and the first bottle of Baileys.

'I have an announcement,' John said at last.

I knew there was something, he'd dropped enough hints over the last week. Was Vanessa pregnant again? Looking at her sitting next to me in her size six jeans and miniscule sweater, it didn't seem likely.

'That's exciting,' I said encouragingly.

'Well, it's been on the cards for a while now, but it's official. We are moving,' John said.

Across the table Vanessa smiled, a flush of colour coming to her cheeks.

'I didn't know your house was on the market,' I said.

'It's not,' Vanessa said, 'we're going to rent it out.'

'So where are you going?' I asked, rather puzzled.

John took a deep breath, trying to hide the grin that was spreading over his face.

'New York.'

I gasped, not quite able to process this information for a few seconds.

New York. But that was America. The other side of the Atlantic. I felt a bit sick for a moment.

'New York, America?' I said at last, rather foolishly.

'That's the one,' John said, evidently very pleased about this, 'for two years. Maybe longer. I didn't like to say anything before now in case it all came to nothing, but this promotion has been on the cards for six months and they've been asking me to go for a while, and now it's all fallen into place.'

'We're very excited,' Vanessa said, her blue eyes wide, 'we

wanted to tell you first, but the girls will be thrilled when we tell them.'

'You're all going?' I said, my mouth dry.

The lasagne suddenly sat like a stone in my stomach.

She nodded. 'Absolutely. The company have fixed us up with an apartment to start with, and suggested schools for the girls. And when we are settled, we can look around for a house, it's going to be so broadening for them, to see more of the world, other cultures, and customs.'

'Yes, I suppose so,' I said faintly.

'It's a bit of a shock, isn't it, Mum?' John said. 'Perhaps you can come out and visit us?'

'I knew it! I said you'd have something to brag about,' Sara said furiously, slamming her napkin down on the table. 'Big promotion, big new life, big everything! Just when my life is falling to pieces!'

'That's a bit unfair,' I said. 'Congratulations, John. I'm sure we are all delighted for you.'

Was I happy? I suppose I was pleased for them, for him. He had done so well, but America. It was so far away.

Sara took her glass, downed the Baileys in one and reached for the bottle.

'You could come and visit us too,' Vanessa said.

'Oh yes, I can just see me springing for airfares when the girls and I will be living in some squalid flat somewhere while Marty moves his bit of stuff into my house.'

I think Sara had been knocking back the Pinot Grigio during the meal with more enthusiasm than any of us realised.

'I'm sure you're wrong. Perhaps Marty will be the one to move out,' I said, 'and you and the girls can stay where you are. After all he is the one who has caused all this.'

Sara scowled, looking exactly as she had when she was thirteen and been refused permission to go out with her friends on a school night.

'You don't think I'm going to stay *there,* knowing what those two have been up to? In my bed!'

I glanced across at John and we exchanged a look.

'You need to take it one step at a time. Go and see a solicitor after Christmas, find out the best plan of action,' he said, 'I'm sure—'

'Oh, what would you know about it? With your perfect life, your perfect wife,' Sara spat back.

'No need to be like that,' he replied evenly.

'Well, you tell me then John, the golden boy who couldn't tie his shoelaces until he was eleven, how should I be?'

The door to the dining room burst open and Mia came in her expression thunderous.

'Mum, *tell her.* Bunny is being mean. She says my hair looks stupid and she says Poppy won't ever get a boyfriend. And Poppy said Bunny was a silly cow, and then Jasmine started crying and she threw a cushion at Poppy and broke a vase, and there's water all over the sofa. And Jasmine said it was my fault.'

We all got up and went to sort the chaos out. Sara doing her best but crying, Vanessa brisk and efficient, John trying to find out the true version of events and me going to get a cloth and the dustpan and brush.

3

I suppose I had imagined Christmas Eve night passing in a sort of golden, Walton-family haze with my four granddaughters bonding, talking, and giggling together in their attic bedroom before falling asleep without any sort of shouting or parental threats about Santa not coming. The rest of us would be sitting in the magical, twinkly light from the Christmas tree and the battery-operated candles, remembering Christmases past, our hopes for the year to come.

We would perhaps raise a glass to the old year and get a bit sentimental, and Sara and John would tell me how marvellously I was getting on with my life. This would then expand into what a great mother I had been, how I was the girls' favourite grandparent, how happy they were to be back in my house. What a lovely day we were all looking forward to in the morning.

And then maybe there would be some fun dealing with the Christmas stockings. John would take the obligatory bite out of the gluten free mince pie and washed, organic carrot left in the fireplace for Santa by the youngest grandchild, Bunny, with a slight rolling of her eyes, making me think she was only doing it for my benefit, and he would knock back the whisky in the special Father Christmas tumbler I'd bought from Woolworths so many years ago when my own children were small.

I'd draw the curtains against the dark night, where ideally it would be snowing, and put on a CD of Christmas music. We'd have a few drinks and delve deeper into the tub of Celebrations, complaining about the coconut ones, and the fire would be friendly and warm, and we would all agree how lucky we were.

Well, it wasn't like that at all.

My granddaughters went off to bed with their electronic devices and there was a fair bit of leaping up and threatening by Sara and John before the girls settled down for the night, presumably with visions of Fortnite and Taylor Swift dancing in their heads.

Sara had deliberately planted herself martyr-like in what was always regarded as the least comfortable armchair. Vanessa dressed in cream, cashmere loungewear sat at one end of the sofa with her bare feet tucked up underneath her. I sat at the other while John leaned back in what had been Stephen's chair, listening out for sounds of screaming and shouting from his daughters upstairs.

We made desultory, whispering conversation about Marty whenever Sara was out of the room. In the New Year John promised to ring his friend Barry who was a divorce lawyer, and I scurried back and forth to the kitchen bringing out snacks and fresh bottles of wine and then at about midnight shoving the turkey into a low oven for its starring role the following day.

'I just don't know how he could do it,' Sara kept saying, 'to me, to the girls. How could he?'

'He's an idiot,' John said, 'just plain stupid.'

Vanessa stirred from her nest of cushions. 'You know we don't use that word, darling.'

'Well for him I'll make an exception,' John said firmly.

Sara was slumped a little in her chair, one hand grasping her wine glass, the other resting on a box of tissues.

'How am I going to get through this?' Sara said, her eyes filling with tears again.

I reached over to pat her hand. 'We'll help, I promise you. We'll give you all the support you need, won't we, John? And Vanessa too.'

Sara sank a little further in the chair that had lost all its support after years of her and her brother jumping on it.

'John's not going to be much use, swanning around New York.'

'I'll be just a phone call away,' he said, 'you can ring me anytime you need a chat. Although there is a five-hour time difference. And you'll have Mum and all your friends.'

Sara took a sulky slurp of wine. 'S'pose.'

'And in the meantime, you can come here whenever you want to,' I said. 'The rooms are always ready. If you need a break or anything.'

Sara shook her head slowly. 'I'm dreading going back to The Old Rectory, I really am. When I slammed the front door behind me, it felt like I was closing the door on my past.'

Vanessa reached out and with the ends of her fingernails took one Pringle, which was very unlike her. They were neither low salt nor additive free. And speaking from personal experience, once you pop, you don't stop until you're shaking the last fragments from the tube into your palm. But then Vanessa was made of sterner stuff than I was.

She leaned forwards. 'One of my friends got divorced in July. She had the best lawyer, he used to say "*don't get mean, get everything*". And she did. Her ex is living in a one bed in Milton Keynes. That will be Marty this time next year, you wait and see.'

'Heating up beans over a camp stove with newspapers over the windows,' John chuckled.

Sara struggled upright again fighting against the flabby seat cushions, spilling some wine in her lap, which she brushed off with an irritated hand.

'But I don't want him to be living in Milton Keynes, I want things to be back the way they were. With all of us living in The Old Rectory and being happy.'

'Were you happy?' I asked.

Sara emptied her glass and reached for the bottle again. I would have to stop her soon or she would head further into the maudlin phase.

'No, not really,' she said at last, 'but we could have been if... if that woman hadn't...'

'Marty's forty-two, he's a grown man,' John said, 'you could never make him do anything he didn't want to. Remember that Saturday when we all agreed to come over to help Dad with the shed roof? Marty turned up in an Armani suit and just stood giving out advice for ten minutes, and then he went in to get a beer and watch the Six Nations rugby.'

'He'd come straight from the office,' Sara said defensively, 'an extraordinary meeting of the directors.'

'And he was an extraordinary waste of space,' John fired back.

'Oh, shut up,' Sara mumbled.

'You shut up!'

'John darling. Be nice. Sara's upset,' Vanessa murmured.

'It's not my fault he can't keep his trousers on, he always was a—'

I could see this degenerating into something that would not be appropriate during *the most wonderful time of the year* and plastered a big fake smile on my face.

'Right, you lot, I'm going to bed. Can you make sure you turn everything off when you come up? And don't forget to take up the girls' stockings,' I said as cheerfully as I could, 'we don't want them to be disappointed when they wake up tomorrow.'

'Actually Joy, Bunny and Jasmine have never believed in Father Christmas,' Vanessa said earnestly. 'We told them years ago that it was just a product of advertising and Victorian sentiment. And Coca-Cola.'

'God, you're such a spoilsport,' Sara slurred.

'Well no, I disagree. I think it's important to tell them the truth, right from the start,' Vanessa said testily.

I stood up, cleared some of the empty glasses and bowls onto a tray and left them to their argument.

* * *

Out in the hall I thought I could still hear the dull thud of music coming from the girls' room, which meant non-existent Santa couldn't arrive at the end of their beds with their despised Christmas stockings any time soon. For a moment I could almost feel my blood pressure spiking.

Never mind. Push it away. I was determined to look on the positive side.

Everyone was safely here, there was plenty of food in the pantry and lots of heating oil thanks to a recent delivery. I'd remembered to buy three sorts of batteries for any toys that turned up, I'd stocked up with spare toothbrushes, hair bobbles and there were organic, vegan, hypoallergenic toiletries in the bathrooms. I'd bought luxury crackers, too, with proper gifts inside, not just horrible plastic tat and paper hats that didn't fit anyone.

Surely tomorrow would be different. Everyone would have had time to get used to being here, each other and of course the prospect of Sara regularly having a bit too much of the wrong sort of Yuletide spirit.

And then there was John's news about moving his family three thousand miles away. My heart did a plunge of disappointment at the prospect. I would miss him terribly. And he would be going soon, too, the middle of January he thought. He would be gone so soon, the idea that I wouldn't be able to just pop over and see them was awful.

But that was weeks away; for now I would make an extra effort to cheer everyone up, to make their stay really special.

In the morning there would be hot chocolate and croissants for breakfast, a delicious, traditional Christmas feast after the King's speech and a day filled with laughter, perhaps a jigsaw and some board games in the evening. This was a strange image really because no one in the family was any good at jigsaws, and Monopoly had been banned for years because of the arguments and cheating.

I'd always wanted to believe there was a special magic about Christmas, something that united people, when all the shops had shut, and I loved the idea that a lot of families were all doing much the same thing as we were.

I seemed to remember John saying something about all of them staying until the New Year, which in itself was unusual. Now that I knew that next Christmas he would be on the other side of the Atlantic, it all made sense.

If I was honest, it was all going terribly wrong, and we hadn't even got to Christmas Day yet.

I got back to the sanctuary of my bedroom after midnight, first tidying away all the shoes and handbags on the stairs and picking up the coats from the floor and hanging them on the coat stand.

I caught sight of myself in my dressing table mirror. I looked old and tired. Well, I supposed I was actually both of those things.

I pulled a face at my reflection.

'Merry Christmas, you filthy animal,' I murmured.

I looked out of the window at the dark, rain-battered night and sighed. I began to wonder if I had been totally unrealistic about how this visit would go. An unexpected and unwanted question came into my head; *when* were they *leaving*?

4

When Sara and John were children, Christmas Day usually started early. Any time after five o'clock and they would come cannoning into our room, shouting with glee. *'He's been! He's been!'* That Christmas was different.

I woke just after six thirty and lay for a moment wondering if there was any noise from my family, if I had missed out on any of the fun. It seemed not.

I dressed quickly in jeans and a lurid Christmas sweater that had been a present from the twins last year and went downstairs. The curtains in the sitting room were still closed, the Christmas tree lights were still on and so were the battery-operated candles, which were flickering less brightly than they had been. There were also several dirty glasses, some empty beer bottles, and the remains of a pizza in a battered cardboard box on the coffee table. For a moment I was catapulted back twenty years, to a time when I routinely came down to find similar debris from which my children had simply walked away. There were probably wet towels on the bathroom floor and empty juice cartons in the fridge too.

I wondered what time they had stayed up until, and whether

they had been just talking, reminiscing over their marvellous childhood, or arguing. For a moment I was about to be rather annoyed, that even now in their mid-thirties they were capable of reverting to juvenile behaviour the minute they came through the front door.

I bet Vanessa wouldn't put up with John leaving his shoes under the sofa and Marty would be more likely to eat one of his silk ties than order in a pizza that had probably arrived in a heated bag on the back of a moped.

Anyway. There was a lot to do, even with all the Mary Berry 'getting ahead' business, so I tied on a clean apron and decided to cheer myself up, open the oven and gloat over the brined, juicy bird within. It was then that I realised that the kitchen was not filled with the lovely, Christmas scent of a roasting turkey. In fact, they had ignored my requests to turn off the Christmas lights and candles, but someone *had* turned the oven off and the blasted thing was still raw.

Instead of the beautifully golden exterior I had been expecting, it was still pink and pallid and really rather distasteful.

Right, I whacked the oven up to full power and consulted Mary Berry for advice. It would take about four hours, so all was not lost, but it was just one more thing to worry about. That's the thing about Christmas dinner, I knew some people thought it was only a glorified Sunday lunch but there were so many pans and bowls and plates to spin, not to mention limited oven and worktop space. I took a deep, calming breath and made some coffee. It would be fine. Perhaps I should write out a timetable.

Having done that and realising that I would now not have a sacred hour mid-morning when I could join in the seasonal excitement, I decided to abandon breakfast in the kitchen and instead laid the dining table with some festive plates and got out the juices and jams. And yes, there was one empty carton of cranberry juice carefully put back in the fridge door and a seriously depleted bottle of Cointreau on the worktop next to some squished-out limes, so I guessed the late-night shenanigans had included several Cosmopolitan cocktails.

I must have got my daily ten thousand steps in before anyone else came downstairs, and then I did the rest of the vegetable preparation, not sure if anyone other than John liked parsnips, and wondering whether the girls – even if some of them rejected the happy, bronze, organic turkey – would still want to eat pigs in blankets? And if so, how many?

Hunger eventually drove my granddaughters downstairs before their parents, and they bounded into the kitchen where I was wiping down the worktops for the umpteenth time and crossing things off my timetable.

'Merry Christmas, Grandma,' they said in unison, all coming over for a group hug, which was wonderful. I felt the brightness of Christmas Day excitement swell up inside me all over again.

'Merry Christmas, girls,' I said, looking down at their bright, pretty faces and dropping a kiss on each head. For a moment I almost felt like the sainted Marmee in *Little Women*. 'Has Father Christmas been? Did you all sleep well?'

'I did,' Jasmine said, 'even though Mia was snoring.'

'I've had a cold,' Mia said, 'everyone snores when they have a blocked nose, don't they, Grandma?'

'Of course they do,' I said, sending a meaningful look at Poppy who was making quiet but unmistakeable pig noises.

Bunny, the youngest tugged at my arm. 'And I only had two teddies, because Mum said that was all I could bring, and I usually have six.'

'Never mind, you had Poppy, Mia and Jasmine in the room to make up for it,' I said, dropping another kiss on the top of her head.

'S'pose,' Bunny said, pouting and looking very much like her Aunt Sara the previous evening.

'Can we open our presents now?' Poppy asked, standing in the sitting room doorway looking hopefully at the piles of lavishly wrapped gifts under the tree.

'We should wait for your parents to come down,' I said. 'Let's have breakfast first.'

'Do we have to?' Mia moaned, 'they won't be up for ages, and I'm not hungry. I ate all the chocolate coins in my stocking.'

'Ah yes! Did you get lots of exciting things from Father Christmas?'

Jasmine gave me a look. 'It's fine, Grandma, we all know it's mum and dad. Apart from anything else, Father Christmas uses the same wrapping paper that they do, and we all got exactly the same things. Except Bunny who got a gluten free gingerbread man and didn't get lip gloss because she's allergic. So how would Father Christmas know that?'

'How about some hot chocolate and croissants?' I said brightly.

'Are they gluten free?' Bunny asked.

'Some of them are,' I said, 'I got them just for you.'

'I bet they're not as good as the real ones,' Mia said, 'I bet they taste like cardboard.'

'Absolutely not,' I said, as Bunny's lip started to tremble, 'and they are much more expensive. Because they are special.'

'Dad said only people with actual coeliac disease need to avoid gluten. And you haven't got that,' Poppy said.

'I might have,' Bunny said.

Poppy laughed rather too hard for it to be genuine.

'No, you haven't. My dad says your mum is a helicopter.'

'That's stupid, how can she be a helicopter? Anyway, where is *your* dad?' Jasmine added, springing to her sister's defence.

'We're not allowed to say, stupid,' Poppy mumbled.

'Right then, I'm going to put some croissants into the oven, they only take a few minutes. Hands up who wants some Nutella?' I said, overly cheery.

Four hands were raised, and the sniping stopped long enough for them to settle at the table, which meant when John and Vanessa came down a few minutes later, all was calm, all was bright.

Sara appeared shortly afterwards, still in her Christmas pyjamas and dressing gown. Ignoring everyone she made a beeline for the kitchen, the coffee, and the paracetamol.

* * *

They spent the rest of the morning in the sitting room, opening presents and exclaiming with delight. Although there was a bit of a problem when Jasmine and Bunny opened matching iPads.

'I wish we had those,' Mia said enviously, the new palette of seven trillion eyeshadows forgotten in her lap.

'Perhaps when you're older and less likely to drop them or leave them on the school bus,' Sara said. She was still sitting slumped in an armchair, nursing her third cup of coffee, and shielding her eyes from the sunlight streaming in through the windows.

'But they are both younger than us,' Poppy mumbled.

'I wish I had that make up,' Bunny said, looking over.

'I'll swap if you like?' Mia offered.

'No, no we can't do that. I've already registered them,' Vanessa said quickly.

'Yes, of course you have, you're so efficient,' Sara replied rather sourly.

'Well now then, why don't you give Grandma your special

present, girls?' John suggested, pulling a flat parcel out from under the tree and handing it to Jasmine and Bunny to give to me.

There was a slight tussle then and the paper was torn slightly, but eventually it was handed over.

'Lovely,' I said, unwrapping a hideous tartan shawl, 'just what I needed.'

'We chose it ourselves. Our headteacher says old people feel the cold more,' Bunny said, 'and they can't afford heating or food.'

'Well, you don't need to worry about me just yet,' I said.

I swung the shawl around my shoulders and instantly felt ten years older.

'What cheerful colours,' I said, stroking the wool, 'red and green and brown; so bright and pretty. They make me feel warmer just looking at them. And so soft too.'

'It's cruelty-free cashmere,' Vanessa said, 'made from soya beans.'

'Really? Isn't that marvellous,' I said. 'What will they think of next?'

'And this is from us,' Poppy said, pulling out a similar sized parcel.

'Ah, how absolutely lovely,' I said unwrapping a similar shawl. 'What lovely shades of grey.'

'Eco-unfriendly, and made from petroleum-based polyester,' Sara murmured.

'Well, they are both lovely, and thank you all so much, I don't know which one to wear first,' I said.

A timer pinged in the kitchen, mercifully releasing me from having to make any choice at all.

'Twelve thirty, goodness the morning is whizzing past. That's my cue to do something,' I said, 'I'd better go and see.'

'Need any help, Mum?' John asked, making no attempt to move.

'No, I'm fine, all under control,' I said, 'perhaps it's time for a sherry? If you want to sort that out?'

'I haven't got a clue where you keep it these days.'

'I'll do it,' Sara sighed, heaving herself out of her chair.

She followed me out to the kitchen and found the sherry in the pantry.

'Can I have my phone back?' she said. 'I feel a bit lost without it. It's all right, I won't text Marty.'

I handed it over and she poured herself a sherry and drank it while scrolling through her messages.

'Nothing,' she said at last, 'not even to let me know he got there okay.'

'Oh, Sara, you poor love, what a horrible thing to happen. I hope you got some sleep?' I said, putting an arm around her shoulders.

'A bit,' she said, sitting down heavily on one of the kitchen chairs. 'Not much, it's just the shock.'

She knocked back the rest of her sherry and refilled her glass.

I took the turkey out of the oven and heaved it onto the worktop to baste it while Sara watched me.

'That's a big turkey,' she said.

'The biggest I could get.'

'Marty loves turkey,' she said, her voice cracking with emotion. 'He always said Christmas dinner was his favourite meal. Even though it's nothing special. Just a Sunday roast really, isn't it?'

Well, it's a bit more than that actually, I thought, looking at all the pans and trays of six different vegetables, two stuffings – one vegetarian, one not – pigs in blankets and the big jug of batter for the Yorkshire puddings everyone expected. And then there was the home-made pudding, steaming away in my biggest saucepan, the dishes of double cream, brandy butter, the jug waiting for the custard. Then the platter of seven different cheeses and assorted biscuits, the bowls of tangerines mixed in with gold-wrapped chocolate coins, the cafetière of coffee and my favourite coffee cups ready on a tray.

'I suppose so,' I said, basting the bird with a splattering of hot fat. 'Now take the sherry into the other two and I'll be just a few minutes. There are some home-made cheese straws in that box, take those too.'

Sara sighed and did as she was told, the glasses rattling together on the tray as she went.

I returned to my task and gave the turkey a huge, teeth-flashing grin that was more of a grimace.

I conjured up the idyllic scene I had imagined, of all of us gathered round the dining table, like some Norman Rockwell painting. Smiling faces, everyone pulling the expensive dinner crackers I had found, the food appetising and steaming hot as though the food stylists from the *Good Food* magazine had got hold of it. Although I'd recently read an article about that sort of thing and as is often the case, not everything was what it seemed. Mashed potato used to make milkshakes, strawberries painted with lipstick, shaving foam used instead of cream cheese frosting, brown fence paint over a roasted chicken.

I looked at my turkey more critically, wondering if it might benefit from the same treatment. No, perhaps a layer of creosote was a step too far in my quest for Christmas perfection.

5

At half past two, I started encouraging Sara to go upstairs and get dressed. Still in her dressing gown, she had been intermittently dozing in an armchair by the fire, while around her the chaos continued.

The twins were plastering each other with eyeshadow, Jasmine and Bunny were quarrelling over their new iPads because one was silver, and one was pink and each preferred the other one. When I suggested they could just swap, I was looked at with incredulity, so I backed off. It seemed they were enjoying the excuse to argue rather than reach a solution. And of course, it kept their ownership of such trophies to the forefront of Mia and Poppy's minds.

Every time Vanessa opened a present from John and told him how marvellous he was, often bestowing a loving kiss on his cheek, Sara looked over with some resentment. After Sara's third sherry and the unwrapping of a Tiffany charm to add to Vanessa's bracelet, her comments became even more acerbic.

'Aren't you the lucky one? Marty bought me a new wheelbarrow for my birthday, and apparently nothing for Christmas, and they say romance isn't dead.'

'I've been collecting these for years,' Vanessa said with a fond smile at John. 'It's a bit of a cheat really, it means he doesn't have to think about it.'

'And of course it's vegetarian. He thought about the pink, soya bean cashmere cardigan though I expect. Which bit of the bean is used exactly?'

'I don't really know,' Vanessa said.

'Let's hope no abused donkeys were used to haul the sacks of soya beans into the factory,' Sara muttered.

'Let's leave it, Sara,' John said.

'It will be time for the King's speech soon. Lunch will be on the table in forty minutes,' I said brightly.

'I'm not very hungry,' Bunny said, 'I've eaten most of my selection box. Can we have it later?'

'I haven't even opened mine. No wonder you're getting podgy,' Poppy said.

'I'm *not*! Mum what does podgy mean?' Bunny wailed.

'Poppy's being silly,' Vanessa said soothingly. 'Now then, let's all go and wash our hands, shall we? Poppy and Mia have a lot of eyeshadow on their fingers, haven't they? What a lot of colours.'

'Can I buy eyeshadow with my birthday money?' Bunny asked.

'Oh, you're pretty enough already. You don't need any,' Vanessa said.

Sara's eyes narrowed as she left the room.

* * *

For just a split second, my dream of a perfect Christmas came true. Everyone sat down in their allotted places with only a minor squabble about whether Bunny wanted a red cracker or a gold one. The candles on the table and the sideboard were lit, brightening up the dark afternoon. The best wine glasses and the posh cutlery sparkled and shone, and everyone let out the required '*ooohs*' of admiration as John carried the turkey in on the china platter decorated with Christmas trees that he and Vanessa had given me the first year they were married.

He then took his place at the head of the table where Stephen used to sit and began the ceremonial carving of the bird.

'Is that an actual turkey?' Poppy said as she watched John pull one of the legs off and start hacking at it, 'it looks like it's been run over.'

John has a lot of talents, but carving had never been one of them. I watched him and wondered why did this always happen? Women, i.e. me, did all the shopping, the planning, the work and then at the last minute a man would steam in and grab the spotlight. It was the same with barbeques. I would make the salads, buy the meat, light the barbeque, put out the cutlery, crockery, glasses, and condiments, and then Stephen would behave as though it was all his doing. And people would complement *him*.

'I don't want any of that,' Jasmine said, as John held out a plate towards her.

'Really? But I thought you loved turkey?' I said brightly.

'No, I'm a vegetarian,' she said, leaning away from the plate as though it was polluted.

'Then just have some vegetables,' Vanessa said.

Jasmine stood up and dabbed at the roast potatoes with a spoon and put two on her empty plate. 'I don't like parsnips or carrots.'

'Those carrots died for you,' Poppy said.

'The carrots are dead?' Bunny said, her eyes wide.

'Everything on this table is dead,' Poppy said, 'absolutely everything. That turkey is just a dead bird, which has been cooked.'

'I wish I'd known; I could have done you a nut roast,' I said, 'or a pie with soya beans.'

'I expect the soya beans have all been used up to make pretend cashmere,' Sara said from her end of the table.

'Let's pull our crackers,' I said as Vanessa opened her mouth to respond to this.

We did, with the usual problem of some of the girls getting two prizes and others getting none. Something that was swiftly resolved by John awarding the handbag mirror to Jasmine and the set of pencils to Poppy, her scowl showed her disapproval.

'I wanted the mirror,' she said, prodding her sprouts.

Vanessa tried to be the peacemaker. 'Let Poppy have it, Jasmine, she needs it to look at all that eyeshadow.'

Jasmine scowled and shook her head. Then of course Vanessa made some encouraging comments about how wonderful the meal was, how happy they were to be all together again, enjoying a proper family Christmas and John agreed, while Sara sat empty-eyed, and staring into the far distance.

'By the way, Joy, do you think we could have some different towels?' Vanessa asked. 'We seem to have the pink ones by mistake, which are a bit rough. Usually, we have the white ones.'

'Yes, of course,' I said, stifling my first impulse which was to scream, tear my paper hat off and throw it at her, 'I'll sort it out after lunch.'

'Oh, no rush. But I thought I might take a nice relaxing bath later,' she said with a sweet smile, 'it always helps me sleep after a tiring day.'

A tiring day? What could she have done that necessitated that? I wondered. Other than get up late, eat half a croissant, sit down with coffee, and open some presents. While I had been flogging myself around the kitchen since dawn.

No, I wouldn't think like that. I would take a deep breath and calm down. I reached for the red wine and filled up my glass. *Oh, tidings of Merlot and joy...*

'I wonder what Uncle Marty is having for his Christmas dinner?' Bunny said.

At that point, Sara stood up with a strangled cry, her paper hat falling to the floor, and dashed out of the room. We all sat looking at each other before I went after her to see if she was all right.

I found her sitting on the stairs, dry-eyed but looking furious.

I put an arm around her. 'Come on, Sara, don't let Marty spoil today for you or the girls. You'll have a lot of difficult days ahead. Let's enjoy this one.'

'I keep wondering what they got up to in my house. When I was down in Cornwall with the girls this summer. The cottage there was horrible, and it looked nothing like the photos. There were exactly four plates, four mugs and four sets of cutlery, but only three teaspoons. And the weather was foul. We didn't have a wonderful sea view, because it was raining all the time, and there was no broadband so when he did arrive, Marty couldn't work at all, so he went back two days early. And I bet he went back to *her*. I bet she had dozens of teaspoons. I bet Vanessa has hundreds, all in a special box.'

I handed her a tissue and she blew her nose loudly.

'Come on, let's go back and finish lunch,' I said, 'the girls will be missing you.'

'No, they won't, I bet they are just arguing. That's all they do these days,' Sara said, her voice giving a little sad catch.

'They're teenagers, that's what they do,' I said, hugging her. 'Remember what you and John were like?'

'We weren't as bad as them. And put the four of them together and it's ten times worse.'

'At least none of them have set fire to the curtains, like you did.'

Sara clicked her tongue in exasperation. 'I've told you so many times, I was just a kid and that was an *accident*.'

'You were fifteen and you were smoking, and you left a fag end on John's windowsill.'

'Oh, bring it all up, why don't you? No wonder my husband had an affair if I am such a trial to everyone. That's what you're saying, aren't you?'

I sighed. 'No, I'm not saying that at all. Look, come back into the dining room, let's have a lovely lunch together and then afterwards we can play charades. Or something. You were always good at that.'

'Yes, the way I'm feeling at the moment, I could knock a couple of my teeth out and cut my own hair with the kitchen scissors and do *Les Misérables* with no difficulty.'

'Sara, stop it,' I said. 'Come on. Cheer up, for the girls if not for me. I've tried so hard to make things nice for you all.'

Sara dropped her face into her hands and took a deep breath.

'Okay, I will. Sorry. But sometimes I just wonder what's the point? What's the bloody point of all this? Of me?'

Welcome to my world, I thought.

'You have everything to look forward to. You're only thirty-six, you probably haven't even got to the halfway point in your life. Look at me, I'm sixty-three, I'm on the downhill slope to old age and dementia.'

'You'd better not be,' Sara said fiercely, 'I'm going to need you to look after the girls if I have to go back to work. I bet Marty will leave me with nothing, and every alimony cheque will be late, and when he takes the girls out for the weekend, he'll send them back high on sugar and additives. It's going to be a nightmare.'

I was a bit taken aback by this. Love them as I did, the prospect of being press-ganged into Sara's parenting schedule wasn't something I had ever considered. I'd done the occasional sleepover and babysitting, but that had been enough for me. I had always been convinced that if anything happened to either Poppy or Mia, it would be on my watch and my fault. And Stephen had been even more resistant. He and small babies didn't ever get on, he said they were like horses; expensive, dangerous at both ends and remembering Poppy's three-month colic and projectile vomiting, he possibly had a point.

* * *

On television the chef produces a fabulous meal and then friends/family come around to eat it. And they are all appreciative, with complimentary and witty conversation and no one gets drunk, argues or pulls a face when presented with beautifully cooked vegetables as Bunny did because the *'parsnips were in the same dish as the carrots.'*

I'd put all the vegetables and side dishes out on the sideboard, too, so that everyone could help themselves. This was a mistake as the pigs in blankets were snaffled up in seconds, leaving only one for Poppy. Of course, this provoked some hissing disagreement from all four girls, when they were asked to share a bit more generously. Even Jasmine's supposed vegetarianism didn't stretch that far, as she *'was allowed to have six because she wasn't eating the dead bird.'*

'But you'll eat two sorts of dead pig,' Mia said heatedly, 'what's the difference?'

'I don't like pigs as much as I like birds,' Jasmine said.

'We did a project in school about pigs, and they are very clean and friendly and just as intelligent as some people. That's what Mrs Spencer said,' Bunny said, sticking her chin out and looking belligerent.

Her face a tight scowl, Poppy looked at her lone pig in a blanket, and turned towards Sara, who was reading one of the cracker jokes and evidently not finding it funny. Honestly, I might just as well have saved my money and got twelve from the supermarket. At least one of them might have had a moving cellophane fish to show how sexy I was. Or wasn't.

'Mum, *tell her...*'

Sara and I exchanged a look as though she was hoping I would sort it all out, and I shrugged, stood up, went out to the kitchen to refill the gravy jug and left her to it.

I had looked forward to this day so much, and even I, with my considerable reserves of patience was getting a bit fed up with the endless bickering and dissatisfaction from my family. I loved them all, and this was my way of showing it. And my thanks to them for their support since their father had bailed out, I couldn't have put a price on that.

What would it take, I wondered, to have the sort of family gathering that Nigella had? Children smiling, grandchildren rosy-cheeked and happy? Everybody laughing like crazy and probably talking about how lucky they were.

Why was it that it had taken me hours, if not days, to produce this meal, and my family were apparently speed-eating as though they had something better to do. I had hoped that my grand-daughters would be talking excitedly about Christmas, their days in school, then going off to play with their new toys or games, or at least, eyeshadow.

Instead, everyone was looking miserable, and my four grand-daughters were glowering across the table at each other, deliberately not laughing at the jokes in the crackers, not answering my questions with anything other than monosyllables and generally being – dare I say it? – rather rude. And there seemed to be little or no parental involvement, which was strange because Vanessa was usually first to spring to Jasmine or Bunny's defence.

I looked across at her, marvelling at how stylish and pristine she was, picking at her food daintily. I looked down at my trousers, which despite the stout apron I had been wearing when I was cooking, had been splattered with turkey fat and flour. Vanessa took a tiny sip of white wine.

'No red for me,' she'd said as the bottles were passed around the table, 'I've just had my teeth whitened, and red wine stains so badly.'

I'd given a merlot-enriched grin at this and passed the Pinot Grigio, which she declared *'not quite chilled enough'* so I'd fetched some ice cubes for her. I was beginning to think I was mad to bother.

Any minute now and I was going to say something.

What I wasn't sure. Perhaps one of those clever comments that sound reasonable but deliver a punchy message. I wasn't very good at those; heaven knows I had tried hard enough while Stephen was around and he had made a careless remark that had sent me off in a huff. I generally came up with one days or even weeks after they would have been useful. In fact, during some sleepless nights, I had come up with the perfect response to the time when Stephen had actually told me my bum did look big in some new trousers. And then insisted he was just joking.

I wasn't staff. It was my Christmas too...

Was that really all I was good for, picking up after people and not protesting that I felt unappreciated? Wanting to feel as though I had a life of my own? That my feelings still mattered? That *I* still mattered. I couldn't go on like this. Something was going to have to change.

6

Boxing Day – when as children, Isabel and I had happily eaten re-hashed leftovers and played with our new toys. We'd always secretly agreed that we enjoyed Boxing Day more than Christmas, it seemed more fun somehow, more relaxed. I suppose I had hopes that the same thing would apply that day.

Vanessa appeared after breakfast dressed in a new waxed jacket, new *Le Chameau* boots, and matching cashmere (ethical) hat, scarf and gloves that perfectly matched her blue eyes. She wanted us to all go out for a *'lovely walk'*, so we could get some exercise and *'blow the cobwebs away'*. She was met with little enthusiasm, evidently everyone was perfectly happy with their cobwebs and atrophying leg muscles, and anyway, it was still raining. She took a cup of coffee and pouting prettily, went back off upstairs to change.

I produced a buffet lunch complete with bubble and squeak, which I had assumed everyone would enjoy and then watched as Bunny picked out the strands of sprout, Jasmine ate nothing but crisps and the twins sulked because the eyeshadow boxes had been overused and subsequently confiscated.

John was in good form, jolly and talkative, telling me all about his new offices in Manhattan and their new rental apartment that was apparently in an area called Midtown and within easy walking distance of Times Square, Central Park, Broadway, the MoMA, and sundry other delights.

Sara didn't appear until lunch had started, confident that someone else would be entertaining the twins, and when she did come downstairs complained that she had a headache and that there was no brie left on the cheese plate.

'There's a pantomime on at the village hall,' I said. '*Cinderella*, I've reserved us all tickets for tomorrow.'

The girls looked at each other and pulled faces.

'Is there anyone famous in it?' Poppy said.

'Probably not. The vicar is playing the wicked stepmother and the milkman and his brother are playing the ugly sisters. It will be great fun.'

'I'd rather stay here and read,' Jasmine said cunningly, knowing as all children do that this was an occupation to which no parent would ever object.

In the end, we didn't go. I didn't notice anyone huddled away with a book, and nor did we get any sort of walk, so after four days we were all getting cabin fever and none of the girls were speaking to each other following a major disagreement about some reality star I'd never heard of.

It seemed that the last bright embers of my Christmas expectations were flickering and dying, and I felt powerless to do anything about it. It was such a shame; nothing was going as I had planned.

I began to feel rather angry too. My granddaughters were

being rude and ungrateful, Sara and John seemed to have abandoned most of their parental responsibilities in the same way they had stopped clearing up after themselves since the moment they had arrived, and I was being treated like unpaid staff. Considering the trouble, effort and expense I had gone to, it was all so disappointing. I felt like a cross between some aged retainer, shuffling around with a damp cloth and a nanny distracting them all from yet another argument and finding something entertaining for them to do.

By New Year's Eve, the weather cleared up and John and Vanessa went out for their walk. Sara buttonholed me in the kitchen as I cleared away after another meal and the girls watched television in the sitting room with the door closed. This apparently necessitated bringing all their duvets downstairs to huddle underneath, even though the heating had been on all day since they had arrived and I, for one, was boiling and had even opened a kitchen window.

'Can I talk to you?' she said.

'Of course you can.'

'Well, will you stop tidying up and wiping the worktops for a moment and sit down? And can you shut that window, it's freezing.'

'Right. This sounds serious,' I said, 'have you heard from Marty?'

Sara nodded. 'He messaged me to say he would be back tomorrow.'

'I'd rather he didn't come here,' I said, imagining Marty planting himself in my hallway bringing with him a supercilious sneer and a pungent whiff of his aftershave.

'God, no. That's not what I meant,' Sara said, her eyes wide with alarm. 'I want to ask if the girls and I can stay on here for a while. They don't go back to school for another few days; I could pop into town and buy them a few things to tide them over. I brought a lot of their stuff with me anyway. Have a think.'

I thought back over the last few days of arguing and disappointment and shuddered. Perhaps it would be easier with just them? But what if it wasn't? What if this awful behaviour just continued?

It was the start of a New Year the following day, a time when a lot of people plan new things. I wanted to achieve something with it, something for me for a change. If nothing else, the last week had showed me that I was turning into a martyr, a domestic drudge who seemed to be putting up with just about anything. Was that really me?

I'd had a good career, been a head of department, had organised people and events. I'd been married to the same man for nearly forty years, I'd produced two children, run my home efficiently and well. Was I going to allow myself to behave like this for the rest of my life?

Sara busied herself making me a conciliatory cup of coffee and bringing me the tin of Christmas biscuits which she placed at my elbow.

'There aren't many left,' she said, 'I think all the good ones have gone.'

I poked about amongst the Jammie Dodgers and broken digestives for a moment and then gave up and put the lid back on the tin.

'Of course you can stay,' I said at last, 'I do understand things are hard for you all. It must be so difficult.'

Sara sighed with relief. 'It wouldn't be for long. Just a few weeks.'

Hang on, we had somehow gone from 'a few days' to 'a few weeks'.

What could I say? I wanted more than anything to be

supportive and helpful because that's what parents did in these circumstances.

'Okay,' I said, trying to sound both of those things, 'of course, if you're sure.'

'I'll tell the twins,' Sara said, smiling for the first time in days. 'Once John and his lot have gone, I'm sure they will settle down. You'll hardly know we are here. And the school is only a twenty-minute drive. And I need to make an appointment with a solicitor. John has a mate who works in town, I could see him. Start the ball rolling.'

'Well, at least have a talk and find out what your options are.'

Standing behind me, Sara swooped down to put an arm around my shoulders and kiss me on the cheek. She exuded an air of bitterness and my Chanel N° 5 bath oil.

'Thanks, Mum. You're the best. I don't know what I would do without you.'

Was I the best? When in my head I was nearly screaming?

'It's fine,' I said loosening her arm, which while affectionate was pressing uncomfortably on my throat. 'We'd need to draw up some ground rules for everyone. What time you'll be eating, what to do about laundry, that sort of thing.'

'Of course,' Sara said.

She came to sit next to me and put one hand over mine. Unfortunately, it was the one holding my coffee mug, and it slopped all over the table. Sara pulled a yard of kitchen roll off the dispenser and dabbed at it ineffectively.

'The twins are out most afternoons after school, with their clubs and extra activities. We usually eat at about six thirty. They're really not precious about food.'

'That's not the evidence that I've seen this week,' I said, 'they've hardly eaten a single meal without complaining about something. I've got a food delivery coming later; perhaps they could let me have some suggestions. And the broadband here is very slow. And unpredictable,' I said, 'you need to tell them that.'

'Oh, they won't mind,' Sara said, leaving the pile of coffee-sodden kitchen roll in front of me, 'and they look after themselves pretty well. Occasionally I have to go and rescue plates and bowls from their bedrooms, but as a rule, they are no trouble. I hardly know they are there most of the time. Gosh, I'm so relieved. I've been dreading asking you. I think I need a drink.'

She went into the pantry and found the bottle of sherry that *someone* had replaced empty on the shelf. She pulled a face and put it back. Then she took out the Cointreau and slugged the last of it into a glass, adding some ice cubes for good measure.

I thought of suggesting that she might be drinking rather too much than was good for her, but we were interrupted by a piercing and heart-rending scream from the sitting room, which suggested that Poppy was trying to take someone's teeth out without benefit of anaesthetic, and the now familiar shout of '*Mum, tell her...*'

'Oh, FFS,' Sara said, putting her glass down as she went in to see what the fuss was all about.

I sat looking at my coffee and tried to organise my thoughts. But suddenly I couldn't. There just seemed to be one problem after another. Perhaps when I was younger, I would have felt differently, but that day I wasn't sure that I had the strength to cope with it all. I had a ridiculous urge to run away from everything, to sit on a beach looking at the sea, or in the middle of some woodland listening to the breeze. Somewhere no one could ask me for anything.

At that moment my mobile rang, it was Isabel. At last, some sanity.

'*Bonjour ma soeur!*' she said cheerfully. 'How's my big sister this New Year's Eve?'

She sounded so happy, and I could almost imagine her sitting in her warm, friendly kitchen on one of the mismatched chairs, her feet up on another. Perhaps she would have a big bowl of *café crème* in front of her. There would be sunlight streaming in through the windows, her husband, Felix, and their two sons would be out somewhere doing something useful and manly. Chopping wood perhaps or servicing Isabel's car.

I almost said, the usual stuff: *Oh, I'm fine, how are you?* But suddenly I couldn't, my throat seemed to close up and to my horror I found myself on the brink of tears.

'We have been having a lovely time, slobbing around doing nothing,' Isabel continued, not waiting for me to answer, 'lots of food, far too much wine because our neighbours all gave us cases of the stuff when they came over, the Christmas tree fell over twice because one of the cats got in and tried to climb it, so there are pine needles everywhere. I really should get the hoover out but it'll only get dirty again, so really what's the point until Felix takes it away? I'll do it when my menfolk have gone back to work. I'm enjoying the peace and quiet. We are having work done on one of the *gîtes*, and we are expecting delivery of a shepherd's hut sometime in the spring, which is going to be very popular. I wouldn't mind moving in there myself. Now, what's the matter?'

My sister had always been able to do this. Swerve away from the subject and zone in on my mood, even though it seemed that she was being blithely oblivious to it. I felt somehow seen for the first time in days.

I took a deep breath. 'Oh, you know. I think I might be all

Christmas-ed out. This gap between Christmas and New Year always is a bit unsatisfactory, isn't it?'

'Are they being terrible? Are the girls fighting? Is Vanessa feeling out of sorts because she can't go shopping? Is Sara moping around because of Marty?'

I stood up and dropped the wad of dripping kitchen roll into the bin.

'All of the above,' I said.

'Poor you. When are they going?'

'John says they are going home the day after tomorrow. Sara has asked if she and the girls can stay on, she can't face going back home if Marty is going to be there. She seems to think he will have the new woman ensconced already.'

'He *wouldn't*?'

'I've no idea.'

'So how long for? Sara and the twins, I mean.'

I lowered my voice to a conspiratorial level. 'She started off saying a few days and then somehow it changed to a few weeks.'

Isabel gasped, and there was a silence which went on uncomfortably long as we both thought of something sensible to say. In the background I could hear a lot of shouting going on in my sitting room. Some argument about the television remote.

'What on earth is that racket? What's happening?' Isabel said at last.

'Sara's sorting out the girls. In her own fashion.'

There was another lull in our conversation and then Isabel gave an excited '*oooh*'. And then an even more excited squeak.

'What? What's the matter?'

'Joy, I've had one of my fabulous ideas. Come and stay with me *now*,' she said, 'have some fun for once.'

For a brief moment it was as though a door had opened up, and through it came the tempting and unrealistic vision of French sunshine, happy people, decent coffee, and garlic scented cassoulet. And the possibility of fun? That sounded very appealing.

'I'm not sure,' I said rather unconvincingly.

I was conflicted, confused by my own feelings. I knew that since my divorce I had been increasingly lonely, I had retired from a busy life teaching, and then almost immediately found myself living alone. Everything I was used to had changed. Where once there had been people, activities, and sometimes hardly a moment to myself, I was now living in a house that needed hardly any work, and occasionally I didn't speak to anyone all day. And yet when the house was full of people and noise and bustle, that left me stressed and anxious. What was the matter with me?

'You were going to come over here anyway, once Christmas and the New Year were over. You promised. Leave Sara and the girls to get on with things in your house, they probably need some time to process everything, things that you can't do for them even if you wanted to. You could stay in one of the *gîtes*, I think there might be one ready by the time you get here, the one you stayed in last time, and the other one that's being renovated, that should be ready too if my sons ever get their act into gear. Oooh, or you could move into the new shepherd's hut when it arrives. It is so cute and cosy, really, it would be such fun. You could be our first guest in there, like a sort of product tester, and then you can let us know what changes we need to make. You could help me with the *brocante*. I've got such a lot of new things that need sorting out. It would be lovely to see you again. You haven't been to see me for so long. Nearly three years.'

'John is going to America,' I said sadly.

'And? You're planning to pack for him and take them to the airport?'

'Well, no. Of course not,' I said, wondering if I should do exactly that.

No, of course I shouldn't, what a ridiculous thought. He was a grown man with a wife, a family and a career. He wasn't a kid needing lifts to football training or scouts.

'Right then, it's all settled. You can get John and his family off and leave Sara and the twins to calm down.'

'She did say she needed time alone to think,' I said, warming to the idea.

'And this would be her chance to have exactly that.'

'I don't think it's quite what she had in mind,' I said.

'No, I bet she thought you would just take over and be your usual efficient self, clearing up after them while she sits around doing nothing at all and the twins run you both ragged,' Isabel said.

Yes, my sister was probably right, I had imagined this scenario already, only too well. But would it be a good thing to do, to leave her in my house while I went off to visit Isabel? Surely that was unacceptable. Bad mother alert.

'I suppose she knows how everything works and where everything is. She says she feels safe here.'

'Then that's all you need to know,' Isabel said, 'stay as long as you like. You could help Felix in the bookshop or give me a hand with the stuff in the barn, I've got a load of marvellous things from a house clearance. Or you could just relax and get over the festive excitement.'

Festive excitement. There had been precious little of that, in fact the whole thing had been hard work and was gradually turning into a test of my endurance and peace-keeping skills, mixed in with huge meals that at least one person didn't like. And what about the Christmas decorations?

I felt a surge of new anger. Sod it; Sara knew perfectly well where things went. She'd done it in the past when I'd sprained an ankle.

'You know what I always say – "this too shall pass." And then some other BS will come along to take its place,' Isabel added.

Well, that was true, I knew that.

I wanted to feel angry, properly angry, just for once. For so many years I had put Stephen, the children, grandchildren and my job first. And myself last.

But like most women, I didn't do anger very well. We hide it in so many ways. Swallowing it down so that other people can express their feelings and we remain the silent peacemakers. Would Stephen have loved me more if I had been more critical? Argued with him? Would John and Sara still think I was a good mother if I had told them what I really thought?

I might be sixty-three, but I surely wasn't just there to be everyone's referee and dogsbody. Was I?

I knew exactly how Stephen would have behaved – he would have huffed a bit and left it to me to sort out, probably with some comment about how he expected to be allowed to enjoy a quiet retirement without the benefit of teenage arguments echoing down the stairs. Well suddenly, so did I.

He'd had absolutely no patience with such a thing as a fussy eater. *Eat it or stay hungry*, had been his motto. The prospect of vegetarianism appearing in our family, of children not wanting parsnips to touch the carrots or sprouts to be picked out of bubble and squeak would not have sat well with him.

'Be strong,' Isabel said, interrupting my thoughts.

I'd heard that voice all my life, persuading me into things I wasn't really sure about, places I didn't want to go, escapades that had got us both into trouble. And yet she had always won me round, by sheer force of her personality. Her boundless enthusiasm for festivals, concerts, adventures, and escapades. I had always been the cautious one, longing to be more like her.

She was still talking.

'You never know how strong you are until there's no option. Take a break, think of yourself for once. Have a few laughs. Have some fun. You were married to a man who refused to wear T-shirts, who bought John a chemistry set for his second birthday, thought tinned fruit with evaporated milk was the best dessert ever invented and considered central heating the work of the devil. I hope you've taken that awful portable gas heater out of your bedroom; I was always worried you were going to blow up or succumb to carbon monoxide poisoning. John and Sara are both fully formed adults now, with mortgages and kids and electricity bills. It's time you started the next bit.'

'What next bit?' I said wearily, wondering if I had any energy left.

'The rest of your life, you twit.'

7

I had imagined it would be more difficult. Like a *Mission Impossible* film, where there is an insurmountable set of obstacles to get past. Guard dogs and minefields and computer passwords to figure out. In the event, I just told them I was going to visit Aunt Isabel in Brittany for an indeterminate stay, and everyone said '*okay, great, have a good time.*'

Two days later I packed up my car and drove off. Leaving Sara and the girls waving cheerfully on the doorstep. I had wondered if I would regret my decision, but I didn't. For the first time in years, it seemed as though some burden had been lifted from my shoulders. I was still able to do this, make a choice, do something different, spend my money how I wanted to. Dare I say it, just for a change, put myself first instead of always last?

I caught the overnight ferry from Portsmouth to St Malo, leaving the rain behind and arriving early the following morning to a bright, French day. Even that made me feel better and more positive. I leaned over the edge of the ship's railing, watching the ferry approaching the quayside while anxious people rushed down the iron staircases to their cars. It felt odd to be doing this on my own, everyone else seemed to have a family or at least a companion.

The air felt fresher too. The sky bigger, and bluer. None of this was probably true, but I felt an unexpected leap of relief that no one was nagging me, asking for anything, or complaining about something. This immediately made me feel anxious all over again, that I was leaving Sara and her daughters to sort themselves out. Although yesterday the three of them had seemed unusually ebullient as they watched me leave.

I had driven a lot in France over the years because Stephen refused to, and I was looking forward to the journey to Isabel's house, where I was sure I would find the tranquillity I needed. Even if a tiny part of my brain reminded me that Isabel was anything but tranquil.

After the first few miles of jangling nerves, I settled into the journey. I had set directions on my satnav, and it piped up from time to time to encourage me on my way.

I was driving along the rather splendid N176, which apparently also liked to be called the E401, but I soon got used to its tricks. And I felt an unexpected leap of happiness that I was doing this. I was proving to myself that I was just as capable and organised as the next person.

The sun was shining, there wasn't much traffic and I gradually relaxed as I passed industrial estates, wooded slopes, and the occasional isolated farmhouse. I even thought about putting the radio on but decided against it. I found that if I was listening to the radio in the car, I sometimes needed to turn it down to see better. And that wasn't something I was prepared to risk in France, where one wrong turn might send me off to Nantes or Bordeaux or any number of towns where I might get completely lost.

The relative quiet and the beautiful scenery were enough entertainment for me then, and by the time I passed Lamballe, I was feeling quite relaxed. Despite it reminding me of the unfortunate Princess de Lamballe, favourite of Marie Antoinette, who came to a very unpleasant end.

After a while I turned off onto a new dual carriageway where the traffic was sparse and the scenery changed to broad, flat fields, with still the occasional farm or garage. It felt more familiar now, and my excitement grew with every mile. It felt as though I was heading for a place where I was going to be able to – what did the twins call it? – chill. Chillax. That was a very encouraging thought.

It was wonderful to be doing something different, not just plodding through the weeks, remembering which bin to put out on a Friday, not just cleaning the house and tweaking the garden. This was an adventure.

Perhaps there would be a cassoulet bubbling away in the oven, a basket of delicious bread and salty butter, some rough local wine from their friends' vineyards. Isabel would hug me and make me welcome. That night I would be sleeping in a quiet, comfortable bedroom, with perhaps just the echoes of the old house timbers creaking contentedly as I slept. Or maybe in one of the *gîtes*, knowing that no one was going to barge in crying or asking me to settle a dispute.

In the morning it would be sunny, with a brisk, refreshing wind coming from the river. Maybe the sounds of a few chickens scratching in the dirt. Did Isabel even have chickens? I didn't remember any but then it had been three years ago. She had been talking about getting some to go with the other animals that roamed around their house. Perhaps by now the dogs would stop leaping up at me every time I appeared in the kitchen...

I went back to my pleasant thoughts. I remembered the kitchen table that Felix had made many years ago out of an old barn door, where I had drunk perfect coffee from a pottery *bol*, the distinctive *café au lait* bowls that Isabel collected and displayed on her dresser. I imagined mounds of organic vegetables spilling out of a trug, waiting for Isabel to work her magic, making delicious meals.

I was distracted from my daydream of huge cushiony croissants and apricot jam by a massive, green tractor veering around the corner in front of me. Just as I was about to honk the horn and let fly with a fruity oath, I realised I was in the wrong, I had drifted onto the left side of the narrow road.

There was a screech of my brakes, a similar but industrial strength noise from the tractor, and then a volley of French words from the driver which I was pretty sure was not a cordial greeting. The tractor passed on, kicking up some clumps of gravel which peppered my windscreen like gunshots. I flinched, came to a spinning, abrupt halt on the grass verge, stalled the engine and sank down in my seat. Then I closed my eyes in relief that the whole event hadn't been worse.

The tractor sped away, probably with the driver's rude language floating behind him like black smoke, and I took a deep breath. I could feel my heart thudding, and all too easily imagine what might have happened. Me in a ditch probably with the airbags deployed and a broken nose, the front of the car crumpled. Then the arrival of the police, swiftly followed by the *Sapeurs-Pompiers* to cut me out of my car, and then an ambulance to cart me off to hospital. And all this in French. It didn't bear thinking about. Where were my insurance documents anyway?

I looked up and took an inventory of the damage. Apart from the fact that I was slewed at right angles across the narrow road, the worst thing that had happened was that my handbag had skidded off the seat next to me into the footwell, disgorging all its contents onto the floor. I heaved a heartfelt sigh, realising how lucky I had been, and got out of the car, going round the other side to open the passenger door.

Head down and bottom up I scrabbled around under the passenger seat to retrieve my purse, passport, various keys, two lipsticks that I hadn't known were in there, a small notebook and three – no four pens, a tin of breath mints, which had spilled out everywhere, a dry-cleaning ticket I thought I'd lost, a folding umbrella with a broken spoke, which had wedged itself into the carpet with the impact and my spare glasses. How could one reasonably ordinary handbag contain so much rubbish? And I thought I had cleared it out before I left home. Obviously not.

I paused from retrieving all the detritus and lay across the seat for a moment with my head in my hands, actually enjoying the break from the drive and the noise of the car engine.

I was startled by the irritated honking of a car horn somewhere behind me, and I jerked upright, banging my head on the door frame.

Stunned for a moment, and actually seeing stars, I rubbed the sore spot and looked around. A red truck sort of vehicle was waiting in the road, blocked of course by my car and the open passenger door. A man leaned out of the driver's window.

'*Dépêche-toi! Qu'est-ce tu fais?*'

Hurry up, what are you doing?

Bloody cheek, I would have thought it was obvious.

I backed out, rear end first, from my less than elegant position across the car seat and stood up. Ooh. a bit woozy there. I rocked gently for a moment and the newcomer beeped his horn again.

'*Seras-tu beaucoup plus longtemps?*'

'I don't know if I am going to be much longer. I've just had an accident!' I shouted, searching around in my memory banks for the right word. '*Un accident.*'

The man rolled his eyes and after a moment got out of his car. He was tall and long-legged, wearing the sort of blue boiler suit a lot of French farmers wear. He pulled off his baseball cap, revealing grey hair cropped close to his head.

'*Êtes-vous d'accord?* Okay?'

'*Oui,*' I said stiffly, not wanting him to take me for a complete fool. What other French words did I know? '*Pas mal.* Not bad.'

'*Alors, je suis pressé,*' he made some encouraging hand signals towards me, and slipped into English, which was a relief, 'I'm in a hurry. Perhaps you could move? Now?'

He sounded very annoyed, and I was suddenly cross. It felt as though a dam of frustration had suddenly burst inside me, and it all came flooding out in a torrent of irritation. It was absolutely not like me at all. Perhaps it was the adrenalin rush. The possibility that I might have been injured, my car written off, my holiday ruined before it had even begun.

I turned and faced him.

'And I've had a very early start, I didn't sleep very well on the ferry and nearly had a bad accident. Which, okay, might have been my fault because I was on the wrong side of the road, but I've only been here for a couple of hours, and everyone knows it takes time to get used to it. And I've had a really difficult time recently, with my family all being considered, and if you farmers didn't try to drive like Emerson Fittipaldi there wouldn't be a problem. And on top of that I might well be concussed, but don't let that bother you, you rude, obnoxious man. I'll gladly get out of your way and then I'll probably collapse in the ditch with a brain haemorrhage. How would that suit you?'

He pushed out his lower lip thoughtfully. I wondered how much of that he had understood.

'I cannot see any blood,' he said after a few minutes.

This made me even crosser. I felt like a stroppy child being admonished for not doing their homework.

'Oh dear, I'm terribly sorry about that. If I had known I was going to inconvenience you I would have bashed myself a bit harder, so it would have made it worth your while.'

He laughed. He actually laughed. The nerve of the man.

'I'm glad you didn't,' he said. 'Do you need an ambulance? *Médecin*? To see a doctor?'

I did a quick mental check on all my limbs and faculties.

'No,' I said, 'I don't.'

'*Bon*. Good. So perhaps you could...?' he made some vague, encouraging motions with his hands and I did some flouncing and slammed the passenger door closed, unfortunately catching the side of my coat and crunching on my favourite reading glasses (which had been in the pocket) at the same time.

I looked up at him and could see him biting back a smile that made me even more furious.

I opened the car door and freed myself with as much dignity as possible, and then I retrieved the mangled remains of my glasses and shoved them into my handbag, scattering some of the breath mints out onto the road.

'It's not funny,' I said.

'No, indeed,' he agreed.

'Right, I'm moving,' I said.

'Thank you,' he said, with a little bow.

I got back into the driving seat and turned the ignition, which mercifully fired up the first time. The last thing I would have needed was for my car to play up in revenge. Then, still very rattled, I forgot to put the car into reverse and jerked forward, nearly catapulting myself into the drainage ditch. I slammed on the brakes just in time and reversed onto the road, my tyres spinning on the mud. And then I pulled to one side, lowered my window and waved him past me. I don't think I trusted myself to move while he was there looking, and I certainly didn't want him following me down the lane.

He drove past me with another toot of his horn and a rather jaunty wave. He was definitely grinning. I resisted the urge to make a rude gesture at the back of his truck and bent and rested my head on the steering wheel for a moment. I'd been in such a great mood too before all this. That sort of outburst wasn't like me at all, and it wasn't his fault that I'd had an accident, I knew perfectly well it was mine. I'd been driving along, dreaming about what a lovely time I was going to have with my sister. Why hadn't I allowed myself to get this cross with my family? I evidently had a lot of pent-up rage and unfortunately that man had been the lucky recipient.

8

I drove on at a sedate pace. I was beginning to recognise things from my previous visits. A deserted barn at the side of the road, the doors hanging open, shreds of blue paint clinging to the hinges. Then a small town with a cute little church and a few shops. A woman in a floral apron was sweeping the pavement outside one of them. A man was walking past her, a newspaper under one arm and two French sticks wrapped in paper under the other. It was so classically French that it made me smile again.

There had been a café somewhere around here, I remembered, which had sold wonderful patisserie from what looked like the owner's front room. My mouth watered at the thought of *mille-feuilles* and strawberry tartlets. Feather light éclairs filled with custard cream, little *tartes tatins,* crispy and rich with buttery apples. Actually, at that moment the thought of them made me feel a bit nauseous, perhaps that was the adrenalin too. I'd never had that sort of reaction to cake before. I must have been rattled.

I turned off into an even smaller lane, which led to Isabel's house. There was an old sign and a large wooden arrow, propped against the hedge:

Ferme de Pommes de Terre

Potato Farm. She and Felix had built up a comfortable, slightly
rackety life between them, Isabel running their *gîtes* and
managing a barn filled with odds and ends of furniture and
random knick-knacks which the French call *brocante,* Felix with
his bookshop.

I reached the rutted driveway where the ironwork gates stood
permanently rusted open, and I was there at last, with no further
mishap. I let out a long sigh of relief.

Before the car had even stopped, Isabel's two dogs came
cannoning out of the house, yodelling their welcome and circling
the car as though they were herding me. Hoping they were
sensible enough to avoid getting run over, I stopped the car and
turned the engine off. Then I waited a few moments for Isabel to
come out of the kitchen door and shoo them away.

'Marcel! Antoine! *Arrêter maintenant!* Stop it!' she shouted. The
dogs slunk away, and she shouted after them '*Dans ton lit.* In your
bed!'

'Does that apply to me too?' I called across as I opened the car
door, 'I wouldn't mind.'

Isabel laughed and came over to hug me. She looked just the
same as she ever had. Her curly brown hair a bit flecked with grey
now, still trim and energetic, her fashion sense obviously as
eclectic as it ever had been too. A pair of reading glasses were
hanging around her neck on a bright red chain, and I remembered how she had always been losing them when she was
younger but refused to use such a thing because she thought it
was an 'old lady' thing to do. At sixty-one she had evidently got
over that.

'You're here at last!' she said. She leaned back and looked at
me. 'What on earth have you been doing? You look terrible!'

'Well, thanks for that, dear sister, you always were very free with the compliments,' I said. 'You don't look so hot yourself.'

She laughed and pushed her curls out of her eyes. Actually, she looked very happy, completely at ease with herself.

'You look very stressed. Is this a result of the cosy family Christmas you've enjoyed?'

'That and nearly having an accident on the way here.'

Her eyes widened. 'Really? Are you all right? What happened?'

'I forgot about driving *à droit*. I nearly collided with a tractor, and then I had a very embarrassing encounter with a farmer. And then I nearly drove into the ditch, and I slammed my coat in the car door and broke my glasses. Apart from that...'

'You twit,' Isabel said, putting an arm around my shoulders. 'Come on, leave your bags for now, you need some coffee.'

The dogs had not retreated obediently to their beds but had slunk out of the kitchen again and were circling us, tongues lolling.

'Take no notice of them,' Isabel said, 'they'll soon start ignoring you.'

I paused at the open kitchen door, remembering the last time I was there, when I had still been getting used to doing so many things on my own.

The first trip without Stephen, the first birthday, the first summer, the first Christmas. It felt very different this time, I supposed that the passing of the years had indeed made a difference. Looking back, the decades we had shared together felt as though they had been a long dream, or someone else's life.

Standing there while Isabel bustled about, sweeping piles of newspaper off the table and looking without success for somewhere to dump them, putting dirty plates and mugs into the sink and then finding two clean ones, I felt quite sad and philosophical for a moment and then I was nearly knocked flying as one of the dogs leapt up to punch me in the back with its front paws.

'Antoine! *Non!*' Isabel shouted, and the dog scurried off under the table where it had spotted something appealing. The other dog followed and there was a brief growling tussle before both of them scooted outside to have a further argument over a bone.

Isabel pulled me inside and closed the lower half of the stable door with a sigh of relief.

'Worse than children,' she said, 'now how about that coffee?'

The kitchen was just as I remembered, a large room with a low, beamed ceiling. There were small windows along one side and the walls been painted a dull russet colour which made it seem smaller than it was. It was also filled with an assortment of mismatched chairs, the huge table I remembered, a painted wooden dresser filled with an assortment of mugs, plates, *bols*, wicker baskets filled with paperwork and a big stone pot containing pens and pencils. There were iron and copper cooking pans hanging from hooks on the walls and rather oddly a branched candelabra in the middle of the ceiling that someone had raised out of the way with a length of orange baler twine and a huge nail. Felix and the boys were all over six feet tall, and presumably at some point one – or all – of them had grown tired of bumping into it.

'Gosh, this place is a mess,' Isabel said, moving around, picking things up and putting them down again, 'I meant to have a bit of a tidy up before you got here but then – well, I didn't. Now take your coat off, sit down and tell me all your news.'

I did as I was told, brushing ineffectively at the muddy paw marks on the back of my coat and Isabel switched the kettle on, found a cafetière and spooned some coffee into it.

'Tell me about this accident,' she said, 'was anyone hurt?'

I shook my head. 'No, and it was all my fault. I was very lucky considering I could have been flattened by a tractor. But then some man in a red truck had to stop because I was blocking the road, and he made me feel like a complete fool.'

Isabel looked up, interested. 'Red truck? Was he tall, about our age and rather attractive?'

'I suppose so,' I said.

Isabel passed me a large mug of proper coffee and I paused for a moment to savour the wonderful aroma. And enjoy the fact that someone else had made it for me.

'Baseball cap?'

'Yes. And he laughed at me, which was very unfair because I think I was in a state of shock.'

Isabel nodded. 'That sounds like the professor.'

'Professor?'

'When he first came here someone said he looked like Harrison Ford, you know the archaeology professor in Indiana Jones, and the nickname stuck.'

I thought about it. Yes. I suppose there was a certain resemblance.

'Jean-Luc Fournier. He's retired, we started off calling him the professor but in fact I think he used to be a doctor. In Paris. He bought a terrible old cottage from us on the other side of the river some years ago. It's a nice spot but we weren't using it and heaven knows we needed the money. It would have cost us too much to restore and no one around here seemed to want it. He's been reno-vating it for nearly three years. He's a nice chap but not what you would call sociable. That's Parisians for you. They are different.'

'Never mind him, tell me about your lot. How is Felix?'

'Back at work in the bookshop, although I think he reads the books more than he sells them. You must go and see the improve-ments he's made since you were last here. There's going to be a whole new section of books in English for the ex-pats. It'll be very popular. Pierre and Sylveste are still doing the landscaping and gardening business. They get a lot of work with the ex-pats too. Only recently they were helping a pair of sisters clear out their garden and sort out a disused swimming pool. They're always busy.' Isabel jumped up and went into the cavernous pantry, returning with a battered tin in her hands. 'I've just remembered, I made a cake in your honour. It's a bit lopsided but still edible. Now, tell me about Christmas. Was it very awful? You sounded so stressed out whenever I rang you.'

I filled her in on the highlights and she was appropriately horrified, shocked, sympathetic, and amused. Telling her all about the endless squabbles, the noise and muddle somehow made me feel better about the whole thing. Saying it out loud made it almost sound funny rather than the exasperating trial it had seemed at the time.

I finished my coffee and Isabel topped it up again, and then she cut me a chunk of cake, which I think was apricot and honey. It looked as though it had been dropped on the floor, and possibly it had, but it was delicious.

'And was Vanessa still as exhausted and limp as ever? How she will cope in New York is anyone's guess.'

'She did seem to need a lot of little naps,' I said, 'and she would spend hours in her bedroom doing her hair. Although she did always look lovely. You can tell John adores her, which is very sweet.'

'And Sara? Still angry? Still drinking too much? I can understand why she wanted some space away from Martin.'

'Marty, he's called Marty now,' I said with a grin.

'Well, we know what that rhymes with,' Isabel said, with a lift of one eyebrow.

'Stop it, they may make up, despite everything. I can't say anything too inflammatory just yet, in case they do, and after all he is the twins' father. I need to tread a fine line between being supportive and sympathetic, and not going off on one about his selfishness and the way he made just about every woman he met feel slightly uncomfortable.'

'That awful back stroking,' Isabel agreed.

'Stop it!'

'So what would you like to do, now you're here?'

I gave a sigh of contentment. 'Nothing in particular. You said I could stay in one of the *gîtes*? Shall I get my bags in and get settled?'

'Ah, well there's a slight problem there. Pierre and Sylveste have been doing some renovations over the winter, and as usual they got side-tracked and I ran out of money, so they haven't finished yet. I thought you could stay here in the house for a few days. Just until they sort everything out, a few minor tweaks.'

'Okay. What are they doing?'

'There's a leak in the roof of one, and the other has no running water at the moment. They are like their father, really good at getting on with a job, but not so good at finishing it off before they start something else. And they have been a bit preoccupied getting the hard standing ready for the shepherd's hut, but we have had so much rain recently they couldn't pour the concrete. It's due to arrive in about two weeks. I can't wait to see it. Perhaps you could stay in there and do a sort of test run before the paying guests arrive in March. At least I think it's March. It might be April.'

'That sounds fun. So, when exactly do bookings start?'

Isabel looked vague. 'I don't know. I think it's all written down somewhere, or Felix might have updated the spreadsheet on the computer. He was messing about with it over Christmas and I'm not sure he got it finished. Perhaps—'

Isabel went over to the dresser and pulled out a sheaf of papers from one of the drawers. A few fell on the floor and immediately one of the dogs raced over, claws clattering on the flagstone floor, to snatch them. There followed a brief tussle, and eventually Isabel retrieved the paper, by then a bit torn, and damp around the edges.

'Yes, here we are. First bookings are the weekend of March 6 or is that 16? It's a bit smudged.'

I shook my head. Yes, it had always been like this when we were growing up. While I had been the methodical, tidy one, Isabel had always been the exact opposite. Her room was permanently a shambles, homework was never done on time, it was a miracle she had managed to pass any exams at all. I remembered the parents' evenings when teachers had all said much the same thing.

'Mrs Cavendish, Joy is a pleasure to have in any class, but Isabel is very different.'

And they didn't mean it in a good way.

'I hope you are going to pitch in and help,' she said, 'you were always better at making a house look pretty than I was. To me all a bathroom needs is clean towels, a new loo roll, and some hand-wash, you were the one who did all the fussy stuff with flowers and roller blinds and stencils.'

'I'd be happy to help,' I said, 'if I'm here long enough.'

'When are you leaving?'

'You're not supposed to ask guests that the moment they arrive,' I said laughing, 'give it a couple of days!'

At that moment, home felt a long way away. Here, in my sister's chaotic house, I was already beginning to relax. I felt suddenly hopeful that here I could find a new strength, sort out a reason to be optimistic about the future. To finally have the time and space to decide what to do.

'So how was your Christmas?' I asked.

'Oh, you know, quiet. We had the Christmas Eve meal and

then we tottered off down the road to Midnight Mass. And when we got back we had a few drinks with the neighbours. And Pierre and Sylveste and their girlfriends. And the local headmaster and his wife, and a couple of their friends who were staying with them, and Eugénie of course, we couldn't leave her out. I think she watches this house with binoculars, and if she sees any signs of a gathering or visitors she's up here like a shot.'

'How old is she now?'

'Eugénie? Eighty-four, but you wouldn't know it to look at her. Felix says his mother is a witch, and she's done some immortality ritual. She still lives alone in the cottage at the end of the driveway. She will have spotted you arriving, so brace yourself, I expect her to turn up at any moment.'

'That sounds a bit worrying,' I murmured.

I remembered Isabel's mother-in-law from my previous visits. She was quite a character, always immaculately dressed, with sharp eyes that missed nothing and a tongue to match. If she had been my mother-in-law, I don't think I would ever have had a moment's peace, but as I remembered, Isabel dealt extremely well with her.

'And then on Christmas Day, we had a big meal, but I expect it was pretty much the same as yours. Smoked salmon to start with, some of our friends do their own, it's absolutely delicious. Roast turkey, with chestnuts, then the famous *bûche de noël*, we have to have that, or Pierre has a sulk. It's supposed to celebrate the end of winter, but somehow, I doubt it's over. And then that evening some of the neighbours came around for a drink and some nibbles, and we ended up playing charades, and I had a terrible hangover the next day because Bertrand from the village brought some *chouchen* – it's a sort of apple mead, and I really shouldn't drink it. And then on Boxing Day, we just hung around, and I did a big buffet and nothing special really happened, but a lot of people dropped in. It was great fun. The glass recycling bin wouldn't close it was so full. I expect you did much the same.'

I gave an ironic laugh. 'It doesn't sound very quiet to me.'

'No, it wasn't, but at least the accordion didn't come out this year, I'd hidden it in the barn.'

Actually, it sounded enormous fun to me, the sort of jolly, family time I had been hoping for over Christmas. It made me sad to think that we had missed out on such an opportunity, and the days had instead been punctuated by disagreements and sulking.

'Have you had snow yet?'

'Rain,' I said, 'plenty of rain.'

'Same here. It's a shame, isn't it? I'm absolutely positive that we had snow every Christmas day when we were kids.'

Isabel stopped trying to clear up the kitchen table and stood with her hands on her hips, thinking.

'Right, that's better. Now then let's take your bags upstairs and then we can think about what to do for dinner. There's so much food in this house, and yet there never seems to be anything to eat. Or at least that's what Sylveste tells me. And I keep telling him he doesn't live here any more, but it makes no difference.'

* * *

Ten minutes later there was a perfunctory rap on the kitchen door frame.

'*Bonjour, c'est moi.*'

Isabel had been correct in her assumption, and her mother-in-law, Eugénie, was there, wrapped in a beautiful red coat, clutching a Hermès handbag in one hand and a pot of jam in the other. She didn't seem to have aged a day since I last met her.

The dogs, who had been frisking around outside obviously recognised a worthy opponent and sat down at her feet.

Eugénie jerked her chin at them.

'*S'en aller*,' she said. Go away, and they did. I would have to remember that for next time they tried to bowl me over.

'Ah,' she said, sounding surprised to see me although I was sure she wasn't, 'Joy.'

We exchanged the obligatory cheek kisses, and she took her coat off and leaned back to look at me.

'You are ill,' she said, her voice gravelly with probably a lifetime of *Gauloise* cigarettes, 'you look terrible. Your skin is *gris*... grey. Perhaps you need some of my Clarins. I have a spare pot of their restorative night cream. I will bring it for you on my next visit. If the Lord spares me. Now sit down before you fall down.'

I did as I was told, feeling as though I was the eighty-four-year-old and not her, and to be fair she didn't look her age. She had that enviable look of some French women, perfect posture, a trim figure, a slick of scarlet lipstick and a certain sparkle in her eyes. Dressed in navy slacks, a striped Breton sweater and an artfully tied silk scarf around her throat, she made me feel as ungainly as an unmade bed. And she was probably right, I did look awful. Bags under my eyes from lack of sleep, travelling and worry, and no one would have said I looked the least bit chic.

'I have brought you some of my home-made *confiture de figue*. Fig jam. It is the last jar, and by the looks of her, Joy needs some decent nourishment. English food is so dull and brown.'

Isabel sprang to my defence. '*Mamie*, leave Joy alone. She has only just arrived, and she doesn't need your opinions.'

I wondered how Eugénie would take this back chat, but she just shrugged and pouted, not at all offended and sat down at the kitchen table.

'I will take coffee if some is offered. Black, no sugar. We all eat too much sugar.' She darted a disapproving look at the cake next to me.

Isabel poured coffee into a porcelain coffee cup decorated with roses and pushed it with its matching saucer across the table towards her. Eugénie picked it up and pursed her lips towards the steaming drink.

'So now then, tell me all your news,' she said.

'I saw you yesterday, *Mamie*, you know it all already.'

Eugénie pulled a *moué* of dissatisfaction. 'Then make something up. Just to amuse me. Or perhaps Joy has more interesting things to tell me.'

She turned her piercing dark eyes towards me, and I wondered how much I should tell her. I didn't really want to go into it all, it was a bit depressing, and I was beginning to wonder – with the benefit of distance – if I had overreacted in running away here.

'I needed a break, after Christmas,' I said, 'and Isabel kindly invited me to stay.'

She nodded and gave me a sympathetic look, which made me feel a bit better.

'So, I understand you had a difficult time, so often one cannot please everyone no matter how hard you try. People with foods they won't eat, personalities clash where once there was friendship. Perhaps too much wine was drunk? Now your son and his family have gone to America, and you have left your daughter and granddaughters quarrelling in your house while her divorce is settled? Do you think that was wise?'

So, she knew just about everything anyway. I looked across at my sister and she gave me an apologetic grimace.

'I did what I thought was best for them,' I said, 'under difficult circumstances.'

Eugénie finished her coffee and put the cup down with a tiny chinking noise on the saucer.

'*La famille est l'un des chefs d'oevre de la nature.* Family is nature's masterpiece.'

I wasn't sure if she approved or not. Or exactly what she was getting at so I decided to ignore it.

'Joy had an accident on the road between here and the village, perhaps that is why she is rather stressed,' Isabel said. 'A tractor nearly ran her off the road.'

'These farmers. Just because they are bigger than you, they drive like maniacs,' Eugénie said.

'Jean-Luc helped her out,' Isabel added.

Eugénie's eyes brightened. 'Ah yes, Jean-Luc. A man like that is always helpful. Which I for one would enjoy. *Les médecins sont fascinants.* Doctors are fascinating. They know so many interesting things, and what they don't know they can ask their friends. If I were ten years younger and didn't need them quite so much in a professional capacity, I would not allow him to be so reclusive. You should invite him over for dinner, in fact that is a very good idea. I insist you do. It would be – *de bon voisinage* – neighbourly.'

I wasn't sure I liked the sound of this. I had come here for some peace and quiet, not to have Eugénie organising my time. But there was another part of me that realised that life here held different possibilities, and if I wanted things to change for the better, it might be a good idea to be a bit less rigid.

9

Eugénie stayed for quite a while, eventually leaving when Isabel made very pointed comments about how tired I must be after my journey, and how I needed time to settle into my room.

This time it was me in the attic because Isabel said it was the most comfortable bed. A space that had been converted some years ago by Felix and his sons in to a large room under the bending beams of the roof. Half the room at the far end was taken up with exactly the sort of stuff one would expect to find there. Cardboard boxes sealed and taped up, a broken lampstand, which apparently Felix was planning to repair one day, some dining chairs with ragged covers and even an old wardrobe propped up on bricks. However, in the area I was to use, there was a beautiful old sleigh bed, which looked as though it was carved from mahogany, a painted chest of drawers and a blue velvet armchair.

'The *gîte* you stayed in last time will be finished soon and then you can move in there,' Isabel said, looking around with some uncertainty, 'but this will be okay for now, won't it?'

'Of course,' I said, looking up and hoping the roof didn't leak.

'The bathroom is at the bottom of the stairs, I will bring you a tray with a kettle and some tea things, so you don't have to go downstairs first thing if you don't want to. The dogs will jump over you if you do. I've got some tea bags for you. I wonder where they are...'

'Brilliant, thank you,' I said.

'Right, I'll leave you to get unpacked. I'll be downstairs in the kitchen trying to get my head around lunch. Although I don't expect Felix back before this evening. What would you like?'

'Nothing much,' I said, 'I'm still full of coffee and cake.'

'Perhaps I'll just get a few things out then, and you can decide. Some bread and cheese or something.'

'Sounds fine,' I said, 'you don't have to go to any trouble.'

'I wasn't going to,' Isabel said grinning, 'you're just as capable of making a sandwich as I am. Just relax.'

Yes, perhaps I should have taken that attitude with my family, instead of insisting I did everything. Maybe I had been my own worst enemy.

I sat on the edge of the bed after she had gone and looked out of the window. The fields stretched out below me, down the slope to where the little river ran. On the other side of it I could see a single house, and beside it a thin plume of blue smoke rising into the still air. It looked like there was a bonfire burning in the garden. Perhaps that was the old place that Jean-Luc was busy renovating.

I wondered what his life there was like. He had come from Paris after all, where presumably he had led a busy life. And yet he had chosen to live here, in the depths of the countryside, with no neighbours nearby. I wondered why he had done that.

And then I remembered how I had shouted at him, and been rude, and I felt my face grow hot at the memory. I hoped Isabel wouldn't invite him over for dinner, and if she did, that he would make some excuse not to come. Or perhaps I could pretend to have a headache and retire to my room. No, that would be silly and childish. I would be complaining about the vegetables touching in the dish next.

And if I was honest, I had been the one in the wrong. I had been daydreaming, not concentrating on the road. It hadn't been Jean-Luc's fault. There was no reason why I couldn't just apologise to him, talk to him in a reasonable way and be a bit braver about meeting new people. Starting with him.

* * *

I unpacked and only put a few things into the wardrobe, after all I was not sure how long I would be staying in this room, and then I found my phone. There were two messages from John telling me something of the glories of Manhattan and attaching a photo of his office, which seemed to have walls made of glass and an incredible view over other skyscrapers. The girls had settled in quite well and had already been invited to two birthday parties. Vanessa had contacted an old school friend called Beatrice and signed up for a gym and t'ai chi classes.

Sara had sent several messages, asking where the spare tea towels were kept, did I have various pieces of kitchen equipment, would I mind if the girls had a couple of friends for a sleepover and telling me that two glasses had been broken and were they very special or could she just get some from the supermarket.

I sent a message to them both and a photograph of the lovely view out of my attic window, telling only the briefest highlights of my journey, and then sent a message to Sara reassuring her that the glasses were nothing special, a sleepover was fine and not to worry about me.

Then I went back downstairs looking for Isabel and feeling surprisingly rather hungry. After so many weeks of full-on housework and activity, it felt very strange to have nothing in particular to do. No meals to prepare, no towering ironing pile, no need to go out for more milk or biscuits.

The kitchen was empty, the top half of the stable door open and for a moment I stood with my hands hanging, feeling rather unsure what to do. Should I go outside? Should I go back up to my room pretending I needed a handkerchief or something?

In the end I sat down at the kitchen table, liking the feel of the old wood under my palms. So many family meals and arguments and discussions had taken place around it, it had been worn smooth by many hands and cloths, newspapers, and dishes over the years, not by polish.

I looked around at the rest of the room, the worktops were cluttered with piles of catalogues, letters, a wooden box of seed packets, a large ball of twine and pieces of a broken coffee pot. There was a screwed-up tea towel in the sink, and two gigantic leeks, their roots covered with mud.

I remembered Stephen on one of his visits here, musing that perhaps we should stay in the *gîte* as this kitchen was a health hazard. But as I looked at it now, I thought it had a certain charm.

I could hear one of the dogs barking outside, an excited frantic noise that grew louder accompanied by the sound of a car coming up the drive. I felt a moment's ridiculous panic, wondering what I would do or say if a stranger came to the house looking for Isabel and rattling away in French at a speed with which my schoolgirl studies would not cope.

Then a face appeared at the door: a man, tall, rangy and smiling, his thinning hair covered by a cotton cap.

'Ah! Joy!' he said.

It was my brother-in-law, Felix, a canvas bag over one shoulder, which he brought in and dumped on the table, spilling out a load of battered books and paperwork. The two dogs followed him in and sniffed around his feet until he nudged them aside with a knee.

'Welcome, welcome,' he said cheerfully, coming forward to kiss me on both cheeks, 'I hope you have had a good journey. Has Isabel abandoned you already? This is very naughty of her.'

'I'm fine,' I said, 'she was here a minute ago. I don't think she can have gone far.'

'Oh, she will be in the barn I expect, trying to make sense of um, um *les nouveaux draps* – the new linens she found in Morlaix. Such things that were going on a bonfire, so she says. You know your sister; she will never throw anything away if she can avoid it.'

'I know,' I said, remembering the state of her childhood bedroom, 'she was always the same when we were growing up.'

'And so, muddle, muddle everywhere, as you can see. And I am just as bad.'

He chuckled and dumped his woollen jacket on the back of a chair.

'I have come home early, to see that you got here safely and also to go through some of the accounts,' he pointed at the pile of paperwork on the table. 'Lisa can cope without me for once.'

'I'm fine,' I said, 'a very smooth ferry crossing.'

'And you weren't hurt when you had the accident?'

Good grief. Did everyone know everything? Were people on the phone all the time to each other – passing on gossip and interesting bits of news? It wasn't like this at home, where everyone kept out of each other's business. We got on okay but sometimes days could go by, and I didn't see any of my neighbours. In fact, it had been three months before I found out the Robinsons two doors down from me, had migrated to New Zealand and the house had been sold to the couple who owned The Cheese Press gift shop.

'It wasn't exactly an accident,' I said.

Felix pulled a face. 'Well Henri said you were all over the place. He wondered if you were ill or had fallen asleep at the wheel?'

'Henri?'

'He was driving his tractor and said you were on the wrong side of the road. He would have stopped but he's been having some trouble with his starter motor and once it stalls he has a devil of a job getting it started again.'

Ah, yes.

'It was entirely my fault,' I said, 'I was just daydreaming, enjoying the scenery. I wasn't concentrating. Anyway, no harm done.'

'No, Jean-Luc said you were fine when I saw him in the village...'

For heaven's sake. Did everyone know everything?

'...Apart from your broken glasses. He said to tell you there is *un opticien* in Landivisiau who might be able to help you.'

Talk about Big Brother is watching you.

'That's fine,' I said, 'I have a spare pair.'

At that moment Isabel came in holding a straw basket that contained several eggs.

Her face lit up when she saw Felix and she put the eggs down on top of his paperwork and came across to kiss him. Felix gave her an affectionate hug and then patted her on the bottom. They had been together for nearly forty years and married for thirty. I didn't know of any married couples who did that after such a long time together. My marriage certainly hadn't been like that.

I felt rather wistful for a moment. What would it be like to be married to a man who looked at you properly, whose eyes twinkled with delight when you came into a room? I couldn't for a moment imagine it.

'Five eggs today,' she said, 'they are doing quite well considering the dark mornings. They'll do better when we get into spring. I was going to make some leek soup for lunch, but the time has got away from me. Shall we just pop out and get something in the café? You remember that place, don't you, Joy? I'm sure you've been there before.'

'Good idea,' Felix said absentmindedly, leafing through his paperwork, 'I can do this later.'

'You said that last week. And the week before,' Isabel murmured.

'*Mieux vaut tard que jamais*... better late than never,' Felix said, jangling his car keys, '*allons-y*. Let's go. I've just remembered, I need to speak to Louis about something anyway.'

We went to the village, Felix driving his old Renault at some speed down the middle of the country road in much the same way that I had done earlier. He said it was to avoid the potholes. I clung to the seat with both hands and hoped Henri and his tractor were not still around.

In the afternoon sunlight, the town looked charming. The bell in the church tower was tolling a single note, there were people queueing outside a shop with a faded red door and newspaper stuck over the windows, which Isabel reminded me was the local bakery; and some were already walking away with three, four or more long loaves from the afternoon bake under their arms. The French really must eat a lot more bread than I had realised.

At last, we pulled up outside an unremarkable little building with '*Bar des Sports*' painted in blue above the door and a couple of iron tables and chairs placed optimistically on the pavement outside, and yes, I remembered it. Stephen and I had been taken there once about ten years ago and the basic nature of the establishment (he had spent some time looking for a hygiene rating certificate) and the food had not gone down well with him. Particularly when he realised that the customer at the next table, white napkin tucked under his neck, was enjoying a couple of braised pig's feet.

Anyway, Felix didn't so much park the car, as leave it half on the pavement a few steps from the entrance, and we went in. It didn't seem to have changed at all from what little I could remember. The interior walls and ceilings were still stained a distinctive nicotine brown, the grey marble tabletops matched the serving counter, and the chairs were a mismatch from several different decades. Behind the counter was a selection of spirit and liqueur bottles on wooden shelves stretching up to the ceiling, and *Monsieur le Patron* was dabbing a cloth at the ones at the front with no particular enthusiasm.

He turned around as we came in and his face broke into an expansive smile. He was evidently so overjoyed to see us that he came out from behind his counter to shake hands all round and even do the cheek-kissing thing with Isabel.

There then followed a long, chuckling conversation in French, most of which escaped me, after that we were encouraged to sit down at *la meilleure table* – the best table, after he had first turfed a fat tabby off one of the seats.

I watched my sister joining in, her French and her understanding of the conversation obviously fluent. I know she had lived here for most of her adult life, but I still found it a bit odd. I suppose parents seeing their adult child in a Hollywood blockbuster or performing at the Albert Hall must feel the same way. I stood proudly watching her, wondering what Miss Travis, who had tried and failed to teach us both French at school, would think.

There was something about her life that some – our parents

and Stephen for example – might have seen as unsatisfactory, but I was beginning to realise it was far more colourful and – yes – happier than mine had been. I had not taken risks, not really stuck up for myself, not lived my life to the full. I felt a new determination growing.

Even in the short time since I had been here, I wanted to change, to feel real connection with my own life again, to have fun, before it was too late.

'Now then, what shall we have?' Isabel said. There was a laminated menu sheet wedged between a glass vase of artificial daffodils and a pepper mill, and she picked it up.

'I don't know why you are bothering to look,' Felix said, 'you know as well as I do, what you are going to have.'

'Onion soup,' Isabel agreed, passing the menu to me, 'it's the best.'

I looked at the menu uncertainly, pulling it back and forwards to try and get it into focus. I might have some spare reading glasses, in fact, I had several pairs, but they were all back in my room.

'I'll have the same,' I said.

Isabel turned in her chair. 'Louis, *trois soups à l'oignon.*'

Louis flapped a hand at her. '*Bien sûr!*' Of course. 'I'll tell Paulette.'

Evidently we were all having the same thing.

'Excuse me, I need a word with him,' Felix said, wandering off to the bar where he was presented with a tall glass of lager.

'So, how are you feeling? I'm so glad you're here,' Isabel said.

I reached across and squeezed her hand, feeling rather emotional.

'So am I.'

'You're not fretting about Sara and the twins I hope?'

'No. Of course not. Well, maybe a bit,' I admitted.

'They'll be fine. I guarantee it. Sara needs time to get on with her life, to be independent. And she's lucky to have found a place where she is able to do that. It was very generous of you to leave them there.'

I laughed. 'Generous or stupid. Except Vanessa told me I'm not allowed to say stupid. So perhaps I'll say foolish instead.'

Isabel chuckled. 'Vanessa is such a *good* mother isn't she. She makes my head spin. We weren't like that, and the kids turned out okay in the end, didn't they? Tell me all about John and his new job.'

Had I been a good mother? Stephen had been the disciplinarian; I had been the soft touch when the children were growing up. His response to most of their requests had been '*no*', mine had usually been '*well, I'll see*', which was usually interpreted as yes.

Should I have been tougher on them? Should I have said something to Sara about her alcohol intake over Christmas instead of making excuses for her? Made a few comments about the rudeness of my granddaughters? Pulled everyone up for their untidiness? Asked for some co-operation instead of being such a martyr? Yes, I probably should, and I felt irritated with myself all over again.

Felix brought us a carafe of local red wine and we sat and chatted about things while the occasional customer came in for a drink or something to eat. Every time, there was a lot of hand-shaking and loud laughter and sometimes, Louis came out from behind the bar and slapped someone on the back in greeting. It was all very relaxed and pleasant, and I thought about the wine bar back home where Stephen had liked to go – The Oak Barrel – where everything was pale grey, coordinated and unremarkable. Much like our lives together, if I thought about it.

They liked to play Vivaldi or in the evenings some cool jazz in order to liven up the proceedings. The food was good but fussy, but that's what Stephen had liked. Many times, I had gone home hungry after a meal there and had some toast and Marmite to fill me up.

We talked about Pierre and Sylveste and their landscaping business, how they had recently bought a new truck and were inundated with work.

Isabel explained. 'There are a lot of second homeowners, who only come once or twice a year, and the rest of the time the houses are rented out to holiday makers. This area is very popular. Not too far from the ferry ports, near the beaches, lots of little towns to explore. Our *gîtes* are nearly always busy in the high season, that's why we are getting a shepherd's hut. Such a cute thing, just one bedroom, a tiny shower room, and everything you need. I wouldn't mind moving in there, except Felix says I would have it looking like a jumble sale in no time.'

'And the barn?' I said. 'The *brocante*. Is that going well?'

'It could be better. I had such a lovely time in the autumn, going to flea markets and antique fairs. You can still pick up such lovely old things for a song around here. I just need to get the barn sorted out and presentable for the spring visitors. If you want to help me do that, I will love you forever.'

'I will,' I said.

I liked the idea of that. It was the one thing I hadn't thought through when I decided to come here. I was so used to having something to do since I'd retired from teaching, even if it was looking after my husband when he was still around, housework, gardening or cooking for the Women's Institute market, and the lead up to Christmas and the weeks that followed had been a lot of bustle and activity. Now I needed something new to focus on. If I didn't, I could imagine myself getting very bored indeed, and while I didn't have the energy of my younger self, I still had a very active mind.

I suddenly felt a surge of optimism. Whatever I did, it would be something different, not something that people would expect me to do. I would try to open myself up to the possibilities of travel or hobbies or people. I wanted my family to look at me with astonishment, perhaps even admiration.

What on earth are you doing, Mum?

Louis' wife, Paulette, came through from the kitchen at that point with a laden tray that she deposited on the table between us. She was a well-rounded woman of about my vintage, with dazzling blue eyes, a beautiful smile and russet curls bound up with a chic, silk headscarf.

'Enjoy,' she said, 'this is my best, my favourite, I make this with love, and it is all the better for it.'

There were three white, china lionhead bowls and the heavenly smell of French onion soup and toasted gruyère cheese rose up, making my mouth water. There was bread too, in a wicker basket, the crust crackled and golden. Paulette clasped her empty tray to her bosom and gave us a rather misty-eyed look before she went back to her kitchen.

'Did I ever tell you she was once a Dior model?' Isabel said.

'Really?' I said, watching her go.

'So Eugénie told me.'

Felix came to join us.

'Louis says he will put the posters up, for the bookshop and the French evening classes I'm going to run,' he said, 'There's always someone coming in wanting to learn basic French, so why not? We could do with the money.'

There was a large, cheese-covered crouton on top of my soup, and everything was the temperature of molten lava. It was delicious. As I ate, I almost felt as though it was the first real food I had eaten perhaps in years. But it wasn't just the food, it was the whole experience of that simple meal. The French-ness of it all.

The modest red wine in the scratched glass carafe, the simple flavours, the unpretentiousness of the place. There was a quiet hum of conversation, none of which I could really understand. Occasional laughter. People coming and going. My sister opposite me, relaxed and happy. And I was there too, enjoying it.

Our parents had despaired of Isabel when she was growing up. She was always so unpredictable, so wilful while I had been the obedient child. When she had announced she was dropping out of university after two years to go and live with Felix Moreau in Aquitaine without the benefit of marriage, they had been horrified. All that promise and intelligence wasted so that she could go and live in some sort of hippy commune, they said.

I, meanwhile, had got my degree, taught in a private school where I had later married my head of department, and set up home in a leafy and respectable suburb. Which one of us had made the better life, I wondered. Perhaps my parents and Stephen had been wrong, it wasn't all about exam results and money. Maybe there was more to life than just using the right cutlery, going to the best places, having the right beliefs. Perhaps there was more to life than that. But what was it? What was missing? I wanted – no I *needed* – to find out.

10

'Delicious,' I said at last, putting my spoon down with a contented sigh.

'Told you,' Isabel said. 'We can always have leek soup another day.'

Felix poured the last of the wine into my glass despite my protests and I took a hefty swig of it, not wanting people (I mean come on, which people?) to notice that I had more than anyone else. At the same moment the door opened and a man walked in. The professor. Jean-Luc Fournier.

He stood for a moment, shrugging off his coat, looking around. He looked so ridiculously attractive that for a moment I lost proper coordination.

I gasped and of course the wine went down the wrong way, making me splutter all over myself and the table.

Like a couple of other customers, he looked straight at me, and even though my eyes were streaming, I could see a little smile crossed his face. Great, now I really did look like a clown.

Felix was on his way to the bar again and he stopped to do some vigorous hand shaking with the new arrival.

'Ah, Luc. *Ça va?*' How's it going?

'*Ça va bien.*'

They started to engage in a discussion where *travaux de construction* was mentioned more than once, which I think meant building work. Then there was some head shaking and a bit of French shrugging, while I mopped my eyes and took a drink of water. Then I realised I had spilt wine down my T-shirt. It was like a Rorschach Inkblot test. And it looked like either a bird or half a poodle. Flipping heck, what next? Perhaps I could tuck my napkin into the neck to hide it? Perhaps he would go away and I wouldn't see him again. Ever. And yet there was something about him that made me feel different, acutely aware of his every movement. Aware of myself. I watched as he ran a hand over his hair, how his face creased into a smile. His broad shoulders moving under his sweater.

Then Felix was leading him over to our table and pulling out a spare chair and encouraging him to sit down. I shrank down in my seat.

'How are you getting on? Are you over all the excitement of your arrival?' he said. He had lovely brown eyes, and they were focused on me. Annoyingly I could feel my face getting rather warm. I hoped I wasn't blushing.

'*Ça va bien,*' I said, not wanting to seem like a complete fool; I knew a lot of French once, perhaps it would all come back to me? Although O level French as taught by Miss Travis in the 1970s was probably not the same as the French actual French people speak. To them with my outdated vocabulary and precise grammar, I probably sounded like someone from a Jane Austen novel.

'Excellent,' he said.

At that point Louis came over holding four little glasses of something that looked like brandy.

'*Offertes à la maison.* On the house,' he said with a broad smile.

I didn't actually think I needed any more alcohol, but behind the bar, Paulette was waving a tea towel at us and smiling so I took a cautious sip. I think it was rocket fuel and I could feel it burning a path down to my stomach where it sat like a hot little lump on top of my meal.

'*Eau-de-vie à la pomme*,' Isabel said with evident pleasure, 'apple brandy.'

'And I am told you are Isabel's sister,' Jean-Luc continued, 'I can see the resemblance.'

'She was always the good one,' Isabel said annoyingly, 'I was the naughty one.'

I sent her one of my best hard looks, but it didn't seem to register.

'Joy was the pretty one, I was the hippy,' she continued.

'How glad I am that you were,' Felix said gallantly, 'or we would never have met. Now then, Luc is having a problem with Gaston. He was supposed to have done the last bit of plastering last week, but he didn't turn up. Luc has asked if I can have a word with him.'

'Your brother,' Isabel sighed, and turned to me to explain. 'You met him once I think, he's nothing like Felix. Gaston takes after his mother, short with a black beard. Not that Eugénie has a beard. I always think there is a touch of the Captain Pugwash about him. Gaston is always late, so unreliable. But he gets the job done eventually. He's very clever, really. His wife Mathilde is such a lovely person. She studied jewellery making at college and now she makes things out of old bicycle parts and broken necklaces.'

Felix and Luc then carried on discussing where Gaston might be and the best way to encourage him to turn up, while Isabel and I finished our drinks.

Then after a brief discussion, I went to pay the bill. If they were having money troubles – as seemed likely from a few comments I had picked up on – I didn't want to add to them.

'Now I am going to take Joy to get some bread if there is any left, and have a look around the town,' she said at last. 'I'll see you back here?'

'*Bien pour moi*,' Felix said, pleased. Fine by me.

I saw Isabel give her husband what I can only describe as a meaningful look, and I wondered what they were up to.

'*À bientôt*,' Luc said. See you soon.

I wondered if I would, and for some reason I was a little bit pleased at the thought. But that was daft, wasn't it? I thought Isabel had said he wasn't very sociable.

* * *

We walked through the town, the early evening light casting violet shadows across the roads. It was chilly now and I shivered in my sensible jacket and thin shoes. I don't know why I had thought I needed to dress up to go to the Sports Bar. I would have been better off in my old duffle coat and furry boots.

There was a dear little church, a small, cobbled market square, two gift shops and Felix's bookshop, all of which were closed. The baker was still selling the last loaves of the day from his quirky shop and Isabel bought some, wrapped up in rather cute paper with the baker's name printed all over it.

There was an estate agent with pictures in the window of *maisons à vendre* – houses for sale in the area. Tumbledown barns, featureless modern houses, a couple of new developments and one enormous old place, which was something like the one on *Escape to the Chateau*. The price seemed very reasonable and the idea of buying somewhere as an investment was quite appealing for a few minutes. I could almost imagine myself in a ballgown sweeping down the ballustraded staircase until Isabel pointed out the cost of renovating it, heating it and the additional problems of paperwork and visa requirements. Perhaps I wouldn't do it, after all.

'Do you still like living here?' I said as we walked down an alleyway leading us back towards the main square.

'Of course, but then I've had a long time to settle in. And we are friends with *le maire* – the mayor. Nothing gets done without his approval. The weather here is not that different from England, but the food is better, the local people are friendlier – or perhaps nosier. There aren't many secrets in a place like this.'

'Back home I hardly know my neighbours,' I said thoughtfully, 'and we moved into our house thirty years ago. I mean, how does someone like well, Luc, for example get on?'

Isabel chuckled. 'I knew it. I knew you would bring him up. He's a source of much interest around here. A handsome doctor from Paris moves into an isolated farmhouse and starts to renovate it. A lot of people would like to know more about him. There have been all sorts of rumours flying around. He was devastated after the death of his wife in a plane crash, he's been in prison for malpractice, he was struck off for drug offences...'

'Perhaps he just retired and wanted a fresh start somewhere?' I suggested.

Isabel shook her head. 'Much too boring. Anyway, now he has actually appeared and been sociable, Felix is going to invite him to dinner one evening soon, so perhaps you can find out. Use those irresistible womanly wiles to discover the truth!'

'I don't think I have any irresistible womanly wiles these days,' I said, 'not at my age.'

'Nonsense. Of course you have. Every woman has a bit of Marilyn in her, whether it's Monroe or Manson is the problem. But I'll bet you fifty euros that you will discover what brought him here. So how are you feeling these days? Have you thought about, you know, dating?'

There it was again, Isabel's ability to turn the conversation on its head.

'No I haven't!' I said.

'Well perhaps you should. Felix said if anything happened to him I was to find someone else.'

'Easy for him to say. Do you know how hard it is for a woman in her sixties to find a man without terrible habits, dodgy health, or boring hobbies? I once went to a quiz night with some friends and got stuck with a man who talked non-stop about photographing weasels. And he asked me at the end of the evening if I would like to see his hide.'

Isabel giggled. 'Oh, I say! Do you think he was flirting?'

'I told him I was allergic to weasels, and that was the end of the conversation.'

'And no news of Stephen?'

'I don't ask, and I don't think Sara or John see much of him. They met the new wife, they said she had a voice like a foghorn and pushes Stephen around. Perhaps he likes it?'

He had moved on with his life, there was no doubt about that. So why hadn't I? I was beginning to see I was stuck in no man's land, between my old life and my future. I should stop thinking of myself as a sixty-three-year-old divorcee and start thinking of myself as a single woman. I needed to be more decisive, allow myself to find a new path, and yes, perhaps find new friends or a new companion to help me out of the rut in which I had been living.

* * *

Just as the church clock was striking five, we returned to the Sports Bar where the lights were shining out into the dusk. For a simple little establishment, it looked very inviting, and obviously others thought so too. The bar was busy with people having drinks after work. There was a young couple sitting at the ironwork tables outside, huddled in their coats and scarves, smoking, the distinctive smell drifting up into the evening, reminding me so strongly of my younger days when everyone seemed to smoke, and it was even seen as cool. How long ago it all seemed.

There was something so poignant seeing them there, they can't have been more than teenagers. Perhaps they were at the start of a new relationship, excited to be out together. She was pretty and giggling, flicking her hair, fluttering her eyelashes at him. She was making a big fuss about being cold, snuggling her little face seductively into her scarf, pretending to be a delicate little girl when really, she held all the cards in their relationship and more than that, she knew it. He looked unsure and yet proud. Perhaps she was his first serious girlfriend. How hard it must be, being young like that nowadays, not sure about anything and yet having to pretend to be confident, streetwise. Not knowing for one second how the world, how life would treat them.

Who knew what the future would send them? How the utter confidence and carelessness of youth seemed to turn to the hesitation and invisibility of old age in a matter of moments. How liking could turn to love, how love could turn so easily to doubt.

For a mad moment I wanted to tell them, to warn them to enjoy every moment of being young and carefree and invulnerable. But my generation hadn't listened, and probably neither would theirs.

I suddenly shivered, realising that so many years were behind me, and who knew how many were ahead. I supposed I could be classed as 'old' and in the years since I'd divorced, I'd started to accept that. But that evening, at that moment, watching a young girl and her boyfriend laughing together in the cold evening, it didn't feel like it. It felt as though the world was still turning. That I could still be a part of it. Not as I had been, but as I was. It was up to me.

I looked through the windows of the Sports Bar, which were starting to cloud with condensation from the warmth within, and felt a silly flicker of something because I wondered if Luc was still in there, drinking apple brandy with Felix perhaps, talking about Gaston and the problems with workmen turning up on time. I remembered the paperwork Isabel had mentioned, the planning permissions, the legal fees and taxes. How sad that he, just like me, was dealing with living alone. Did he mind that? Was he as reclusive and full of secrets as everyone in this well-informed town seemed to think?

Just for a moment I wondered what his life was like. Where did he sleep? Did he have running water and heating? Well, he had been there for a couple of years, he must have achieved something during that time.

I realised Isabel was watching me as these thoughts went around my head.

'What are you thinking about? Your face is a picture.'

'Nothing,' I said, forcing a smile, 'I'm just tired, it's been a long day. I think I need an early night.'

11

I woke the following morning just after eight o'clock. The high and stately sleigh bed might have been old and the mattress slightly uneven, but I think I slept better than I had for years. The sheets were embroidered with white thread and were probably some of Isabel's vintage treasures, the cotton smooth and soft after years of washing and drying outdoors in the French sunshine. No practical duvet here. There were faded blue blankets and a quilted bedspread, which held the faint scent of lavender. Perfect pillows and a little gilt clock lay on the bedside table next to a ceramic pin tray decorated with May blossom. I'd thought I had been good at making my guests comfortable, but this was on another level.

Perhaps it was those things that led to an uninterrupted night's sleep, or perhaps it was the effect of the apple brandy, or the deep peace of the old attic where the walls were so thick that no sound really penetrated.

I turned my head to look at the window and through a gap in the curtains I could see the sun had risen, and the sky was the delicious misty blue of a winter morning. Perhaps I should get up? Then I caught sight of the tea tray Isabel had given me, and instead – after a quick trip to the bathroom – I made a cup of tea, pulled back the curtains and got back into bed.

From my bed I could see out of the window and the fields below, which were still swirling with early morning mist. In the distance I saw a van looking as small as a toy, travelling along a road, busy with a delivery of newspapers perhaps, or taking vegetables to market. I wondered which vegetables they would be, and I didn't have a clue. In my supermarket there was no seasonal rotation of vegetables and fruit. Everything was there all the time.

I drank my tea and relaxed. I spent a good ten minutes watching the branch of some climbing plant outside my window, the new leaves only tight buds against the dark wood. Sometimes my mind was busy with questions and thoughts, other times it seemed completely empty, which felt very strange. But then I was beginning to realise there is a certain value to just occasionally doing absolutely nothing, like giving my brain a rest from all those years of worrying and thinking.

It was nearly nine o'clock when I finally got dressed and went downstairs. In the kitchen the stable door was half open and there was the usual chaos of newspapers, paperwork, and the remnants of someone's breakfast on the table, but no sign of Isabel.

I wondered if I should start to tidy up a bit while I was waiting for her. There was nothing that made me twitchy more than work-tops covered in random stuff. The place would look so much better if a few things were tidied away and the washing-up in the sink – which was still jostling for space with yesterday's muddy leeks – was done. I noticed there was even a cute wooden box on the table, with 'Lettres Importantes' written on the side in curly script, but all it contained was a bottle opener and some elastic bands.

There was, however, a pot of coffee keeping warm on a hotplate, and I poured myself a cup. I went to stand looking out of the kitchen door and spotted Isabel in the distance at the bottom of the garden with the two dogs zooming around her.

She saw me as she came closer to the house and waved. Not just her hand or her arm, but it seemed with all of her; her enthusiasm for the day – perhaps just for being alive was so great.

'It's a lovely day,' she shouted.

I waved back and was suddenly filled with affection for my noisy, disorganised, and generous sister. Last night she had voiced the opinion that we had been apart for too long, and at that moment I felt she was right. Over the last few years, I could have done with some of her energy, her optimism, her ability to see the funny side of just about any situation. How were we so different, I wondered. Two years younger than I was, she had been the unpredictable one, always late, always trying to add some personal and unacceptable touches to the school uniform, fond of taking risks and speaking her mind. And yet despite the fact that she constantly seemed to be in trouble, she had always seemed happier than I had. I might be more financially secure than she was now, but which one of us had found the better life?

'Coffee,' she panted as she reached the door, 'I've been out with this pair for a good long walk along the river in the hope that they will be too tired to jump all over you. *They* might not be worn out, but I'm pooped.'

We sat at the kitchen table drinking coffee and eating some more of her honey and apricot cake out of the tin because she said she had run out of clean plates.

'I want you to come and have a look at the *gîtes*. Like I said, they are going to need prettying up before the first guests arrive, and you're better at that sort of thing than I am.'

It was on the tip of my tongue to mention the delightful place she had created in the attic bedroom and disagree with her, but then I realised she just wanted us to do something together and it gave me a warm, fuzzy feeling.

'And come and look in the metal storage unit at the new *brocante* things I have collected over the winter. They've been in there because the actual barn is a bit damp, but I'll be setting things up in there because it's more attractive and has that rustic charm. People like that.'

'Has Felix gone to work?'

'About an hour ago. But the boys should be here sometime this morning. They still have the water to connect up in the *gîtes* and they promised they would be here,' she glanced around rather vaguely, 'I've got to find a couple of invoices for them... I wonder where they are.'

'Well, shall we tidy up a bit?' I said. 'We might find them.'

Isabel looked around as though she was seeing the muddle for the first time.

'I suppose so,' she said at last, 'I hate doing that. Do we have to? It only gets in a mess again.'

It was all the encouragement I needed and after we had finished our *petit déjeuner,* we set to.

I moved the leeks onto the only empty space, which was the windowsill, and then I collected up all the dirty crockery.

'Have you got a washing-up bowl?' I said, looking around.

'No, I turned mine over one day and it was disgusting, all sorts of random stains and things on the bottom. I chucked it out.'

So, I filled the stone sink with hot soapy water and started on the washing-up. Isabel meanwhile sat at the table looking through the piles of paperwork and exclaiming in amazement when she found something interesting or important. Then she found a long letter from someone and sat with some more coffee reading it. Occasionally she read out snippets to me, insisting that this person had been at school with us although I couldn't remember anyone called Sylvia Anders who used to be good at netball.

'Listen to this bit. *"I went to the latest school reunion even though my arthritis was playing up and saw Jackie White – who is in a wheelchair – Susan Peacock who has just retired from some high-powered job and looked a million dollars, and Lesley Tims who doesn't seem to have changed at all, apart from having blue hair."'*

I shook my head as I rinsed off the last plate. 'They don't ring a bell.'

Isabel sighed in exasperation. 'Jackie White had more detentions than anyone in my year, even me. Susan Peacock was in your year, she was the one who pushed Miss Coyle into the swimming pool, accidently on purpose, and Lesley Tims was in my year. She got pregnant. She did her O levels swathed in a huge jumper because everyone knew but none of the teachers did. You must remember that?'

'I don't remember any of them.'

Isabel huffed. 'Well, that's your fault, you're the one that left school and was never heard of again. Did you ever go to a school reunion? They happen every five years or so.'

'No, I don't think I did.'

'You should. I didn't go this time because things were a bit frantic here, but usually I do. You must come with me next time.'

'I doubt anyone would remember me,' I said.

'No, probably not,' Isabel agreed absentmindedly.

I was a bit annoyed at this. 'Why not?'

'Because you never did anything bad or rebellious, did you? That's what people are remembered for. You know what they say, well-behaved women seldom make history.'

Was that what I had been? I took a moment to think back. Had I spent the whole of my life so far being so well-behaved that no one would remember me? How tragic.

'I certainly don't remember anyone getting pregnant,' I said, 'I'm sure I would remember that.'

'They probably didn't tell you because they thought you might rat on her and then she would have been expelled.'

'I would never have done that!'

'Oh well, it's all ancient history now. Lesley married some red-faced landowner near Oxford and her son is an MP. Sylvia says he's been on *Question Time*, talking about potholes, so it all came right in the end. Which just goes to show, it's not where you start, it's where you finish. What are you doing?'

'I'm putting the plates away in the cupboard. This one is empty so I'm assuming that's where they should go?'

'Brilliant guess! And the small plates and mugs go in that big drawer.'

'That's empty too. Why don't you just put stuff away?'

Isabel looked puzzled. 'Because then people want them, and they have to get them out again.'

'It's not exactly difficult,' I said, 'and why haven't you got a dishwasher?'

'The boys kept offering to put one in but then somehow, we never got around to it. And then we would run out of plates and mugs.'

'And at that point, you switch it on,' I said.

Isabel raised her eyebrows. 'Ah, I see. Anyway, it's done now. Do you think I need to keep these catalogues?'

I took a look, flicking through the pages. 'Not unless you are planning on ordering a lilac fleece jacket with hamsters embroidered around the bottom. But look, you could also buy a matching hamster scarf and hat and then you would be sent some fleece hamster mittens, free of charge.'

We exchanged a look, and I dumped the pile of catalogues into the recycling, along with booklets on sheds, fire extinguishers and lawnmowers.

We spent the next half hour tidying things up and Isabel managed to file the unopened letters without reading them all and put the envelopes in the yellow recycling bin. Miraculously some space on the table and worktops was beginning to appear.

Just as Isabel was voicing the opinion that we had probably done enough for one day and she was getting bored, there was a perfunctory knock on the door and Eugénie came in, bringing a cloud of floral perfume with her and a wooden box that she dumped on the table.

'*Läderach* Pralines,' she said, 'they were a gift from Charles. There are two layers, which is far too many. I have allowed myself only one, but now I am passing them on to you, because otherwise I will get fat and then probably die. I might fall over and lie undiscovered like a beetle on its back. With no one to hear my cries for help.'

Isabel ignored her, obviously used to this sort of maudlin comment, opened the lid and we both gasped at the exquisite selection of chocolates inside.

'Contains nuts,' Eugénie added, looking at us in a marked manner, 'which seems appropriate. What has happened here? Have you been burgled?'

'We have been tidying up,' Isabel said proudly. 'It's what Joy loves to do.'

'Thank heavens someone does,' Eugénie said with an arch of one eyebrow.

I thought about this. Did I love tidying up, or had I just got into the habit?

Isabel made fresh coffee and poured one for Eugénie in her special cup, and then she pulled two pottery *bols* from the dresser.

'Remember these? We bought them years ago, in Quimper.

With our names on them. I did get one for Felix, but he never drinks *café crème*. Only you are allowed to use this one.'

I felt quite emotional for a moment thinking of my special *bol* left on the dresser unused for so long. And then we sat drinking it and eating some of the first layer of the horribly expensive chocolates as though they were Maltesers, while Eugénie watched us over the rim of her espresso, her mouth pursed like a cat's bottom, and talked about her cholesterol levels.

'We are going to look in the barn later,' Isabel said, 'start to get the *brocante* ready for the spring.'

'*C'est ridicule*,' Eugénie sniffed, 'ridiculous that people want all that stuff. I cannot believe they give you money. Linen sheets no one wants to launder. Old milk bottles, metal watering cans that no one can lift when they are full and *les torchons* – nobody needs tea towels these days, everyone has dishwashers. Everyone except you. It is like living in the Middle Ages in this house. A washing machine that doesn't wash properly, a vacuum cleaner that doesn't clean—'

'Yes it does!' Isabel said outraged.

Eugénie gave a very French pout and a *pouf*.

'Well, it doesn't look like it. I swear there is tumbleweed under this table that has been there since Halloween.'

'I didn't know your eyesight was so good. Anyway, people value old things these days,' Isabel said completely unbothered by her mother-in-law's words. That, in itself, was an eye opener for me.

How marvellous to be able to say what one thought, to be honest about opinions and preferences. Isabel had evidently found the right way to handle her mother-in-law, instead of Eugénie being in command, they spoke to each other as equals, and underneath it all I could sense the mutual respect and affection as a result.

'No one values me, and I am an old thing,' Eugénie grumbled.

'I feel very old today, I think there may be something wrong with my liver. I may not be around much longer and then you will regret not appreciating me.'

'And how is Charles?' Isabel asked sweetly. She turned to me. '*Mamie* has an admirer, Charles Verdun. He's a retired bank manager and he used to be a very fine tenor.'

'He still thinks he is,' Eugénie muttered, her fingers drumming on the table while she resisted the chocolates, 'he never got over being in *The Lisbon Story* at the town hall in 1977. He was outside my window the other night singing "Pedro the Fisherman", and let's be honest, he's no Richard Tauber. I had to close the curtains and pretend to be asleep before he launched into "Donkey Serenade".'

'I would like to have heard that,' Isabel said.

'*Non!* Not at three in the morning you wouldn't!.' Eugénie replied with feeling. 'He thinks it is so clever, but the shock could have killed me. And sleep evades me at the best of times.'

I bit back a laugh and went to the sink to start washing the leeks.

Eugénie drank another cup of coffee and then, when Isabel asked if she would like to help us out in the barn, decided she had some urgent letters to write and left.

'She's quite a character,' I said, slicing off the thick, green leaves from the leeks.

'She's a guinea a minute when she's had a couple of Dubonnets,' Isabel agreed. 'Come on, leave that, let's go and have a look at my latest treasures. I bet you don't think they are a load of junk, and the American visitors love *brocante*. They are some of my best customers. They will spend fifty euros on some things and then spend three times that shipping them back to Boise, Idaho. I have one customer with a chain of stores, who comes back to France twice a year for her winter *Cozy Momentz* collection and then her summer one, *Sunny Delight*.'

'Isn't that orange juice?' I asked.

Isabel looked blank. 'No idea. I just know she likes decorated egg racks and bread bins. She bought six with *"Merci mes Poules"* written on the side and twelve bread bins with *"M Gustav – Boulanger au Roi"* stencilled on the top. She sold them all in a week, apparently. So everyone was happy. That's what I need, more customers like her. The trouble is, we are a bit out of the way here, I wonder if there is a way to get more noticeable.'

Instead of wittering on about making the soup, I dropped the half-chopped leeks, dried my hands and followed her outside. And I didn't feel in the slightest bit concerned about leaving a job unfinished, instead I was enjoying being spontaneous, being with my sister, being a part of her life.

12

The metal storage shed was huge, with an old tractor and some bales of straw taking up a lot of space at one end, and wooden crates and metal trunks at the other. Plus there was a number of carboard boxes, several terracotta pots and garden ornaments, and some bulging black bin liners hung from the rafters.

Marcel and Antoine, far from being worn out by their morning walk, came too and as soon as Isabel opened the doors they shot into one corner of the barn and started barking.

'Mice I expect, although there are a couple of semi-feral cats somewhere. Minou and Chou are pretty good hunters, or of course, it might be rats,' Isabel said, 'which is why some of the things are hanging from the ceiling. I think both those dogs have lurcher or terrier in their ancestry. They love coming in here.'

Glad to not be the focus of the dogs' attention for once, and ignoring the sounds of scuffling and excited yipping, I went with Isabel to start investigating the contents of her new boxes.

'How will you fit all this into the barn?' I asked, amazed at the amount of things she had collected over the winter.

'Oh, I won't do that. I like to put out a really good display to start with, of course, but if a customer says they are looking for bed linen or lace, I tell them I shouldn't be telling them this, but I am expecting a new delivery, and they should come back in an hour. And then I find what they are looking for and put it out.'

'And do they come back?'

'Nearly always.'

'My sister the entrepreneur,' I said, full of admiration.

'The one thing I'm not very good at is display, you know, making things look enticing? Some people can make a pile of crockery look good, but I'm not one of those people. And you are. You only have to compare our dressers. Yours is a beautiful display of Spode blue and white china with a couple of quirky touches, mine looks like a Saturday night drunk has thrown stuff at it.'

'You did a lovely job in my bedroom,' I said.

Isabel pulled a face. 'That was mostly Margot, Sylveste's girl-friend. She's very artistic and clever.'

I pulled out a length of hand-stitched bunting from one of the boxes, it was absolutely delightful in shades of blue and cream. I was sure I could do something with that. And then there were exquisite lace panels and crocheted throws. Admittedly, they were rather grubby and scrunched up, but they could be laundered. I began to feel rather excited at the prospects.

There were some lovely old patio pots, with cherubs and lions' heads on the side. A miniature three-shelf *étagère* made out of curly ironwork and behind that a proper auricula theatre of faded painted wood. The possibilities were endless. And there was nothing I liked better than tidying things up, making rooms look attractive and welcoming. I'd always been like that, even my student room had pictures of Alphonse Mucha's four seasons on the walls and a new lightshade. And I'd found a fabulous patchwork bedspread in the local market for 50p, which had been perfect once I had washed and mended it.

The scenario in front of me suddenly stirred something I had almost forgotten. Yes, I had done all I could to make my home 'family ready', but no one ever seemed to notice it. Look at the Christmas I'd just had. No one but me bothered to turn on the battery illuminated nativity on the mantelpiece, or the fairy lights strung up the bannisters. And I don't think my granddaughters had switched on their own little attic Christmas tree once. Surely people other than me liked such things?

I peered inside a plastic crate that contained twenty-four miniature milk bottles with *'Lait de campagne'* on the side in a suitably rustic, faded green paint. I could almost see it; a long table set with a red gingham cloth, the wicker baskets open to show off delightfully pretty teacups and saucers (I'd noticed some in a box), the milk bottles (minus the dead spiders) arranged artfully around. Perhaps a couple filled with wildflowers, or ears of wheat. And that hand-made bunting would be ideal as a backdrop.

Just as I was letting my imagination spin off into creating a tableau of French rural life, using the ornamental enamel pails to hold some shining red apples and the faience bowl decorated with a man in bloomers, perhaps full of lemons – the bowl not the bloomers – there was a terrific racket from the corner of the barn, and a lot of growling from the dogs.

'Sounds like they have got something,' Isabel said.

'Do you have a lot of rats here then?' I asked rather nervously.

'No more than anyone else,' Isabel said, 'they do say you are never far away from a rat. Or mouse. And we have bats too although I haven't seen any yet this year. It's been too cold.'

We then went over to the display barn, leaving Marcel and Antoine barking happily over something, and Isabel opened the doors. It didn't look too promising. There were a lot of dead leaves blown in over the winter, one dim light bulb in the middle of the ceiling, no windows of course, and a lot of spiders' webs. There was also a musty smell of dust and possibly damp. But there was a wonderful long oak table covered in pigeon droppings, the surface gouged with scratches and even a chunk missing from one corner, which after I cleaned it up, could be perfect for the sort of display I had been imagining.

'So, what do you think?' Isabel asked after a few minutes.

'I'd love to have a try,' I said, dragging my mind away from the old enamel signs for *Mobilgas* petrol, *Le Train Blu* and *Grand Marnier* I had seen propped up against the wall.

'You're hired,' Isabel said, pleased.

Marcel and Antoine suddenly raced past the door, barking loudly and a moment later, we heard a truck pull up outside.

'That must be the boys,' Isabel said, 'they were supposed to call in the other day but didn't. Come and say hello to your nephews.'

Outside there was a truck, the back of which was covered with a tarpaulin and had '*Travaux de Jardin*' inscribed on the bonnet.

'Pierre! Sylveste! *Tante Joy est arrive!*'

Aunt Joy has arrived.

Well that made me feel positively ancient, especially when the two very tall and well-muscled young men jumped down from the cab. They were very welcoming, coming to give me a hug and the obligatory double-cheek kiss, and they seemed genuinely pleased to see me.

Pierre swept off the woolly cap that was pulled over his dark curls respectfully, and Sylveste was very muddy, something for which he repeatedly apologised.

'*Nous avons creusé des fossés.* We have been digging ditches, for the professor,' he explained.

My ears pricked up. Did they mean the Harrison Ford looka-like from the other side of the river? It seemed they did.

'He was in a good mood today,' Pierre said, pulling out a tin and rolling a cigarette, 'and he paid us without any argument.'

'This is not always the case,' Sylveste added, 'Luc is sometimes *grincheux* – grumpy. But today, even a smile. He said he saw you both in town yesterday. And he asked about Aunt Joy.'

Luc had asked about me? It was on the tip of my tongue to ask for details, but I didn't want to appear too keen, because undoubtedly someone would tell him.

Sylveste gave a meaningful nod towards his mother who raised her eyebrows in surprise.

'Perhaps you made an impression,' she said.

'Don't be silly,' I said. 'You're both looking very well. Is business good?'

Pierre took a long puff at his cigarette.

'Pretty good, now the better weather is coming. But today we need to finish off the *gîtes,* otherwise *nous serons grondés* – we will be in trouble.'

'Indeed, you will,' Isabel agreed, 'would you like some lunch first? I am making soup.'

Unsurprisingly they said they would. We left them shouting at each other and unloading their tools from the back of the truck and went back into the house.

When we got there, Isabel paused in the doorway to admire our handiwork of earlier that morning.

'This is amazing,' she said, 'I can see the table, it doesn't look like my kitchen at all. And all the washing-up is done and put away. You are a treasure, Joy. I wish you had been here over Christmas; I could have done with someone clearing up.'

'I was a bit busy doing that at home,' I said.

'Didn't anyone help at all?'

'Not really. Vanessa had just had a manicure and said she couldn't help because I don't own a pair of rubber gloves, and Sara was too busy making wine glasses dirty and leaving them all over the house. I even found one in the downstairs loo. And I'm afraid none of the girls or John for that matter, would have thought about it. I am only now realising what a doormat I was, so really, I should blame myself.'

Isabel went to resume the leek chopping, putting a big pan onto the stove, and melting a sizzling lump of butter.

'I'm not expecting you to clear up,' Isabel said quickly, 'I'm just grateful you do.'

'I don't mind doing it, I just didn't like being taken for granted.'

And that was the truth of it, I guessed. When I was doing all those meals and all that food preparation, I didn't necessarily want anyone to help me, I just wanted the occasional offer or acknowledgment, perhaps a thank you.

Isabel tipped the chopped leeks and garlic into the pan and there was a wonderful aroma which filled the kitchen in seconds. Moments later there was a familiar brief knock on the door and Eugénie – dressed in a very smart, navy-blue coat and red gloves – came in.

'Did you get your letters written?' Isabel said from her place at the stove, 'and did you go into town to post them.'

Eugénie sat down and pulled off her gloves, which she laid neatly on the table.

'I changed my mind. I thought it possible I would have a trip or fall. I was about to go out and I saw those lovely boys arrive. What are you making?'

'Leek soup. Without the potatoes before you ask.'

'*Bon*,' Eugénie said, 'everyone is fat enough. I will join you if I am invited?'

'*Bien sûr*. Of course,' Isabel said.

* * *

Half an hour later the soup was made – with a running commentary from Eugénie and interference from Pierre and Sylveste – and we were sitting around the table enjoying it. There was a large *pain de campagne* loaf too with a criss-crossed, crusty top, and a big wedge of brie, which Eugénie looked at as though it was poisonous.

A lot of the conversation was in French, but I was beginning to remember quite a bit, and I was even beginning to understand more than I thought I would. Still, I was grateful that out of politeness to me, they spoke English too. And even though it was quite a simple meal everyone was being pleasant and appreciative. Why couldn't it always be like this?

'We will start on connecting up the water,' Pierre said, 'it won't take long. And the work on the roof is nearly finished.'

'Knowing how you two get distracted and wander off, I will believe it when I see it,' Isabel said, cutting herself a slice of brie under the disapproving gaze of her mother-in-law.

Eugénie was quick to come to their defence.

'These boys are hard workers,' she said, 'you have nothing to be cross about. They are just like their grandfather, my Bastien, God rest his soul. Now there was a man who knew what hard work was.'

Sylveste grinned at her across the table. '*Mamie*, thank you.'

Eugénie fished in her handbag, pulled out two five euro notes and pushed them over the table.

'*C'est pour les bonbons.*'

Buy yourself some sweets.

Nothing changes, not really.

Pierre and Sylveste got up from the table and put their bowls in the sink.

'*Mamie*, you don't need to give them pocket money,' Isabel said, 'they are grown up. They earn more than enough, mostly from me at the moment, if they ever get on with the job.'

Eugénie ignored her.

'*Du café* if it's convenient, and then I must get on with my day.'

'What have you got planned?' I asked. 'Anything exciting?'

Eugénie gave me a look. 'I need to post my letters and then see the priest about my funeral. I want to be sure it will all be done properly.'

'A bit premature, don't you think?' Isabel said.

Eugénie gave a look at the ceiling as though she was St Joan at the stake waiting for the flames.

'It's as well to be prepared. *On ne sais jamais*. We never know...'

Pierre went to give his grandmother a hug and her face creased into a delighted smile.

'My good boy, I will remember you in my will.'

'Nonsense, *Mamie*, you are as strong as I am,' Pierre said, 'you can come and help us move the pipes if you want?'

Eugénie giggled rather girlishly and flapped a hand at him.

'Terrible boy,' she said dotingly.

She watched them go, a fond and proud smile on her face, and for a moment I rather envied her. She evidently was, and always had been, a caring grandmother, and her grandsons loved her despite her prickly nature. But I loved my granddaughters, too, and yet they were not like that with me.

Perhaps I spent too much time worrying about them and clearing up after them and not enough on actually getting to know them? That was an interesting thought. But now two of them were thousands of miles away. I would have to go and see them in New York, that was the answer.

It must be quite a change for them if I thought about it. They had left everything and just about everyone they knew. And in the same way, Sara's daughters had been through a life changing event. Despite their bravado, it can't have been easy for any of them.

I felt a sudden pang of regret and picked up my mobile.

'Sara, it's Mum. How are you getting on?'

13

Isabel suddenly remembered she had forgotten all about the Twelfth Night celebrations the previous week and she had promised to make a *Galette du Roi* ready for Felix's return to make up for it. She waited until Eugénie was safely away so she couldn't make some comment, and then pulled out some ready-made puff pastry from the fridge. Then she mixed up the frangipane filling with almonds, sugar, eggs and cognac.

'And I mustn't forget this,' she said pulling a little china figure out from a drawer and putting it inside the galette, 'the *fève*. Whoever gets this in their slice is king for the day, which the boys used to like when they were little. And the paper crown. Now we just say the winner gets a wish for the New Year.'

She shoved the *galette* into the oven and set a timer on her phone, then we went back out to the barn and watched as my nephews stopped squabbling and turned into two competent workmen, confidently moving bits of pipework and big bags full of tools. There was even a bit of welding going on as they restored the pipework that apparently had been leaking. I was well impressed.

After rescuing the *galette* from the oven, Isabel did a bit more sorting out in the storage shed, taking a few things out of crates and putting them into piles and then putting them back again. She said she was just reminding herself what was there. Marcel and Antoine ran about, seemingly inexhaustible, tussling with a shred of canvas. One of the feral cats watched us with a sour expression from its perch on top of the tractor. Perhaps it didn't like having its personal space invaded.

As the sun set and the dark evening shadows lengthened across the fields, we locked up again and went back into the house. Pierre and Sylveste had declared themselves happy with what they had achieved and would return *à bientôt*, sometime soon, to finish off the last things that needed doing.

'I suppose I should start thinking about the rest of the dinner,' Isabel said. She held out her hands black with the dust and dirt from our afternoon's work. 'But first I think we should get cleaned up. I always get filthy working in the barn. And you have spiders' webs in your hair.'

I looked down at my grimy clothes, which were bad enough. The possibility of webs in my hair were a different matter, one I hadn't anticipated.

We went off to clean up and I enjoyed a scalding hot shower in the downstairs bathroom where the water pressure was reasonable but not exactly forceful.

Back up in my attic bedroom, I picked out some comfortable clothes for the evening. After all I wasn't expecting to do much more than have dinner, drink wine and chat. A pair of joggers and an old but clean sweatshirt would do. I tied my wet hair back with a scrunchie and slipped my feet into my slippers, which were a joke pair of gorilla feet complete with claws that the twins had bought me for my last birthday.

Downstairs, my sister was sitting at the table leafing through the last of the catalogues and papers, and cheerfully consigning them into a large paper sack to be recycled. She looked very cheerful.

'I'm beginning to see why you like throwing things away,' she said as I came in, 'it's sort of cleansing, isn't it? Getting rid of old rubbish.'

'I remember what it was like when our parents died, having to sort through all the things they had kept. That's when I found all our old school reports. I sent yours to you and I chucked mine away.'

'Sacrilege!' Isabel laughed, 'I've probably still got mine. I bet yours all said the same thing. Works well, never late, a valuable member of the class. Mine on the other hand were terrible. The teachers must have hated me. "*Isabel should be ashamed of this exam result. Isabel has not worked to her full potential except to be disruptive. Isabel would do better to listen in class and not voice unfounded opinions on the Tudors.*" I know what that was about. I said I thought Margaret Beaufort had an unhealthy and rather distasteful relationship with her son and asked Miss Betterson several times about the rumour that Anne Boleyn was actually Henry VIII's daughter. I kept that one going for ages. Just out of sheer devilment because I know it annoyed her so much.'

I shook my head. 'Troublemaker. The thought I had was that one day my kids would have to sort through all my collected stuff and decide what to keep, so I've been doing it for them. I've sent a lot of things to the charity shop and thrown a lot of things away. After all, you never know.'

Isabel pulled a face. 'You sound like Eugénie, prophesying your imminent demise. You're pretty fit and healthy, aren't you?'

'Of course I am,' I said, 'I just don't want to leave them the burden of sorting it all out.'

'Very considerate.'

'But it does make me wonder what I *will* leave behind. Who will remember me when I go? The house will be sold, and I can't believe Sara or Vanessa would want any of my clothes.'

It was true, I could see the distinct possibility that like a lot of ordinary people, I would hardly leave a trace. My children would miss me, I supposed, but in the long run stuff didn't matter, nor did exam results or my organisational skills. What mattered was the here and now. Kindness, support and positivity. I didn't need to win a Nobel prize or invent something. The best thing I could do was live the best life I could, one day at a time. And in a way that was a good thing because it was achievable.

'What do any of us leave behind?' Isabel said gloomily, waving a sheaf of papers at me. 'Bank statements back to 1980? Receipts for gadgets, which broke years ago? A few bits of jewellery? Even photographs aren't as important as we once thought they were.'

'Memories, I suppose,' I said, feeling more optimistic, 'people remembering us, things we said or did.'

Isabel laughed. 'I hope people will forget all that sort of thing where I am concerned. And I've had some terrible photographs taken over the years. It's okay for you, you never sneezed or blinked when pictures were taken. For heaven's sake, Joy, this conversation is much too serious. Let's have a glass of wine.'

She rummaged around in a cupboard under the stairs and came back with a bottle of red wine that she opened and poured into two glasses.

'This feels naughty,' I said, 'it's not even six o'clock yet.'

Isabel darted a look at the clock. 'Damn. I forgot about dinner. Felix will be back soon. I'd better chuck something together. You'll be seeing French cuisine at its best. Said no one ever.'

Eventually she found some chicken in the freezer, which she bashed with a meat hammer to separate some pieces and then defrosted in the microwave. Then she boiled up some penne pasta, cooked some garlic and mushrooms in butter, fried the chicken pieces, mixed everything together with a good slug of white wine and covered the whole lot in a jar of some sort of sauce. Then she hesitated and shredded some of the remaining brie from lunch over the top.

'That'll have to do,' she said as she shoved it into the oven, 'Felix will be glad to get anything, after all these years he knows what I'm like. And to be fair he's not a fussy eater. No good marrying me if he was! I suppose we could have a salad too. I bought a load of fresh stuff at the market garden up the road, I'm sick of all the winter casseroles.'

'I'll do that,' I said, keen to help.

She found a big platter decorated with radishes and passed it to me and I started to construct a salad with the ingredients she found in the fridge and the cavernous pantry. This was something I had always enjoyed doing, taking a pile of basically ordinary things and making them look good. I even spent some time turning the tomatoes into flowers and thin slices of cucumber into roses. I looked up at one point to see Isabel watching me with an incredulous look on her face.

'Do you usually do that?' she asked.

I grinned. 'No. Well... sometimes, I just thought I'd make a bit of an effort.'

I've always thought the secret to a good salad was to add more things, so I did. Some grated carrot, a few halved green olives, little cubes of feta, a sliced apple, some toasted pine nuts, a few tiny, sweet peppers, and then I made some croutons. In the end I was pleased with the result, instead of a boring plate of green it looked colourful and appetising.

'Marvellous,' Isabel said, topping up my wine glass, 'you're an artist. I wonder where Felix has got to. It's nearly seven o'clock and everything is ready once we set the table.'

There was a knock on the kitchen door at that moment, which set the dogs off barking, and Isabel pulled a face.

'That can't be Felix. It better not be Eugénie again; she normally doesn't go out after dark.'

She wiped her hands on a tea towel and went to open the door.

'Ah,' she said, 'hello. What—? I mean— do come in.'

I looked up to see Luc standing in the doorway, holding a bottle of wine in one hand and a bunch of flowers in the other.

'I hope I am not too early. Felix did say seven,' he said.

He was looking very cool that evening in a heavy wool coat, jeans, and a black sweater. And outrageously attractive. As we stood open-mouthed, he slowly unwound a soft red scarf from around his neck. He looked very uneasy, his eyes looking uncertainly at us, as though unsure of his welcome.

It was a good job I was sitting down because I think I felt a bit wobbly for a moment. I don't think I had felt that way for years.

Isabel recovered her composure with remarkable speed, which was more than I did.

'Not at all! Come in, make yourself at home. Let's get this wine open, shall we? What is it? Not that it matters. Ah, a lovely Bordeaux! You are spoiling us.'

'My favourite,' I added hastily.

Luc and I stared at each other for another uncomfortable moment and then I busied myself tidying away the chopping board and knife I had been using. I think I was even blushing. Which at my age was absurd.

'*Madame* Chandler,' he said.

'Please call me Joy,' I said.

'Joy,' he said, holding out a hand for me to shake.

I liked the way he said my name, his accent softening the hardness of the J.

At what point did the French go in for *la bis,* that cheek-kissing thing?

'Luc,' I said, my voice a bit shaky.

I then remembered I was in jogging bottoms, a sweatshirt, had wet hair, no make up and gorilla feet slippers.

He looked down at them and pressed his lips together, presumably to stop himself from smiling.

By then, Isabel had whipped the cork out of the bottle and poured him a glass of wine.

'*Santé,*' he said, raising it towards us, 'your good health.'

There was an uncomfortable silence and then Isabel started finding things for a fourth place setting. I could see she was trying to be discreet, even stealthy but those weren't qualities at which my sister was skilled.

Luc nodded as she slipped some extra cutlery onto the table. He wasn't fooled for a moment.

'Felix didn't tell you I was coming this evening, did he?'

Isabel rose to the occasion. 'Probably, but when you get to know me, you will understand I am a bit scatter-brained. I forget things. Perhaps it's my age.'

She then placed a couple of plates and a water glass onto the table with the stealth of a rather unsuccessful pickpocket.

'I wonder where he is?' she said at last, 'dinner is ready. Heat proof mats that's what I need. I wonder where they are. We've been having a tidy up.'

'On the dresser,' I said and went to get them.

Luc hesitated. 'I can leave, if it's not—'

'Absolutely not!' Isabel said cheerfully. 'It's lovely to have you here. I wanted to introduce Joy to the locals. People we know. Friends.'

He looked thoughtful. 'Well, I am local. I am not sure I am a friend...'

'Not yet perhaps, because you've been a bit— well—'

'Distant?' he said.

I was feeling very uncomfortable at this point although Isabel seemed to be okay with the situation. Perhaps all her years of managing Eugénie had helped.

'Private,' she said at last, 'although I am sure you have your reasons. It must be very different from life in Paris.'

'I've never lived in Paris,' he said frowning.

'But everyone around here said you were from Paris. And when we sold you the house, I'm sure Felix said something about that?'

'Then everyone is mistaken. Although my solicitor is in Paris.'

'Ah, I see. I didn't read all the paperwork, not properly I'm afraid. I do feel a fool. Honestly, Felix. He's hopeless. Which reminds me, I wonder where he is.'

'Look, perhaps I should go. I can see there has been a mix up,' he said.

He actually was fidgeting and moving towards the door, and I realised he was feeling just as uncomfortable as we were. He was still holding the flowers and he hesitated for a few moments before he handed them to me.

We exchanged a glance, and I wasn't sure who felt the more awkward. Which was a shame because I loved being given flowers and it hadn't happened very often.

I went to put them in a glass vase and made some sort of attempt to arrange them.

'Do sit down,' I said, 'and tell us about your progress with the renovations. It must be a lot of hard work.' I took a sip of my wine.

'This is delicious, I love red wine and Bordeaux is my absolute favourite.'

There were an uncomfortable few seconds when I don't think either of us were sure if he was going to stay or not, and then the kitchen door crashed open and Felix came in, stamping his feet on the door mat and looking as though he might have stopped in the Sports Bar for a couple of apple brandies.

'Ah! *Mon ami!*' he said cheerfully, shaking Luc by the hand. 'Good to see you. Excellent. My apologies, I am late. I met up with Gaston and you know how things are. Never mind, we are all here now. What a treat. And something smells wonderful. Did I tell you my wife is *une cuisinère exceptionalle*? A wonderful cook.'

'You might have told him that, but it would be a lie,' Isabel murmured.

'A drink, my friend. I see we are eating in the kitchen. What a fine idea. *C'est plus convivial, plus intime,* more friendly. Now then, a toast to what I am sure is going to be a wonderful evening. With two elegant ladies.'

I shuffled my feet nervously and the claws on my gorilla slippers scraped against the flagstone floor.

Not entertaining any sort of dissent, he urged Luc to sit opposite me at the kitchen table and went to the sink to wash his hands, while Isabel hissed something to him about his failure to tell her she should have been expecting a guest.

It might not have been an elegant meal, but it was delicious. The chicken pasta dish was brought to the table bubbling away like a dish of molten lava, the beauty of the salad was much praised, and the bread was, as is always the way in France, wonderful.

'So tell us how you are getting on, Luc,' Felix asked after people had finished helping themselves.

'I would be getting on faster if Gaston came to finish off the plastering,' Luc replied.

Felix slapped himself on the forehead. 'I forgot to tell you, I saw him just an hour ago, he had just found a broken bicycle chain in the street, and he was taking it back for Mathilde. I expect she will make some earrings. I told him he must get to you tomorrow, or Friday at the latest, or I would publish the photograph I took of him in the bath when he was a baby on the village information page. He was such an ugly baby; you would not believe it. He thought I was joking, I assured him I wasn't. I think you will find him on your doorstep tomorrow morning.'

Luc laughed, and his face relaxed out of his usual serious expression into something rather lovely. I took a large gulp of wine to settle my nerves. This was the sort of occasion I had been thinking about; meeting new people, taking opportunities to broaden my horizon. Not just sit there as I might have done in the past, dumb with discomfort.

'When that is done, I can finish the painting and get the last of the electrics fitted. After that the worst will be over.'

'How long has it taken you?' I asked.

'Two years, two and a half maybe. It was slow progress at first for many reasons. I was not then fully retired, I still had work to finish off.'

'And do you miss it? Your patients I mean?'

Luc looked confused. 'My patients?'

'Yes, you know, the people you were treating, helping them through their various illnesses. I'm guessing you had to hand them over to someone, and that must take time. Their prescriptions, and their notes, and operations – that sort of thing. I know when the doctor at our local clinic retired, it took quite a while, and the receptionists were furious. Not that they weren't usually because they seemed to think anyone wanting an appointment was deliberately annoying them...'

I realised I was babbling under his gaze and shut up.

'I am not a medical doctor,' Luc said.

Isabel chimed in. 'Everyone around here had the impression you were a doctor.'

'Well once again, everyone is mistaken,' he said at last, slowly and very patiently.

We waited to see if he would elaborate, but he didn't. Isabel broke the silence.

'Now then, I have a special treat for you, *Galette du Roi*, for Twelfth Night. I know it's late, but I forgot. I wonder who will get the *Fève*. It's the Baby Jesus in the manger, one Eugénie passed on to me so don't bite it in half. And it's porcelain so you would break your teeth. Whoever gets it, make a wish.'

She cut some generous slices and passed them round.

'I know you are supposed to serve it all at once, but I am saving some for Eugénie, although she will complain I didn't make the puff pastry, and for the boys, who wouldn't care if I'd bought it frozen from the supermarket.'

'You did that on purpose,' I said a few minutes later when I found the little china figurine in my slice.

'No, I didn't. Now make a wish,' Isabel said, 'but don't tell us what it is.'

I closed my eyes and tried to think of something to wish for.

Good luck? Good health?

In the end I wished silently for happiness, and when I opened my eyes Luc was looking at me. I had the strange feeling he knew what I was thinking.

14

Despite the awkwardness of not being dressed for entertaining, not knowing Luc was coming and accidentally revealing that he had been the subject of much erroneous local gossip, the evening had passed pleasantly enough.

He wasn't one to give away a great deal about himself, no matter how hard Isabel asked leading questions and dropped hints about his family. But he did discuss his love of English history and evidently was very interested in us.

When we analysed the evening afterwards, Isabel and I agreed that he had been very good at diverting attention away from himself. He had wanted to know all about the bookshop, the repair of the *gîtes,* the imminent arrival of the new shepherd's hut, and how bookings were going for the new season. By the time he wound his scarf around his neck and shrugged himself back into his coat, I don't think we knew an awful lot more about him than we had when the evening began. Which was very odd and unsatisfactory because Isabel is usually very good at getting information out of people, and I wasn't too bad at it either.

'Perhaps he's reluctant to share personal information because he's a retired CIA agent,' she said after we had waved him off, 'or a sleeper in an FBI cell.'

We went back to sitting around the table, this time with large glasses of Calvados which Felix has insisted on gently warming in a metal ladle over a candle. This had taken several attempts because he kept leaving it too long and the whole thing would burst into flames that nearly took his eyebrows off.

I took up the thread. 'Or perhaps he is an amnesiac, like Jason Bourne, and he has all these skills that he didn't know he had. So he can retile a bathroom and put window blinds in without them falling down, but he's forgotten he has a wife somewhere. She would be a spy, too, living undercover in Marseille. And I bet she is wondering where he is.'

Isabel looked excited. 'Exactly. She will be searching for him, using a computer she keeps hidden in what looks like an airing cupboard. And scouring Interpol and face recognition software in the hopes of seeing him getting on a train. I bet he has built a false panel under the floor where he hides all his fake passports and bundles of cash.'

We roared with laughter, Isabel rocking back rather dangerously on her chair until I grabbed her arm. Which brought her back down with a bump and a crash waking both the sleeping dogs under the table. Marcel and Antoine raced around the table barking until Felix let them out of the back door. I think both of us were probably slightly tipsy from the Calvados. I'd forgotten how it felt to have moments like that, where I could be silly and say daft things.

'You watch too much television,' Felix said, letting the dogs back in again, 'it's much more likely he is a retired professor of English history who is perfectly happy to be left alone.'

Isabel tutted at him. 'You're such a killjoy. I think that was a successful evening, don't you? All the food went anyway, so that's a good sign. Although I would have made a bit more of an effort if I had known he was coming. What must he have thought of us?'

Felix sniffed appreciatively at the last of his warm Calvados. 'I did tell you. I'm sure I did.'

'And I am equally sure you didn't.'

I stood up, slightly lightheaded from the apple brandy, and started clearing things away, before Isabel stopped me.

'Leave it, I'll do it in the morning.'

'If you had a dishwasher, you could load it and just turn it on,' I said.

'I keep telling you this, *chèrie*,' Felix said.

'Yes, yes okay. Put in a dishwasher, take away my one reason for living,' Isabel said dramatically, and then burst out laughing. 'Golly, I think I'm a bit squiffy. Perhaps I should go to bed.'

* * *

We spent the next few days pottering about, exploring the contents of the storage unit and sweeping all the winter dust, cobwebs and debris out of the old barn. Once we had done that, I could see what the space really looked like.

'I usually just pull that thing out and put things on it,' Isabel said, pointing to something under a couple of old wine crates and a broken umbrella stand.

We had lugged the old table outside. It was a cold morning and there was a breeze coming off the river. Having lost interest in the whole event and as we could only find one scrubbing brush, Isabel was checking her phone and watching me use a bucket of hot soapy water to clean off the winter coating of dirt and bird poo. And then I went to fetch some clean water to wash the suds away.

On my return I swung the bucket back as far as I could,

intending to throw it over the table. Just at the last minute I realised that Eugénie, warmly wrapped up in a thick tweed coat and matching hat, had scuttled into view and was standing in the direct line of fire (or water in this case), gazing at the table, looking rather wistful.

With commendable reflexes, I thought, I span around on one leg rather dramatically, nearly fell over and managed to throw it over myself.

'My Bastien's father made that table,' Eugénie said, ignoring me as I stood dripping and trying not to swear, 'just after he and *grandmère* were married. They were so poor; he said every day was a struggle. They had terrible health that nothing could cure. Both dead now of course, their lives cut tragically short by war and poverty.'

Isabel threw me a look. 'But they both lived to be over ninety, *Mamie*.'

Eugénie took no notice. 'What are you doing out here?'

'I told you; we are getting the barn ready for the new visitors.'

'So, there is no chance for an old woman, who has walked all this way in the freezing cold and with weak ankles, to be given coffee?'

'Of course.'

Eugénie turned and gave me a puzzled look, sweeping from my red, sweating face to my soaking wet trousers.

'And what on earth are you doing? Did you know you are very wet? It's very bad to have wet shoes, you will catch *pneumonie* – a bad chest – and then you will need to go to hospital. There used to be nuns at the hospital, I remember them well. They were very fierce. I knew someone who went there with suspected appendici-tis. The nuns said he was a fool, he had indigestion and was to go home and stop wasting their time, and he did.'

'Goodness me, what happened?'

Eugénie shook her head sadly and crossed herself.

'A terrible tragedy. Only twelve years later he was dead. He was run over by a milk lorry.'

I choked back a laugh and squelched after her and back into the house to change.

* * *

Back downstairs again I found Eugénie busy interrogating my sister about Luc.

'Why a doctor needs to build his own house I do not know. Surely he makes enough money from his patients to pay someone?'

'He's not a medical doctor,' Isabel said, 'he told us was a professor of English history.'

'*Ne sois pas ridicule!* How will he know how to treat me when I'm ill? Read me Baudelaire or Shakespeare? The world has gone mad. I said as much to Charles last night.'

'Is he still singing under your window?' I asked.

'If you can call it singing. He has tried something new. Half past one and he has brought his portable record player and starts up with Edith Piaf, "Sous les Ponts de Paris". Do I look like the sort of woman who would like to sleep with the vagabonds under the bridges of Paris? I should have thrown a bucket of water over *him*,' she added with a look at me.

'He means well, *Mamie*,' Isabel said, 'he can't help himself.'

Eugénie nodded. 'He is *amoureux de moi*, in love with me. I can't blame him for that. He says he has felt this way for years, ever since he saw me dressed as *Marianne* on the float on Bastille Day in 1965.'

'Well, of course,' Isabel said, 'I saw the photograph.'

Behind her back I mimed a question at my sister. The famous

painting of *Marianne* generally showed a bare breasted maiden, gallantly leading the revolutionary forces towards freedom. Which personally I would have thought would have been far too much of a distraction for the *sans-culottes*. Had Eugénie done that too? Isabel bit her lip to stop herself laughing and shook her head.

'I have something for you,' Isabel said, 'I know it's late, but I saved some especially.'

She brought out a plate with the slice of *Galette du Roi* on it and placed it in front of Eugénie with a little pastry fork.

Eugénie looked at it and then leaned forward to peer at it.

'It is very bad luck to be late with such a thing. I expect we will have a terrible year. And then I will be ill. This is bought pastry, isn't it?'

Isabel and I exchanged a knowing look, and she rolled her eyes.

'Well yes, I didn't have time to make it myself,' Isabel admitted, 'but it turned out very well.'

Eugénie took a tiny taste of it and then prodded the rest with her fork.

'Hmm. No *fève* for me then this year. And I would have wished for better health, an end to my circulation problems perhaps. Or my palpitations, which are very bad at the moment. Who had it?'

'Joy,' Isabel said.

I gave an apologetic smile.

Eugénie pushed the plate away and finished her espresso. 'It seems God does not wish to bless me. I may not be here next year. I'm not blaming anyone. I cannot stay here entertaining you and doing nothing all day. I have a hairdresser's appointment at eleven. I was hoping you would drive me there, but if you are too busy with your *brocante*, then I will ask Charles. I don't want to do because it just encourages him. He will get funny ideas.'

'Why don't you just marry him, *Mamie*?' Isabel said, sighing.

Eugénie gave a disgusted *pouf*. 'Why would I do that? *La chasse* – the hunt is part of the fun. Once I am caught, I will be like a trembling doe trapped in a net.'

'More like a Tasmanian Devil wedged in a tree stump,' Isabel murmured.

I turned away to hide a laugh and pretended to be washing up some mugs. She was hilarious, but the relationship between her and my sister was even funnier.

'The secret is to keep running, men cannot resist that. And I don't want to be caught, I just like to be pursued,' Eugénie said.

'You are *méchant* – unkind,' Isabel said, 'keeping Charles' hopes alive for all these years.'

'Men like to chase,' Eugénie said, 'it is intoxicating.'

I thought about this; yes, she was probably right. Perhaps I should take a leaf out of her book. I was actually enjoying getting to know Luc, and I knew he was feeling the same way. There's just something that I think most women can pick up on. I knew he was aware of me, there were subtle things that couldn't really be described. The tilt of his head towards me, an inflection in his voice the occasional look that didn't involve anyone else. It was indeed, intoxicating. I hadn't felt anything like it for years.

'Now then are we going or not?'

'Of course,' Isabel said, 'I'll just get my keys. Joy, do you want to come too?'

After days of sorting through watering cans and fabric scraps, I was eager to get out and about, and now that my feet were dry, I was keen to go along too.

* * *

The little town looked lovely in the sunshine and there was a small, early morning market in the square, which by the time we arrived, was starting to pack up.

We deposited Eugénie outside *Madame Julie – Coiffeuse* just after midday, and she went in with much ceremony, and was welcomed by a doughty looking woman with a floral overall and an aggressive perm. There followed much cheek-kissing and fuss as Eugénie was ushered through the doors. I think it must have been like when the Queen Mother in her heyday arrived at the London Palladium.

Isabel parked the car in front of Felix's bookshop where there was a sign saying:

Parking Interdit.

'Don't take any notice of that sign, Felix made it out of an old tin plate and a broomstick. Right, we have time to go and buy some bread and perhaps grab a coffee. There is an absolutely lovely café just around the corner, you might remember it.'

'I do,' I said, rather excited, 'I remember the cakes anyway.'

We went first to the *boulangerie* where the afternoon loaves had just been put out on the shelves. Despite the small size of the shop there were so many different types of bread that it was hard to decide what to buy. And the aroma was bewitching. Eventually Isabel selected a *boule* and *un gros pain*, which was like a fat baguette. When the bread was this good, it didn't seem too much of a hardship to get it every day. Then we made our way through the little streets to *Le Café de Mimi*, where Mimi herself was sweeping the pavement outside and keeping an eye on everything.

'Ah, *c'est ton soeur*! Joy!' she said as we arrived. 'And 'ow are your family?'

'Very well, thank you,' I replied.

'It's good to get away from them sometimes, *n'est ce pas?*' she said with a grin.

Hmm, not only did she remember who I was, she evidently knew something of the reasons that had brought me back in the first place.

I made a sort of head wagging gesture that was vaguely French, and as the sun was shining, the wind had dropped, and all the spaces inside were taken, we sat down at an empty table outside. Isabel gave our order and moments later, two coffees and two vast *Religieuses* pastries arrived. They looked like heaven.

'No wonder you like living here,' I said, through a mouthful of choux pastry and crème pâtissière. 'But don't you get tired of everyone knowing everything about you?'

'No. It was odd at first, but then I realised that actually no one is that interested. If everyone knows everyone else's business, there is nothing to find out. Which is why Luc was a bit of a hot topic when he arrived. He was difficult to get to know, I suppose he still is. He seems nice enough though, don't you think?'

'Yes, from the little I know,' I said.

'I expect you to find out everything,' Isabel said with a wicked gleam, 'I think he likes you.'

Did he? I felt a bit odd – and dare I say it? – nervous at the thought. For most of my adult life, I'd assumed that this sort of thing wouldn't happen. I'd been a wife and mother by the time I was in my early twenties, and since Stephen and I had divorced, the prospect of any man looking at me with interest again hadn't crossed my mind. Until now.

I feigned indifference. The moment Isabel got a whiff of my interest in him, she would want to sink her teeth into it and would never let it drop, like Marcel with his rubber banana.

'You can't possibly know that.'

'Maybe, maybe not. We'll see.'

'So, when will the boys finish the base for the shepherd's hut. I thought they were supposed to be starting the concrete this week.'

'Who knows? There's no point trying to chivvy them along. It just puts their backs up, and then I get irritable and then Felix gets irritable. It's much better to accept that they will get it done in time. I can't wait to see it. It used up all my savings. It's pale green, with the sweetest little kitchen and bathroom. Perfect for one person, or two people, if they get along.'

'You should advertise it as a romantic getaway and put a little table and chairs outside. I saw some in the storage unit, which would be perfect once they are cleaned up. And some solar lights. And perhaps a chiminea.'

Isabel nodded. 'Good idea. I knew you would be good at this sort of thing. Now then, I suppose we should go and see if Eugénie is ready to go home. It's been nearly an hour since we dropped her off. Well, good heavens, speak of the devil, which actually we weren't, and who should I see...'

I turned in my chair to follow her gaze and saw Luc coming towards us, carrying a brown paper parcel under one arm.

Remembering our very recent discussion on the subject of him *liking* me, and my own thoughts about him, I felt very awkward.

Isabel hailed him and pulled out a chair, encouraging him to sit down. After a moment's hesitation, he did.

Mimi came out like a shot.

'*Du café, m'sieur?*'

He agreed that would be good and she scuttled back inside, her eyes bright with excitement to fetch it.

'So what are you up to?' Isabel asked, 'anything interesting?'

He dumped the package on the floor by his feet.

'Just a few things. Nothing interesting at all. A new spirit level because I ran over mine in the car. Some *ruban de masquage* –

masking tape. I will be painting soon, as Gaston has finished the plasterwork.'

'Then you are nearly finished,' Isabel said, 'well done, you. Do excuse me I need to just pop inside to – you know.'

Luc and I looked at each other for a moment. And then I started babbling with nerves.

'You'll enjoy that part I expect. Moving in and making the place look nice. That's always my favourite part. Do you have a lot of things in storage? It will be like Christmas when your things arrive, won't it?'

'I wouldn't go that far,' he said.

'No, perhaps not. Well, if nothing else it will be good to have your home looking nice again, won't it?'

Mimi returned at that point with a large cup of coffee with a couple of little macarons in the saucer.

'*Ceux-ci sont gratuits.* On the house,' she said, with a winning smile. 'Always nice to have customers returning, you have stayed away too long, *m'sieur.* And 'ow is your building? I hear Gaston was finishing off the plastering. That's a relief. Tell him I am still waiting for him to do my back passage. It has been months and still he does not return.'

'I will be sure to mention it,' Luc said.

He sipped his coffee in silence for a moment.

'They are very good,' Mimi said, pointing at the macarons, 'I made them.'

'Thank you,' he said.

'Almond,' she added.

She pulled a cloth out from the pocket of her apron and wiped a crumb off the table.

'You should come on a Friday, I make *madeleines.*'

'Perhaps I will,' he said.

He gave her a charming smile and then flicked me a glance. There. It was moments like those that I recognised.

Mimi fidgeted for a moment and then luckily Isabel returned, and Mimi went back inside, obviously disappointed that she hadn't managed to prolong the conversation with him.

'Thank you for a delightful dinner last week,' he said. 'I enjoyed it.'

'Anytime,' Isabel said cheerfully, 'you must come again. It can't be easy for you to cook at the moment. I should have invited you earlier.'

'I manage,' he said, taking one of the macarons. 'Yes, these are good.'

'Tell me about your building work,' I said at last, wondering if that would draw him out a little.

'It's been harder than I thought, but I feel I have achieved something.'

'Felix's great-uncle, Jacques, used to live there. He had nine children,' Isabel said.

Luc raised his eyebrows. 'Really? Nine? But there were only two bedrooms. I wonder where they all slept?'

'Perhaps he should have had a hobby or bought a radio to take up his spare time,' Isabel said, and gave a nervous giggle. 'Oooh, I've just remembered something.'

She stood up again and went back into the café, leaving me and Luc to our non-conversation.

At last, he finished his coffee and put the cup down with a decisive chink into the saucer.

'I think your sister imagines we are going to talk,' he said, 'so you can find out all about me and she can ask for the details later.'

'I'm not sure,' I said, 'are you that interesting?'

He laughed then, a proper laugh, which was rather lovely, and I felt myself relax a little.

'No, I think when you get to know me better, you will find out I am not.'

He really was tremendously good-looking but unlike many handsome men, gave the impression that he was unaware of it. Which was unexpected and very attractive. I wondered if he did have a wife somewhere, or even children. And if so, where were they? Perhaps he was divorced, or he had spent his entire life ploughing through academic tomes in university libraries. And *'when I got to know him better'*? Was that even a possibility? Considering the conversation had been so stilted up to now, it didn't seem likely.

I realised I was having very inappropriate thoughts and tried to think of something to say.

'Sorry. Isabel just said that when everyone knows everything about everybody, no one takes any interest in them any more. You ought to think about that. I was surprised how everyone knew about me. People I'd never met seemed to know all sorts of things.'

He leaned forwards slightly and fixed me with his beautiful brown eyes. I think I heard myself give a little whimper, and I cleared my throat to hide the fact.

'So what brings you here, have you just come to visit your sister? Or is there more to it than that? You don't have to tell me, but perhaps I can just ask the postman when I see him next?'

I laughed too and the atmosphere between us warmed up a little. Out of the corner of my eye I thought I saw Isabel coming outside, but then she made a sharp 180 degree turn on her heel and disappeared again.

'Of course I wanted to see Isabel, and Felix and my nephews, but I also needed a change of scenery. Christmas was – shall we say – hard work this year. For a lot of reasons.'

I had a sudden flashback to the day after Boxing Day when I

had made yet another huge meal, pasta with home-made bolog-
naise sauce for most of us, and pasta with cheese for Jasmine and
Mia. Halfway through Jasmine had told Bunny she was eating
minced up cow and Bunny had started crying. And then there had
been a spirited discussion about personal choice and bullying,
which had degenerated into Jasmine being sent out of the room
for a time out, and not allowed back until she apologised to
Bunny. Not to me, I'd noticed.

My resentment had resurfaced at that point, and I had
stamped about for a bit, fetching yet another bottle of wine and
the pepper mill, and slamming them down on the table and no
one had clocked my ill humour at all. It really had been as though
I was invisible. I don't think I would put up with that now, I think a
certain resolve had started up inside me.

Luc nodded and ate the second macaron after first offering it
to me. I politely declined, referencing the remains of the crème
pâtissière on my plate. I didn't want him to think I was a complete
pig.

'Christmas can be difficult,' he said, 'I went to see an old friend
in Marseille.'

Ah yes, that was exactly what Isabel had suggested. What a
coincidence. Perhaps he was a spy after all. For a split second I
imagined a beautiful blonde girlfriend draped over a pale chaise
longue, the boats bobbing suggestively behind her on the dark
sea. It was possible she had a *Sobranie* cigarette in an amber
holder too. Or perhaps he had gone to visit his missing wife, who
would be chic and intelligent with wide, beautiful eyes and a sexy
laugh.

'He was a colleague of mine, now he is a professor, he's writing
a book about the Wars of the Roses, very interesting indeed.'

The imaginary blonde and the wife disappeared in a puff of
smoke.

'Ah yes, York against Lancaster. That didn't end well for a lot of people,' I said.

His eyes lit up. 'And the relationship between Margaret Beaufort and her son was always interesting—'

You should hear what Isabel thinks about that, I thought.

'—and the fact that she was descended from an illegitimate line in the first place. English history is so fascinating.'

'It didn't seem that way when we were being taught it in school, I can assure you,' I said.

'No, I suppose not.'

We talked for a while about various things. School and travel (he wanted to revisit London and York) and were just getting on to family when Isabel came outside again, looking at her watch.

'Sorry, but we do need to collect Eugénie from the hairdresser,' she said, 'there's only so much gossip that can keep her occupied for this long.'

I stood up, feeling unexpectedly disappointed that our meeting was coming to an end, and I knocked against the table, making the cups rattle.

'Of course. Well, perhaps we will see you again soon,' I said.

Luc smiled. '*A bientôt.*'

* * *

'*So?* What did you find out. I left it as long as I could,' Isabel said as we walked back to the car.

'He spent Christmas in Marseille with an old friend.'

'Girlfriend?'

'Old history professor.'

Isabel pulled a face. 'That doesn't sound very interesting.'

As we walked back to the car I constructed a rather pleasing mental picture of Luc and another historian, who possibly smoked a pipe and wore a tweed jacket. They were sitting on a sun-drenched balcony (so perhaps the jacket wasn't needed) overlooking the Mediterranean, discussing the Battle of Bosworth or something like that.

There were tumbling cascades of bougainvillea on either side, perhaps a little table with some glasses of cognac, a dish of perfect green olives. And there was some point in the conversation when Luc laughed, and he looked relaxed and happy.

I wondered what it would be like to go somewhere new like that, to live like a local person, to find out more about the world and no longer be constrained by memories of a husband who had thought every stranger posed a threat.

Perhaps marriages didn't have to be one person in charge and the other person scrabbling round trying to please them all the time? Although life after Stephen left had been difficult and sometimes frightening, I think I was beginning to realise that I was, after all, capable of running my own life, paying my bills, sorting out my days without him telling me what I was doing wrong.

And then I allowed myself a dangerous thought – what would it be like to go to Marseille with Luc, to be on that balcony, the bright light reflected off the sea, flowers everywhere, colour and fragrance? Fishing boats in the distance, a heavenly blue sky.

Would it be like that at Christmas in the South of France? I didn't know, but suddenly I wanted to find out.

15

I would have been happy to start sorting out the barn that day after we had collected Eugénie who had been looking very pleased with herself, her white hair having been given a fresh, faintly apricot rinse and set into a rigid-looking French pleat.

Isabel was having none of it.

'Remember that poem by Rudyard Kipling we had to learn for speech day? "If you can fill the unforgiving minute, tumpty tumpty tum". Well I would say fill the unforgiving minute with a nice sit down, a good book and a few biscuits. There will always be another unforgiving minute coming along later.'

'I see the boys have poured the concrete at last,' I said, 'I saw them early this morning from my bedroom window.'

'See? I told you they would, they are good boys really. And how are your two getting along? Any updates?'

'I had a long email from Vanessa. They have had heavy snow, but the roads get cleared in no time. John is working hard, she has had lunch with a couple of the company wives, who are called Betsy and Tatiana. I expect they spent the whole time pushing salad around their plates and complimenting each other. Vanessa would have loved it. The girls are horrified because they have to wear tartan kilts as part of their school uniform, but Bunny is thrilled that she has a real celebrity's daughter in their class.'

Isabel took down a couple of the bin liners and prodded about inside them. 'Anyone we know?'

'I can't remember, apparently he is in a band and the girl gets delivered to school by a chauffeur and a bodyguard every morning. Sara says she is doing well, the girls are fine, too, and she has started divorce proceedings. Marty is outraged. She sounded quite upbeat actually.'

'Right then, so nothing for you to fret about,' Isabel said, 'you did exactly the right thing.'

I nodded. 'I suppose I did. Now then, let's have a look in these boxes.'

I ripped off the packing tape and opened the cardboard flaps.

'Don't get your hopes up, that stuff was from a house clearance,' Isabel said, 'and I got there late, and only got a few things. They were a job lot because the trader wanted to finish for the day. No Fabergé eggs or old masters.'

Inside was a lot of what I think could only have been described as junk. Some kitchen utensils, a couple of iron doorstops, an old biscuit box filled with bits of glass jewellery, and a couple of painted, tin buckets and spades. The sort of thing any French child might have taken to the beach in the 1960s. I opened another box, which was filled with much the same sort of thing. Remnants of someone's life that had once meant a great deal to the owner but had now ended up in my sister's shed. If that wasn't a life lesson, I didn't know what was.

'I hope you didn't pay a lot for all this,' I said.

'A few euros, I think. Nothing much.'

We worked away for a couple of hours, putting some things back into the boxes and others into piles to be transferred to the display barn and then predictably Isabel got bored and wanted to do something else.

'Let's go and see how the concrete is coming along,' she said, 'it should be setting by now, surely.'

Outside we found Pierre and Sylveste standing admiring the new concrete base, which looked very smooth and smart. A big cement lorry had come and gone that morning, disgorging the contents into the structure they had created. We stood respectfully admiring it, it looked very professional, and I was impressed.

'Oh, it is nothing,' Pierre said modestly, lighting his roll-up, 'the drainage was all done, and then the compacting and the gravel and sand. And we used up some old flagstones too. Then we built these wooden shutters to get the right shape, we just need a few days without rain for it to finish setting properly although it's firming up nicely. We're going to prop a canvas over it too this evening, just in case it rains. I'm really pleased with it.'

Sylveste chimed in. 'And we just need to keep the dogs off it – *non!* Antoine! Marcel! *Non!* Stop them!'

Unusually quiet, the two dogs had snuck up behind us and were watching. Marcel had moved forward to give the concrete a sniff and had raised one paw, trembling over the surface. Antoine was just a dog's length behind him.

We all adopted the same rather ineffective position; knees bent, crouching, and holding out warning hands towards the pair of them, making encouraging noises.

'I told you to shut them in the house,' Sylveste hissed at his brother.

'And I told *you* to,' Pierre hissed back.

'It's okay, I'll get them,' Isabel said confidently, and took a step forwards.

It was too late.

A pigeon flew low over our heads, hotly pursued by Antoine

and Marcel, who barking with joy chased after it, straight through the setting concrete, leaving a pattern of paw marks across the middle.

'*Je te l'ai dit, idiot*! I warned you!' Pierre shouted.

'*Ne me blâme pas*!' Don't blame me. The perennial cry of the older brother. 'Look out! Catch them!'

Splattered with cement from the dogs' flying paws, Isabel stood helplessly, calling to them and for one moment they both stopped, paws planted in the concrete, looking at her with interest, presumably wondering what the four of us were up to and were there any treats to be had.

Isabel succeeded in catching hold of Marcel's collar and Antoine followed but then he doubled back to see what Pierre was shouting about and ran across the concrete again, causing further mayhem and another fresh set of paw prints.

Marcel meanwhile broke free and did some zooming around on his own, barking at the pigeon who had landed in the branches of a nearby tree. Unfortunately, one of the cats was already up there, having an afternoon nap, and it took a swipe at the pigeon causing it to fly off again in a flurry of feathers. Marcel followed it down the field and onwards, barking all the way, while the cat slipped off the branch, dangled meowing and complaining, until it fell into the bushes below with a startled yowl. This new excitement caused Marcel to do a speedy U-turn and he raced back through the concrete yet again, his paws slipping.

'Blasted animals,' Pierre shouted at him, '*arrête ça*! Stop it!'

Unexpectedly, Marcel stopped obediently in the middle of the churned-up concrete, tongue lolling, one front paw raised. I put both hands over my mouth in horror, and then I couldn't help myself, I burst out laughing and after a moment Isabel joined in.

At last we caught both of them and Isabel washed their paws and fur under a hosepipe while I hung onto their collars. The water was cold, and I don't think either dog appreciated our efforts. It was a process, which meant that, of course, there was a lot of vigorous shaking from them both, and all four of us were soaked.

Pierre and Sylveste meanwhile shouted a lot of abuse at the dogs and each other. Luckily, it was all in rapid fire French and I couldn't follow what they were saying. We dragged the dogs off, roughly towelled them dry and shut them up in the house while the young men set to work, trying to smooth out the surface again.

'It's going to be underneath a shepherd's hut, no one will see if it isn't perfect,' Isabel said encouragingly.

'You won't be saying that when it starts to crack,' Sylveste grumbled.

'I'm sure it will be fine,' I said, still trying not to laugh.

Behind him the cat slunk back into the barn, its belly low against the ground.

'And I bet it's going to rain later,' Pierre added gloomily, '*c'est un désastre* – a disaster.'

'It will be fine, I have absolute faith in you,' Isabel replied, wringing water out of the sleeves of her coat.

Pierre and Sylveste glowered at each other and carried on smoothing out the paw marks.

'Let's go and get changed, and then you know what I always say; if in doubt, make food. I'll sort out some sandwiches for them, that always cheers them up,' she said.

The following day, Pierre and Sylveste, having called in to inspect their work, pronounced themselves reasonably satisfied, removed the tarpaulin and drove away, still not really speaking to each other.

We spent the morning sorting out more of Isabel's junk finds and then I took out my laptop. The broadband was surprisingly good in some rooms of the house, particularly the sitting room, which was a long, low-beamed room with an enormous inglenook fireplace at one end.

Isabel finished clearing up the lunch and came to see what I was doing.

'Just doing some research on a couple of things that we found this morning in the *brocante*,' I said.

She pulled a face. 'You're wasting your time. And I can assure you if you did find a lost Leonardo da Vinci, we don't have many art collectors dropping in on the off chance.'

'Still, it's worth checking,' I said.

'At least the *gîtes* are finished. We should go and get them ready after lunch; the first visitors arrive in a week according to Felix's new spreadsheet. You were so clever making him do that. Want to help?'

'Of course,' I said.

We found umbrellas and coats and went out to see what state they were in.

I was pleasantly surprised. They looked pretty much as I remembered, two tiny farm workers cottages that had been reno- vated some years ago when Isabel decided she wanted to make some money from the holiday makers. The paint had been fresh- ened up and there were new blue and white curtains at the windows. It just needed a bit of dressing up to make them look appealing.

Isabel made up the beds with crisply ironed bed linen and I hoovered and dusted. The kitchens were fairly well stocked with enough basic crockery and cutlery for two people in each, but it all looked as though it had come from the nearest supermarket.

'Why don't we put some of your finds in here instead?' I said.

'You have all that rather nice china, all the floral plates and cups. We would only have to find a few matching ones. It would look more rustic and appealing. And then I can put in some of the ornaments you couldn't sell last year. A vase or two, with some flowers. And I saw some lovely brass candlesticks in a box in the attic, which I could polish up and put on that sideboard. And I noticed two rather nice lampshades decorated with shells. They've obviously never been used. I could replace those boring ones on the bedside lamps if you like?'

'Okay,' Isabel said, 'but that would mean I can't sell them.'

'You can tell your guests that all the decorative things are for sale if they like them. And then we could replace them with new things for the next people. That way you would have twice the chance of selling things.'

Isabel agreed this was a good idea and we set to.

By the time Felix returned at about six o'clock, we had just about finished our work, and Isabel was delighted with what we had achieved and dragged him out to have a look.

'Very good,' he agreed, 'but I liked it the way it was before as well. *C'est chic*, very fancy. *Ça a l'air* – seems very girly.'

'I don't suppose men would even notice,' I said, 'but your female visitors will. And I think they will like it.'

'I notice lots of things,' Felix protested, 'particularly how beautiful my wife is, and also how hungry I am.'

'You have no soul,' Isabel grinned.

We went back inside, and Isabel brought out a defrosted coq au vin out from the pantry where she had hidden it away from the dogs and put it into the oven.

'How is business?' I asked Felix.

He pulled a face. 'Not too bad, because some of the holiday makers are starting to call in. But today was quiet and Lisa has broken up with her boyfriend, so she is *misérable*. It won't encourage the customers in to see her sad face behind the counter. She says she wants to go and see her mother in Nantes, but I don't want to be there on my own, it gets boring on days like today.'

'You could always do a stocktake,' Isabel said as she set the table, 'or get your papers in order for the accountant.'

Felix gave a groan. 'What I could do and what I want to do are two separate things.'

'I could come and help you,' I offered impulsively, which surprised me and both of them I think, 'Isabel and I have sorted out the *gîtes* ready for the first visitors, and we have been through the *brocante*, we are going to make the barn look pretty tomorrow, but that won't take more than a day.'

Felix looked more cheerful. 'If you're sure. I have a delivery of books in English arriving one day this week, which you could sort out, if you didn't mind? *Je suis daltonien* – I am not good with colours.'

'He means colour blind,' Isabel explained.

'Absolutely, I'd love to help out. And Isabel wanted some time in her greenhouse, which I can't help with, because my gardening ability is nil. So it would work okay.'

'Good idea,' Isabel agreed, 'when I go to help out in the bookshop—'

'You are no help at all,' Felix interrupted, 'you just sit there reading the paper and telling customers they could go to the public library in Morlaix for free.'

'I only did that once!' Isabel protested.

'I don't tell your customers they could stay at home for free, do I?' he said.

'It's not the same at all! You are ridiculous!'

'You're impossible,' he said.

'You are!'

Felix went behind her to fetch a bottle of wine from the fridge and slapped her bottom as he went past.

'And you are a bad wife who does not feed her husband!'

'*Tu es un cochon gourmand*! A greedy pig!'

I watched my sister and her husband squabbling and just for a moment it triggered a memory in me. I had been party to a lot of bickering when Stephen and I had been married, but then I realised that – as they always did – Isabel and Felix were doing it with humour, that they didn't really mean anything by it, and this was just a part of their relationship. Underneath it all they thought the world of each other. How lovely to feel that way, even after so many years together. It made me a bit wistful, and it made me smile too.

I was beginning to realise that I had missed out on something like this in my own marriage. I must have been mad to put up with it. No wonder my children took me so much for granted; their father certainly had. Well not any more.

16

We had enjoyed a very late night after Felix opened a bottle of *Eddu Breton* whisky, given to him by one of his suppliers to try and tempt him to stock a range of notebooks.

I wasn't a great lover of whisky, but I was prepared to give it a try.

'Listen, I will read you the tasting notes,' Felix said, '"*complexe*, floral, with heather and rose. Chocolate and smoky notes, with a hint of pepper."'

He swirled the golden liquid in his glass and took a sip.

'It's very good,' he said at last, 'very good indeed.'

Isabel looked at the label. 'And 43 per cent proof. So even if I didn't like it, I probably wouldn't remember.'

'I like it,' I said, 'it's sort of smooth, isn't it?'

'I'm not sure,' Isabel said holding out her empty glass, 'let's try again.'

The evening then passed into a blur, which as I recall ended with Felix trotting out to the storage shed, finding the accordion behind the tractor, and trying to play *La Vie en Rose* on it and sing. Very badly. Despite that, it was fun. And I think I laughed more than I had in a very long time. I had to go out of the room at one point, my sides aching, and Antoine had followed me, hoping for treats.

Isabel looked thoughtful as he finished. At least we thought he had finished; it might have been that he just got fed up with it.

'Is that it?'

'*Bien sûr*, yes, that is it,' Felix replied.

'It's hardly Sacha Distel, is it? It reminded me of the time I got Chou's tail caught in the barn door,' she said, 'that was very complex too. With several high notes. A combination of a yowl and a shriek. No hints of heather though.'

'You don't understand,' he said, dropping the accordion onto his foot. It made a wheezing, grumbling sound that set us both off laughing again.

'You are right, *chèrie*, I don't,' Isabel said, blowing him a kiss.

'I hope you agreed to stock the notebooks,' I said, wiping away my tears with a tissue.

'I can't see the point. Who needs such things?'

'Any woman you talk to,' I said, 'I have at least ten notebooks.'

'So you don't need any more then,' Felix said, his tone indicating that he had proved his point.

I gave a spluttering laugh. 'We don't buy them to write in, we like to have them, in case we want to write in them.'

'S'true,' Isabel nodded, 'and the nicer the notebook, the less likely I am to write in it. They are for special things, not just shopping lists.'

Felix gave this some thought. 'I have seen your shopping lists; you usually leave them on the table by mistake when you go out.'

'We get them as presents, we give them to friends as presents,' I said.

'But why?' Felix was genuinely puzzled, or perhaps it was the whisky.

'Because we do,' I said, 'and that's all there is to it.'

Felix shook his head slowly, trying to understand.

'So when you get another one, do you think "hurrah, what a lovely notebook," or do you think "oh dear, I already have ten"?'

'Always hurrah,' Isabel said, 'and then I put it with the others, for when I need them. Eventually, the right moment will present itself.'

'I bet you ten euros you will sell them all. Especially if they have gold swirly bits on the cover or peacock feathers. And if they have a little magnetic clasp, even better,' I said. I stabbed the air with a finger for emphasis.

I was surprised to hear myself talking like that, expressing an opinion, trying to convince someone I was right. Having my feelings seriously considered. It made a change. Perhaps it was the whisky. Maybe it was just me feeling more confident than I had in years.

'Well, okay, but I will never understand women,' Felix said, picking up the accordion, 'now shall I play something else?'

Isabel had slumped over at a slight angle, and she struggled upright in her chair.

'I will give you ten euros not to, *chèrie*. Fifteen if it will convince you.'

* * *

After that we had a late start to the following day, and so we were sitting at the breakfast table having waved Felix and his headache off to work, when there was a familiar rap on the kitchen door, and Eugénie came in. She looked very chic in tailored trousers, a white sweater (no dogs in her house then; I wasn't sure I would ever get the splatters of concrete out of my jeans) and a checked blazer, while we were still in our dressing gowns.

I think she was appalled at our slovenliness.

'*Que se passe t-il ici*?' What's going on?

Well, I suppose she had a point, it was nearly ten o'clock.

'Coffee, *Mamie*?' Isabel said sweetly.

Eugénie sat down at the table and gave a gracious nod.

'You always look so elegant,' I said, trying to persuade her out of her evidently bad mood. In fact, I didn't think I had ever seen her wear the same outfit twice.

She looked at me with a meaningful expression and tapped the side of her aquiline nose.

'I have – how would you say...? – contacts. Now then, the reason for my visit. That wooden box of pralines I gave you. I would like them returned. Charles wishes to see them and perhaps try one.'

Isabel and I pulled the same agonised expression, which said that this would not, and could not happen.

'I'm not sure where they have got to,' Isabel said.

At the same moment I blurted out, 'We've eaten them all, I'm afraid. Ages ago. They were very good though.'

Having given the unacceptable answer, Eugénie focused her gaze on me. 'You have eaten them? All of them?'

I nodded. 'But... that was quite a long time ago,' I added, 'and it wasn't just me.'

She took a sip of her coffee and stared at the far horizon, while behind her Isabel rolled her eyes and pretended to hang herself.

'I've never known such greed,' Eugénie said at last.

'Well, you did give them to us,' Isabel said.

'To *have*. Not to *eat*,' Eugénie said, 'do you know that gift was over one hundred euros? I looked them up. You have made me feel very unwell. I need some medication. There is some seriously wrong with me, my heart is fluttering.'

'Sorry,' we said in unison.

'I still have the box,' I said, knowing somehow that I was treading on dangerous territory but unable to stop myself, 'it was too nice to throw out. I was going to do something clever with it.'

My voice faded at the look in Eugénie's eyes. I think I knew how the dogs felt.

'Ah yes,' Eugénie said, her voice silky and slightly dangerous, 'I know how this will go. I will set my table with my best china, which was left to me by a dear friend in her will. It is *Sèvres* in case you wanted to know. *Chateau de Fontain Bleu* pattern. Charles will arrive at six because *il est toujours en avance*, he is always prompt. He and I will have a Dubonnet *frappé* and he will admire my hair. He notices such things. Then we will eat our supper by candle-light, I am going to make pasta. He has new teeth that will not cope with anything challenging. Afterwards we will perhaps talk about the old days, and he will pay me some extravagant compliments, which I will enjoy. Then I will make coffee, pour a small glass of cognac for each of us and say, "Look Charles. Look at this empty box. Joy assures me you can do something clever with it."'

I slumped a little, feeling very foolish.

'Perhaps you'd like a biscuit?' Isabel suggested, with a weak smile.

'I will tell Charles what has happened to his wonderful gift. My evening is in ruins. Instead of discussing his chocolates I suppose I will have to listen to him singing.'

'Can he play the accordion?' I blurted out, trying not to laugh at the memory of Felix the previous evening.

Isabel widened her eyes at me.

Eugénie sniffed. 'I don't know, and I have no wish to find out. I will take one biscuit now if it is offered.'

* * *

Later that day, we made our way to the barn and began making it look beautiful. At least that was the intention.

I pulled out the table, which newly polished with several coats of beeswax, looked wonderfully rustic. Then Isabel began bringing out all her treasures while I set the scene with the garlands of blue and cream bunting, several strings of fairy lights and the old, enamelled petrol signs which – having done some research – I was sure were worth more than the twenty-euro price tags Isabel had stuck on them.

I put out a few of the little milk bottles with red and white paper straws stuck into them, a couple of decorated tin plates, some faience pottery dishes, embroidered tablecloths and napkins and a slightly battered wicker hamper made a charming pretence of a school picnic on a side table.

'It's awfully good,' Isabel said when we stopped for a drink of water, 'I'd buy it all, I swear I would.'

'Daft thing, you already did,' I laughed.

'Yes, but do I really want to sell these things? Couldn't I just keep a few?'

'And put them where?' I said, 'all your cupboards are full. And that's not what you are trying to do here. You're trying to make a profit.'

Isabel picked up a little china figurine of a hunter with his dog and stroked it regretfully.

'I suppose so. Now then the watering cans, what shall we do with those?'

We lined them up, and I filled some with greenery, others with dried flower heads. Then I tied some of the scraps of lace ribbon around some of the handles, and tricolour ribbons, left over from some Bastille Day celebration, around others. It looked really colourful and attractive.

There was a small, wooden cupboard painted with flowers that

Isabel had found in a skip and repaired. We put that by the entrance and, to hide the worst of the scratches, propped the door open with a cast iron doorstop in the shape of a cat. Then we filled it with artfully draped linen sheets and embroidered hand towels.

'Marvellous,' Isabel said, 'much better than I could have done. Now we deserve a treat for all that hard work. Let's pop into town and buy something nice for dinner. The supermarket stays open until seven. And on the way I want to stop off somewhere.'

'Where?'

'You'll see. It's a surprise.'

* * *

We locked up the barn, gloating over our new display, Isabel picked up a sturdy brown paper bag of tiny new potatoes she had collected, and then we drove up the drive, turning left when we would normally have turned right.

'I'm not sure I like your surprises,' I said after a few minutes, 'I remember my tenth birthday when you gave me a frog in a shoebox.'

Isabel laughed. 'But you still remember it after all these years, don't you? I bet you've forgotten all the bath cubes and handkerchiefs you were ever given.'

'Stephen gave me three tins of undrinkable tea and a new iron for Christmas once,' I said.

Isabel roared with laughter.

'Romantic fool,' she said, 'didn't he know you should never give any woman a present with a plug?'

We turned off again after a mile, and headed down a rutted road with grass growing down the middle, until we reached a gateway, and Isabel drove confidently in.

'You've brought me to a building site?' I asked, looking around at the cement mixer, the random piles of stone and the skip, filled with pieces of broken wood.

'Here we are,' she said. 'Surprise.'

As we got out of the car, Luc came out of the front door, in the familiar blue boiler suit, which was splattered with white paint, and I felt myself blushing.

'What on earth are you playing at?' I muttered.

'Felix had the idea,' she said.

'Look, I'm just going to say something stupid, I know I am.'

'Naughty! We don't use that word, don't you remember what Vanessa said?' Isabel grinned. 'And anyway sisters and friends don't let you do stupid things alone. Hello there, Luc, I promised you some of my new crop, so here you go. Potatoes from Potato Farm.'

She handed over the paper bag and stood looking hopeful.

'Can we come in and see how you are getting on?'

Luc looked at first bewildered and then slightly worried.

'Of course,' he said, stepping to one side. 'But please be careful, some of the paint is still wet.'

Inside there was the crisp, clean tang of new plaster and paint, and underneath, the more subdued smell of old stone. A small hallway led into a large room painted a restful green, where there was a wood burner tucked into the chimney breast already set with paper and logs. It would just take a match to start the fire, and in minutes the thick stone walls would ensure that the room would be warm and welcoming. Two candlesticks on a large wooden beam above it served as a mantelpiece. There were shelves built into the alcoves on either side, empty, but ready for his books.

I could easily imagine the room furnished with a comfortable sofa, perhaps a leather armchair next to the fire where he would sit in the evenings, reading a book perhaps, a glass of whisky on a small table next to him.

The floor was still covered in canvas dust sheets and there was a folding workbench in the middle of the room with an impressive toolbox on top of it.

Stephen had possessed something similar, because he said a man should have such a thing, but I don't remember him ever really using it. Other than to put a couple of nails in the wall to hang pictures. This sort of activity was on another level.

Actually, I had always thought that simple DIY was something I would quite like to do, but Stephen had insisted it was his job, which meant that more often than not it wouldn't get done. Perhaps when I got home, I would watch some YouTube videos and at last fix the window blind in the bathroom that kept falling down and replace the grouting behind the sink. Why shouldn't I? It couldn't be that difficult.

'I hope we are not interrupting anything,' I said.

'Not at all, I'm delighted to see you both,' he replied, 'I would shake hands but...'

He shrugged and held out his hands that were spotted with paint. He pulled a rag out of his pocket. His hands were large and tanned, a graze across the back of one, the hands of a man who didn't mind getting them dirty. I watched as he wiped the paint off, almost mesmerised by it.

Isabel nudged me back to awareness.

'So you're making progress,' she said, 'do show us what you've been doing.'

He took us through, under an archway and into the kitchen, where he apologised for the mess and muddle although it looked fine to me. Just for once, I felt absolutely no urge to get a cloth and do any wiping or cleaning. That was a new feeling.

It was fitted with pale, painted cabinets and a stone worktop.

Everything looked new and fresh. And well planned. I'd wanted to change my kitchen back home for years, the badly designed layout, the dark wood that I had never liked, but I never had. It seemed too much of an effort, not to mention the expense. And yet as I ran one hand across the smooth surface, feeling the dust and tiny fragments of grit under my fingertips, I realised that I could organise this sort of thing if I wanted to. I wondered how he had managed to get this huge worktop in, no YouTube video could deal with that.

'I put the cabinets in myself, but I had help with the stone,' he said in answer to my unspoken question, 'a firm from Morlaix, who were very good.'

'And what else have you been doing?' Isabel said.

For a moment I was terrified she was going to ask if we could all take a look around upstairs. I imagined his embarrassment as we poked our heads around doors, looked at his camp bed, or perhaps a mattress on the floor, with his clothes spilling out of suitcases and bags.

'The bathroom is finished,' he said, 'and there are three bedrooms where once there were two. You can take a look if you like. I will make tea.'

While his back was turned, Isabel took me by the shoulders and mouthed 'stay there'. I mouthed back 'no', and she gave me one of her looks and raised her eyebrows in a menacing way. And then she went off, her footsteps echoing up the wooden stairs, leaving me in the kitchen watching as Luc filled the kettle and opened cupboards to find three mugs.

'I still don't know where everything is,' he said apologetically, 'and everything gets covered in dust.'

'That will settle for months, I expect,' I said, 'I know what it was like when we had a bathroom put in. I mean we already had a bathroom, but it was bright turquoise and absolutely hideous. I needed sunglasses to go in there. It's not like we had a tin bath hanging on the wall, it wasn't as bad as that. And the loo didn't flush properly, we had to jiggle the handle in a particular way.'

Oh yes, that's a really good topic of conversation, I thought.

'Ah, so you know about these things. And did your husband do the work?' he asked.

I laughed at the very thought of Stephen with an electric drill in his hands.

'Ex-husband, and no, he wasn't that sort of man, we used some local builders. They were excellent. They did a good job. It's difficult to find good workmen these days, don't you find? I'm always afraid they will take the money, and then run off with the job half done. Although, my ex-husband was good at keeping them to schedule. That sort of thing. He used to do spreadsheets. And he was always interfering.'

I was aware I was babbling on, talking a lot of nonsense. Why had I mentioned a tin bath? And a loo that didn't flush? He would think I was crazy.

The kettle boiled and he made the tea, even using a proper teapot, which wasn't something I thought French people went in for.

'A habit I developed when I was working in London,' he said in answer to my enquiring look, 'my friend sends me over proper tea bags occasionally.'

So he had worked in London, that would explain his excellent English, and he had a friend who sent him tea bags.

He took a milk jug out of the fridge (he had a milk jug?) and passed it over to me. I wondered what on earth Isabel was doing upstairs, and inwardly cringed as I imagined it. Was she poking about? Being nosey as she usually was? There were only three bedrooms and a bathroom up there, it wasn't as though she was exploring Downton Abbey and had got lost in some endless corridor.

'Thank you,' I said, and took a sip, 'that's the best cup of tea I've had since I came over. Isabel only seems to drink coffee.'

He looked pleased. 'You are welcome to tea anytime.'

Well that was unexpected. Was that some sort of invitation? Perhaps it was.

He opened a tin that looked as though it had once contained biscuits, and then closed the lid and put it down again.

'Sorry, I seem to have run out. So what have you been doing since you came here?' he asked. 'Have you been enjoying yourself?'

Yes, I supposed I had.

'I've been helping Isabel get the holiday *gîtes* ready for the spring visitors. And she has a barn filled with *brocante*, which I have been helping her with. You know, making it look nice, so that people can see what she has in the best way.'

'Good, that sounds like fun,' he said.

There was a loud thump from upstairs and we both looked up at the ceiling. What was she doing? Was she rummaging through his cupboards, if he had any? Had she knocked herself out on a beam and fallen to the floor unconscious?

I went to look out of the kitchen window at the view down to the river, and of course beyond it the distinctive outline of Potato Farm with the two chimneys. Maybe he stood and looked out and pondered what we were doing, just as I did with him.

'I wonder what Isabel is up to,' I said at last, 'I can't believe she has got lost.'

'I expect she has a plan,' he said.

'Nothing she has told me about,' I said.

He looked down at his feet, slightly uncomfortable, or perhaps nervous?

'The truth is, Felix told me that you are on your own – he thought I should ask you out to dinner. I'm guessing Isabel is giving me some space to do so, trying to encourage me.'

'Oh, for heaven's sake!'

I gave a careless laugh to disguise my feelings. Even Felix was in on this. I think I felt slightly annoyed, and yet there was something exciting about it too.

He smiled. 'Silly, isn't it?'

What did he really think?

I thought about going out with him, trying to imagine him in some smart clothes, a suit and tie perhaps and me in an elegant outfit. I liked the idea of that. But I probably didn't have an elegant outfit with me. Perhaps I would have to buy something. I tried to control my thoughts, he hadn't even made the suggestion, I was three steps ahead of myself.

'Anyway, you don't like people,' I said foolishly. 'I'm told you prefer to be left alone.'

'I did for a while, for my own reasons. But now, well...'

'Oh, I see.'

'You are an interesting woman, I'll admit that. But—'

But I don't find you attractive, was the unspoken end to that sentence.

It was on the tip of my tongue to laugh, to correct him, to tell him that I wasn't at all interesting. That after I retired from teaching, my life had been filled with other people being interesting while I did the washing-up and the ironing. I'd sorted out family squabbles and problems. I'd helped with babysitting and sewing on name tapes to school uniforms, that sort of thing. Just for once I found the pause button and didn't say any of that.

Then I wondered what it was about me that made him come to that conclusion in the first place. I believed I was kind, evidently had some artistic talents if my sister's praise was any indication, I was a good cook and I liked to look after people, but was I interesting?

'Oh dear, I'm making a mess of this,' he said at last.

'No, not at all.'

I tried to sound as though I didn't care, but all of a sudden, I realised I did.

I would have enjoyed having dinner with him, getting to know more about him, maybe even making friends with him. But now the possibility seemed remote.

How did women manage this sort of thing? I knew nothing about the rules of dating for people my age. Not that this was dating, but it was the closest I had come to it for a very long time. And I'd blown it. Not so long ago I would have felt relief, but at that moment, I didn't. There was something about him I liked, and it wasn't just his good looks, or his dark eyes, or the way he smiled.

'Would you like more tea?' he said.

Probably not because then I would need the loo, but it would have been nice to carry on chatting to him, finding out more about his plans for the house and the neglected garden.

At that moment we heard Isabel coming back down the stairs, far more noisily than was probably necessary. She came into the kitchen with an innocent look on her face.

'You've done a lovely job up there. The bathroom is glorious. Nothing like it used to be.'

The moment between us was broken, and for some daft reason I felt a bit annoyed with her.

17

'So, you *don't* have a date with Luc!' Isabel said gloomily as we drove away ten minutes later. 'After all that effort. I knew it. I knew my plan wouldn't work.'

'You had a plan? Don't you think you should have told me?' I said.

'I just thought that as you are on your own and so is he, you might sort of – pair up? There aren't many good-looking, unattached men around here.'

'I think I have been ambushed,' I said, 'and why are you so determined to pair me off with someone?'

I sounded annoyed, but I was looking out of the car window and feeling rather confused and disappointed with the way things had turned out. Even at my age I didn't want to be thought of as some old bird who might be interesting *but...*

I hadn't been on a proper first date for decades. I hadn't spent any time alone with a man who wasn't Stephen, a doctor, dentist, or solicitor for years. I'd just spent a lot of time on my own. And much as I enjoyed relative peace and quiet, being lonely was a very different thing.

I spent the rest of the journey listening to Isabel recommending various cafés and restaurants where we could have gone, and then berating herself for coming back downstairs too soon.

'I'm not looking for anyone,' I said, 'and nor is he. Stop trying to tidy me away; married couples always do that, a woman on her own seems to make them twitchy for some reason. You're wasting your time.'

I didn't volunteer much to the conversation after that. As always with my sister, it was easier to let her get on with it. But I did think about it a lot. I wondered if it was as hard for men his age as it was for women. How did they know what the dating rules were these days? I certainly didn't. And I was beginning to see that he was just as nervous about it as I was. Perhaps I should do something to help myself, to help both of us over the first stumbling steps. And if it all went badly wrong, so what?

The supermarket was stuck on the side of a new industrial estate, which I didn't remember at all from my previous visits, and it was huge. In fact, it seemed far too big for the small, scattered communities I knew about, but Isabel said it was very popular, although the local traders in town had been predicting doom and disaster for their businesses ever since it had opened.

We took a big trolley and headed off down the aisles.

I loved visiting foreign supermarkets; they were full of unfamiliar food and unexpected things. Even the sight of the price cards, written in the classically French way, with curly script and sevens written differently were exciting. Back home I knew my local shop so well, I could have navigated it blindfolded; here things were different.

There were dozens of different jams and spreads, scented

honeys, boxes of rounded sugar cubes, a whole aisle devoted to various mustards and flavoured salt, hundreds of chilled desserts. The shopping cart was half full in no time.

I added a few things, proper English tea bags, some lavender soap in a beautifully rustic block, a new comb, because I'd mislaid mine, and some *Mère Poulard* butter biscuits. I didn't much care what the biscuits were like, but the square tin was delightful, with vintage writing and a picture of Mont St Michel. Then I added some rather more exotic chocolate cookies.

'We'd better get back,' Isabel said at last as she threw a new dog toy into the cart. 'I didn't actually plan on buying half these things, I just need some of those brioche rolls, I'm going to make burgers.'

'Just one thing before I forget, or it's too late,' I said as we loaded our shopping into the car, 'please don't go spreading this nonsense with Luc all around the town, will you? I know how gossip works.'

'Absolutely not,' Isabel said, rather outraged, 'as if I would! I am discretion personified!'

* * *

'So, you have a date with Jean-Luc,' Eugénie said the following morning when she called in unannounced for coffee.

I gave my sister an exasperated look, and her eyes slid away from mine.

'No, I don't. I don't know where you heard that,' I said, trying to sound outraged.

Eugénie sat down and took off her gloves, which were dark blue leather. Underneath her hands were, as always, beautifully manicured, with just one large diamond ring sparkling on her left hand.

'Goodness me,' I said, seeing an opportunity to deflect the conversation, 'what a beautiful ring, are you and Charles engaged?'

Eugénie flared her nostrils at me. '*Ridicule!* Of course not. What an idea. I am married to Bastien.'

'He has been dead for twenty-three years,' Isabel muttered, 'poor Charles.'

Eugénie bridled. '*Pas le pauvre Charles!* Not poor Charles at all. He is the most fortunate of men to spend time with me, and he knows it. This is a friendship ring. He gave it to me a long time ago. It was his mother's. I expect it is glass, and worth nothing. But it is pretty, I'll admit.'

'Is he still wooing you with romantic songs?' Isabel asked.

'He has taken to singing "Boum", all about his heart beating with love for me. But he pronounces it "Bum", which spoils the effect. Charles Trenet sang it much better. Now then, Jean-Luc. Tell me about that.'

'There's nothing to tell,' I said, at last realising it was pointless to lie about it. 'Felix suggested Luc should ask me out to dinner, but it was obvious he didn't want to. Which is fine by me.'

Eugénie pulled a face and then sighed.

'Men never know what they want until we show them, don't you know that? Bastien told his friends he didn't want to ask me to the Bastille Day dance in 1958. But I knew better, I knew he was the man for me. So handsome, with a wonderful head of hair. Three years later we were married with two sons, and I was digging rows of potatoes. So what do you know of him?'

Men never know what they want until we show them.

Yes, that was an interesting thought. Perhaps my idea to be a bit more proactive was worth considering.

'He seems very pleasant; we went to visit him and see how he is getting on with his house. And that's all.'

'You should have taken me,' Eugénie said, 'next time you go, if the Lord spares me, I wish to be included. I will ask him about my liver problems and ask if there is some new treatment.'

'I did tell you, he's not a medical doctor,' Isabel said, handing her mother-in-law her coffee in its special cup.

Eugénie took a sip. 'I will ask him anyway.'

'By the way, that special box you were asking about,' I said.

'The one you were going to do something clever with?'

I went to get it off the dresser. In Isabel's collection of things, I had found some vintage photographs, and some sentimental old Valentine's cards. I had bound them up with faded pink ribbon and put them inside.

'This was what I thought might be nice,' I said.

Her voice softened. 'Yes, that is very romantic. My Bastien used to give me cards like that. So pretty. I wish I had kept them all.'

I watched her as she examined the cards, a little smile on her face, her hands gentle on the ribbon. It was evident she liked what I had done, and I felt happy for her and rather proud.

At last, she re-tied the pink ribbon carefully around the cards, and put them back into the box, closing the lid with care. She was deep in thought, and her expression was unusually tender.

'Perhaps romance is what the handsome doctor needs. To take his mind off illness and death.'

'He's not that sort of doctor,' Isabel murmured again.

Two days later the first people came to stay in the *gîtes*. One was a young couple, Marcus and Cathy, who were celebrating their first wedding anniversary. They arrived in a battered old VW Beetle, laden down with cases and boxes of food. They seemed delightful, said polite things about the countryside and the *brocante* and then giggling, disappeared into the *gîte,* presumably to enjoy each other's company, so to speak. We didn't see anything of them for the rest of the day.

Later that afternoon the second renter, Bill, arrived; a man of about seventy, on his own who had come to '*finish his work*'. He made a lot of fuss about the broadband speed and wanted to know if there would be much noise, because he needed to concentrate.

'Not really,' Isabel said, handing over the welcome pack of leaflets and maps, 'the countryside is quiet, the dogs may bark a bit occasionally, but I don't think there is anything that will disturb you too much.'

'That's good,' he said, pushing his glasses up his nose, and looking earnest, 'because I am on a tight deadline. And I am hoping my two weeks here will sort things out.'

'That sounds interesting,' I said, 'what are you doing?'

'I am finishing my book,' he said proudly, 'my debut. I have nearly completed the first draft, it's already over two hundred thousand words, and I need to think about killing someone.'

'Not actually killing someone?' I said.

He gave a short, barking laugh. 'In my book. They do say that when you come to a tricky part, the best thing you can do is kill someone. The problem is, I have already killed off three people, including the main character. I'm wondering if another one is a good idea.'

'You won't have anyone left at that rate,' I said.

He looked thoughtful.

'Yes, I was sorry to lose my hero because I quite liked him. But then over Christmas I got fed up with him, he used too many adjectives, and he kept shrugging, so I had him shot. I did think of poison but then I couldn't decide who would do it and how. Poison is hard work, you know? Not for the faint-hearted. I'd already spent two weeks down a rabbit hole of research learning about cyanide. I hope the authorities never search my browsing history.'

'So it's a murder mystery?' Isabel asked.

'A murder-romance-steampunk crossover,' he replied, 'with elements of police procedural. I'm creating a new genre. And I do wonder if I did the right thing – shooting Simon at the end of chapter forty-seven, but then I was really pleased with the way that scene went.'

'Perhaps you could invent an identical twin brother to make a surprise appearance,' I said.

'I didn't know Simon had a twin,' Bill said, looking worried.

'But he could have if you wrote one,' I said.

'Hmm.'

Bill disappeared into his *gîte* and slammed the front door behind him.

'He's either furiously angry or inspired,' Isabel said. 'Come on, we have two customers at the barn. Let's go and encourage them.'

There was a middle-aged couple in there, poking about and admiring the watering cans. They also seemed to like the vintage farm implements and the milk bottles, but as the woman said, they didn't have room for much in their car. In the end they bought two tea towels with pictures of the iconic stripey beach tents of Dinard on them.

'Well, it's a start,' Isabel said, 'I always think it's lucky to have a sale on the first day we open.'

'Even luckier to have two,' I said as another car pulled up outside.

Two women got out and went towards the barn with a determined tread. One turned as she got to the door.

'Have you got any Beanie Babies? We are looking for a Princess Diana. Or Star Wars figurines?'

'No, I'm afraid not. But we do have some lovely vintage—'

They turned smartly around and got back into their car and were gone in no time.

'—pillow cases,' Isabel called after them. 'Oh well, can't win them all. You should go into the bookshop and help Felix out tomorrow; it would give you a change of scenery and I know he can do with the help. And Saturday is always the busiest day of the week, particularly now the holiday season has started. I could give you a lift. Or I suppose you could go in with Felix?'

'Do you think I would be any use?' I asked.

'Of course you would. If you can sell tea towels, you can sell books.'

'I don't think it's quite the same thing,' I said, 'particularly as most of the things will be in French.'

'But you could persuade him to stock those notebooks, I think that's a great idea.'

I suddenly felt rather unsure about the prospect. What would I know about the notebook-buying habits of the French?

'Oh, I don't know, Isabel, old dog, new tricks? I might say the wrong thing and then Felix might lose a lot of money. I'd hate to be responsible for that.'

Isabel looked exasperated. 'Look, I was reading about something called Kanreki the other day. It's a thing the Japanese do, a big celebration when people turn sixty. You wear red and get a party and presents, which sounds great to me. I'm annoyed I missed out on that. It's all about rebirth and new beginnings. And passing on the ghastly, adulting responsibilities to the next generation. Which if you think about it is what you and I have both done with our own children, isn't it? Although Pierre and Sylvie do live in a flat above Sylvie's parents' garage, so perhaps that doesn't count. Sylveste and Margot are living in a flat in town and are buying their first house soon, so that's definitely first-rate adulting.'

'I suppose so, although I'm still not convinced I did the right thing where Sara was concerned. But she does sound quite cheerful and positive in her emails.'

'Well there you go. But it means we've both missed out on a party. But when you get to seventy there's also a celebration called Koki when you're supposed to wear purple. And eighty is called Sanju. And you wear gold. So, the Japanese don't think that people our age are past it, do they? And nor should we.'

'I don't know. Sometimes I feel I am, and other times I'm not so sure. My hearing isn't as good as it used to be. I can't stay up as late as I used to, and I don't sleep as well either. I think I need stronger reading glasses too.'

Isabel put an arm around my shoulders.

'I like to think that although my eyesight might not be as good as I'm getting older, I can certainly see through people much better.'

I shook my head. 'Getting old is a pig of a thing.'

'Yes, but the alternative is worse. I used to be able to do handstands against the garage wall when I was younger, now I've been known to fall over putting my pants on.'

We both laughed and she hugged me.

'Okay, with that image seared into my brain, then I'll do my best. I'd quite like to drive actually,' I said, 'otherwise my battery is going to go flat. I haven't been out in my own car since I got here.'

'Always the practical one,' Isabel said. 'I'll tell Felix when he gets back, he'll be so pleased. And tomorrow is market day in the square, which is eternally interesting, and you know where you can park already.'

'By the tin plate sign?'

'Absolutely. Felix parks round the back of the shop, and he will tell the local *gendarmerie* it's your car, anyway they never make a fuss. His nephew, Andre, married one of the sergeants two years ago. I don't think you've met her, Mireille, she looks like a long-distance lorry driver but she's very sweet really. And her father is the mayor. That counts for a lot over here. You have to keep on his good side.'

I imagined myself driving into the town the following day, knowing where to park and the prospect was rather fun. I had opened my mind to the possibility of doing new things and found another one. It wasn't something for me to lie awake all night worrying about, it was exciting.

18

The bookshop was called *Le Livre Ouvert,* meaning The Open Book, and it was absolutely delightful. The window frames were painted blue, and there were ornamental white shutters on the outside. Two flower boxes underneath had been filled with plants and looked as though they would spring into colour before too long. There was also a small table and two ironwork chairs outside in the morning sunshine, tempting customers to sit and read for a while. Inside, the room was quite narrow but it stretched a long way back, with shelves which nearly reached to the low ceiling, and two racks of second-hand paperbacks, all marked very cheaply.

Inside was the distinctive smell of books and paper, which was just the same as the bookshop at home, 'bibliosmia' I thought it was called. Felix was sitting at his desk near the back of the shop, drinking coffee from a cardboard cup and eating a chocolate éclair out of a paper bag.

'*S'il te plait*, please don't tell her,' he said when he saw me, 'she makes me eat yogurt and fruit for my breakfast. It is not enough to keep a man going through a hard morning at work.'

I laughed. 'I won't. Now tell me what I can do to help?'

'I have a box of English print paperbacks just arrived; you could put them out on that empty shelf by the front door? And perhaps label them so people know what they are.'

It didn't take me long because there weren't that many. The usual best sellers on one shelf, sagas and romances on another, and a couple of books about the English countryside and French travel guides in English on a small low table in the window.

I spotted an old and very worn red tapestry armchair halfway down the shop covered with some old pamphlets and Felix's coat and scarf. I cleared it all away and moved the chair into the window and dusted it, to make a tempting reading area. The faded fabric somehow worked; it looked – what was the expression – shabby-chic.

'Yes,' Felix said when he came out of his office an hour later, 'that orange chair looks good. I don't know why Lisa didn't think of that.'

'It's red, actually. You could have done it too,' I said.

He looked thoughtful. 'I don't have those sorts of ideas. I have all the paperwork to do and the ordering. That takes up a lot of my time.'

'Which reminds me, those notebooks. You really should have some. And some pens and pencils too. I'm sure they would sell to your visitors.'

'Right then, against my better judgement—'

He went back into his office and brought out some booklets.

'This is what the man left me, and looking at them is driving me mad. They all look the same to me. I cannot decide between the colours. You choose what you think we should have. But don't get carried away, we don't have much space as you can see.'

Felix might not have liked looking at them, but I did. There were so many attractive colours and patterns, although they all seemed to have squared paper in them not the lines I was used to. I picked out half a dozen and went to ask for his opinion. I found him in his office, half hidden behind a computer screen and a pile of documents, eating chocolate. There were books everywhere; on the floor, under the desk, even piled up on a spare chair in one corner.

'These,' I said showing him the ones I had chosen, 'and if you buy enough the company will provide you with a little display stand. It says so in the small print.'

'I never noticed that, but where would that go?' he said gloomily.

'I thought we could move the small shelf with the guides to this area nearer to the front door, to catch people new to this area, and then behind that put the notebooks and the pens.'

'*Je ne suis pas convaincu...* I'm not sure.'

'Then I will buy them,' I said, 'then if they don't sell you will have lost nothing.'

We discussed this for a while, as Felix wasn't sure he liked the idea, but when I said that I would take any unsold ones back home with me, he agreed.

'Though what you will do with them, I can't imagine,' he said.

'I've already told you, give them as presents to my friends and family.'

He shook his head and did some muttering about the risk and all the terrible upheaval, as though I was planning to bring in a three-ring circus. Then he declared he needed another cup of coffee before he felt strong enough to place the order, and I walked to Mimi's café around the corner.

She greeted me as an old friend asking about Isabel and Eugénie until I left with a spring in my step, feeling quite the local. I hadn't felt like that at home for quite a long time, probably years, if I thought about it. Just a simple interaction, with some nodding and smiling. *Deux cafés et deux tartlelettes aux fraises, s'il vous plait.*

In the grand scheme of things, it wasn't much, but somehow it felt significant. Since I had arrived here, I had found myself doing new tasks, helping my sister, learning more of a language I thought I had forgotten, meeting new people and interacting with them. It was all very unexpected and rather exciting. Perhaps I had consigned myself to the scrap heap too soon; there might be more out there for me than I had anticipated.

I returned to the bookshop a few minutes later with coffee for both of us and two beautiful strawberry tartlets in a cardboard box to cheer us up.

'I have sold three of the English paperbacks already!' Felix said triumphantly as I walked in. 'Two women who wanted to know if we had anything about Star Wars and I said no, but we did have a vintage Tintin annual, and they bought that, even though someone had coloured in Snowy the dog to look like a spaniel. *Je suis ravi...* I am very pleased indeed. And you have brought me *une petite friandise* – a little treat! This is excellent news. Perhaps you are right about the notebooks after all.'

After we had finished our snack, I brought out a few more of the English paperbacks to fill the spaces, and by the end of the afternoon we had sold six and Felix had placed my order for fifty notebooks in different colours and patterns. He seemed quite jaunty by the end of the day.

'Lisa was very resistant to anything new, perhaps that was the problem. But you have persuaded me that perhaps I should do something exciting and unexpected,' he said. 'It's like Isabel told me, you can't *change* the people around you so change the *people* around you. I didn't know what she meant at first, but I think I do.'

'I wouldn't get too excited, Felix. It's only a few notebooks.'

'We'll see how they sell. And if they don't, you'll still take them, right?'

'Absolutely,' I said, wondering what I would do with them but not willing to admit it.

'*Bien*, you go home, and I will close up the shop. I won't be long,' he said.

* * *

Feeling incredibly positive and happy, I drove home through the dusk, and reached Potato Farm where the lights were still shining out from the barn, and there was a car parked in front of it. I could see Isabel inside, and a couple walking around, picking things up and putting them back again.

Getting out I shivered, there was a cold wind blowing my jacket open, and a few drops of rain fell onto my head.

'I'm glad you're back,' Isabel murmured as I looked in to see how she was doing, 'I've sold nothing all day and I don't think these people are really interested in anything other than the auricular theatre, and they can't fit that in their car. Even if I dismantled it, and then it would probably fall to bits, and they wouldn't be able to reassemble it. I don't think a pile of vintage French firewood would be very appealing to many people.'

'Where are they from,' I asked, 'perhaps I could take it back when I go and get it to them somehow?'

'It's a kind thought but they live in Glasgow,' Isabel said, 'it would cost you more in petrol than the thing is worth.'

I went forward. 'If you wanted something to put some small plants on, perhaps a few pots of herbs for your kitchen windowsill, maybe this would be suitable,' I said, pointing to the miniature *étagère*.

The couple looked at it very doubtfully.

'It's really lovely, I noticed that when we came in, but I don't think it would fit in the car, we have quite a bit of stuff already,' the woman said, although her eyes looked longingly at it. She reached out a hand and touched it regretfully.

'But if you did this...' I said. During our sort out of all the new things Isabel had collected over the winter, I had cleaned up the ironwork and oiled the bolts that kept the *étagère* together. Which meant that in moments I had unscrewed them and the whole thing folded flat.

The woman's face lit up and she darted a hopeful look at her companion.

'Lenny, I'd really like that, and she's right, it would hardly take up any room.'

Lenny rolled his eyes, and the deal was sealed.

'You said you were going to pace yourself, Jess. We've only been in France two days. At this rate you'll have to travel home on the roof rack.'

They drove away a few minutes later with the *étagère* in the boot of the car.

'Marvellous!' Isabel said happily, 'who knew you were such a salesman? And how did you get on at the bookshop?'

'Really well I think – it was fun, actually. I had such a great time. And yes, before you ask, Felix did put in an order for those notebooks.'

'Fantastic. Anyway, I have some exciting news. I had a phone call about the shepherd's hut. It's being delivered tomorrow. Probably in the afternoon because they are bringing it from Nantes. On the back of a low loader, so we'd better get the dogs in, and for now, looking at the cloud coming in, I think we'd better close everything up and get indoors. The weather forecast isn't looking good.'

19

That night a storm blew in from the Channel, and in my snug bed up in the attic, I could hear the rain thundering on the roof tiles. The wind was howling, too, it really was a bit eerie. The windows were shut tight against the weather, but being old and a bit rotten in places, I could see the curtains puffing out slightly when a particularly fierce gust caught that side of the house.

At some time in the middle of the night, I heard a worrying noise of something crashing about in the yard below me, but looking out into the darkness I couldn't see anything other than what was probably the recycling bin, tipped over and probably disgorging its contents onto the garden.

By the morning, the storm had eased off a bit, but a quick look outside showed I had been right. There was waste paper, plastic wrappings and bottles strewn all over the place and it looked as though the familiar outlines of the trees had changed. Perhaps some branches had been dislodged.

I dressed quickly and went downstairs just in time to see Isabel, shrouded in one of Felix's waxed jackets and a tweed hat, battling her way in through the back door.

It was obvious she was very upset.

'What's happened?' I said, 'are you okay?'

She wiped the rain from her face with a tea towel.

'Oh, I'm all right, I've just been picking up some of the rubbish from the bin that was knocked over, but my greenhouse isn't. Absolutely typical; I spent hours cleaning it out and washing all the glass, and now a damn great branch has come down and blown into the side of it. It's just about wrecked, and everything in there will be ruined. All my lovely plants, and they were starting to do so well. And the garden is full of rubbish and recycling. It's awful. I just came in to ring the boys and see if they can help.'

'I'll get my coat on,' I said. 'Where's Felix?'

'He's gone to work. Apparently there's been some damage to the bookshop, I don't know how bad, but Lisa rang him about half an hour ago because she lives in a flat just round the corner, practically hysterical. She says there are trees down across the road too.'

The kitchen door banged open at that moment, making us both jump, and Marcel stood there looking very dazed and confused. Holding a branch in his jaws, which was wider than the door frame, he had tried to bring it into the kitchen and crashed into the wall.

'Oh, for heaven's sake, Marcel, *chien stupide,* have you no sense at all?' Isabel shouted and then she burst into tears.

I took both of her hands in mine and rubbed them.

'Look, sit down for a moment, you're frozen. I'll make some coffee.'

'There's no time for that,' Isabel said, 'there is still rubbish all over the place. Luckily the *gîtes* are undamaged, but the site for the shepherd's hut needs clearing up because they will be arriving at some point today, and I can still see the dogs' paw marks all over it. And what I am going to do about the greenhouse, I don't know. I'm going to ring Sylveste again. He didn't answer ten minutes ago, knowing him he was probably still in bed. Honestly, considering he didn't sleep through a single night until he was three years old, he's certainly making up for it now.'

She found her mobile and stabbed at the keys again. I went to open the back door for another look at the damage outside, and Marcel triumphantly tried to bring his tree branch in again, nearly knocking me over.

After a brief tussle, I persuaded him back outside and threw his branch as far as I could, something that I could tell he thought was an excellent idea by his wagging tail and pricked ears. I watched as he ran round the yard with it in his jaws, scraping the side of my car with one end of it. Great.

'Still no answer. And I can't get through to Felix either. Perhaps it's the storm?' Isabel said after a few minutes.

'I hope Eugénie is okay,' I said, 'can you ring her?'

Isabel tried. 'Nothing from her either, there doesn't seem to be any signal. I'd better drive down and check on her. I'm not walking.'

'I'll come too,' I said.

'No stay here. Just in case the boys turn up. Or, heaven forbid, the shepherd's hut. Although they did say the afternoon. Oh dear, this is awful.'

I went to give her a hug. 'It'll be fine, we'll get everything cleared up in no time, you wait and see. And if the men arrive to deliver the hut, I'll entertain them with the accordion and songs from the shows.'

Isabel laughed and then jammed her tweed hat firmly over her eyes and refastened her coat and then slowly set off in her car towards Eugénie's cottage, Antoine and Marcel chasing after her, barking fit to burst.

If I was a dog, I think I would have preferred to be indoors, in my rather chewed basket under the kitchen table, gnawing at the new rubber pineapple Isabel had bought for them in the supermarket. I supposed that was just dogs, always wanting to be part of everything. Perhaps I should get a dog, or a cat. People did say they were good company.

For the moment, I stood wondering what else I could do to help Isabel and started off by doing the washing-up from the previous evening and putting things away. I might not be able to do much about a smashed greenhouse, but I was, after all, an expert in clearing up, wiping down the worktops and the kitchen table. Then I made a pot of coffee, ready for Isabel's return.

There was a knock on the kitchen door.

'That was quite a storm. I came to see if you were all right.'

I stood with my mouth unattractively gaping for a moment. It was Luc.

He was wearing a dark waterproof coat and a broad-brimmed hat, which at that moment made him look even more like Indiana Jones.

'Would you mind? Could I come in? It's still a bit wild out here,' he said.

'Oh gosh, of course, please do,' I said, rather flustered.

He stood on the doormat, water dripping off his coat.

'Coffee?' I said at last.

He nodded. 'That would be good. Thank you. Have you had much damage?'

'A lot of rubbish blown over the garden, I'm going out in a moment to pick it up. And Isabel says some glass in the greenhouse has been smashed. Were you okay? Any damage?'

'No, I am fine,' he said, 'just a couple of old tarpaulins blown down the garden. I have a small greenhouse, too, but it was sheltered behind an old wall, and didn't come to any harm.'

'Felix has gone into town, apparently there is some problem at the bookshop, and Isabel has gone to check on Eugénie. There doesn't seem to be any phone reception.'

'It must be the storm. I'm sure it will be fixed soon.'

We stood sipping at our coffee for a few minutes.

'Perhaps I could help clear things up?' he said at last.

'I'm sure Isabel would appreciate it,' I said.

'And I wanted to apologise,' he said, 'I was thinking about you.'

I felt a bit wobbly at that point; he'd been thinking about me?

'Whatever for?' I said trying to sound slightly amused and unflustered.

'The other day when you called in, I think I was rather rude.'

Well, no, not rude exactly, I thought. A bit crushing, perhaps.

'I could have handled it better,' he added.

'I don't actually need much *handling*, as you put it,' I said stiffly, 'and I certainly don't need my brother-in-law trying to organise my love life – no, I mean my *social* life. Or you for that matter.'

He looked worried. 'No, I am sure you don't. But possibly—'

He was interrupted by the back door crashing open and Isabel came in. Eugénie followed, crouched down in a position she kept up as she walked across to an armchair. It was like a Marcel Marceau mime, walking against the wind.

'Goodness me, it's still rather wild out there,' Isabel said, panting slightly, '*Mamie* has a couple of tiles off her porch roof, and she said she would feel safer here.'

Eugénie reached the armchair in the corner of the kitchen, with a lot of fuss and groaning, as though she had just run a marathon, not just been driven up the road.

Marcel and Antoine followed and with one look from Eugénie, slunk under the table and got into their basket. That woman had quite the authority, there was no doubt about it.

'I think she saw that Luc's truck was here, and she was very keen to come,' Isabel murmured in my ear.

'I have not slept a single moment,' Eugénie said in a wavering voice, 'everything banging about, the wind howling. I'm not sure I shouldn't have a cognac, to get over *le traumatisme* – the trauma. I have a tile loose.'

'Can't argue with that,' Isabel muttered.

'It was quite a storm,' Luc agreed.

'Perhaps you could suggest something to help me recover,' Eugénie said, 'something for my *crise de nerfs*. Nervous breakdown.' She held out one hand, and the diamond ring sparkled. 'Look, *mes mains tremblent*. My hands are shaking.'

Isabel opened her mouth to remind Eugénie yet again that Luc was not a doctor.

'*Thé à la camomille*,' Luc said kindly, 'camomile tea.'

Eugénie's face brightened. 'And do I need a prescription for that? Or do I need to see *un spécialiste*?'

She removed her plastic pixie hood and started to unbutton her raincoat.

Meanwhile Isabel went into her pantry and brought out a box of camomile tea bags which, with quite some dexterity, she passed to Luc behind his back without Eugénie noticing.

He bit back a smile and presented them to Eugénie, producing them with the skill of a conjurer.

'Happily, I have some here,' he said. 'I recommend you try them. You may not like the taste at first, but that is the way of all good medicine, *n'est ce pas*?'

'*Alors*,' Eugénie said with a triumphant look at Isabel, 'I knew the good doctor would be able to help me.'

'Pierre rang me when I was down the lane, he will call in to fix *Mamie's* loose tile. Now then, we must go and take a look at the damage to the greenhouse. The dogs can stay here with you, *Mamie*, I don't want then trampling through a lot of broken glass.'

'Perhaps you could dispense my medicine before you go?' Eugénie said in a pathetic voice, holding up the box of tea bags.

'*Permettez-moi*? I will do it for you,' Luc said, and Eugénie closed her eyes in satisfaction and sighed happily.

'*Je me sens déjà mieux.*'

'She says she feels better already,' Isabel said, and rolled her eyes at me.

* * *

Having settled Eugénie with her camomile tea, a blanket over her lap and a hot water bottle at her feet, the three of us went out to the vegetable garden to see what had happened to the greenhouse. The wind had dropped now, and the last of the storm clouds were blowing away over the horizon. We could see that a branch had landed on one corner and several of the glass panes were smashed.

'This can easily be fixed,' Luc said, 'the frame looks to be undamaged. I have some spare panes left over from when I was building mine, which may be of use. I have learned to do these things, it's not that difficult. I have some special gloves, which my brother advised me to buy.'

So, he had a brother! At last, some basic information about him. Isabel and I exchanged a look.

'That would be great. Pierre and Sylveste are so busy fixing other people's problems, and my poor plants... all those little seedlings... what am I going to do about them?' Isabel said sadly. 'I just know the rabbits will be in here the moment my back is turned.'

'I can take them over to my place,' Luc offered.

'Really? I could always move the trays into the barn or something. Although it's not very warm in there, and there's no light either. And despite Marcel and Antoine's efforts, there are probably rats too.'

'It's no problem,' he said, 'I can sort it out very quickly, and then when everything is mended, I will bring them back.'

The three of us hummed and haahed about this for a few minutes, and Luc tried to reassure her.

'Of course, I haven't started doing much in my greenhouse yet, it's the first time I have had one, so apart from anything else I would appreciate your advice later on. There's plenty of room. And you would need to clear away some space, while the repairs are underway. There is still a lot of broken glass in there to sweep up. And I would like to help.'

'That would be marvellous, if you're sure?'

'*Pas de problème* – no trouble. I can put them in the back of my truck.'

Isabel's eyes brightened, presumably as another of her cunning plans struck her.

'And maybe Joy can help you. I have the barn to look after, the shepherd's hut will be arriving, and I need to make sure the people in the *gîtes* are okay. I'm going to be terribly busy.'

I sent my sister a hard look and she smiled innocently back.

'Thanks so much, Joy.'

20

We spent the next couple of hours clearing up after the storm, Luc and I moving all the trays of seedlings and plants out into the back of his truck and Isabel and Pierre cleaning up the broken glass. Eugénie meanwhile remained in her armchair, sipping camomile tea, dispensing advice and occasionally shouting at the dogs when they edged nearer to the back door.

At last, we stopped for coffee. Felix had returned briefly to tell us that Lisa had been exaggerating, only one window had been cracked by flying debris and would be mended in a day or so, but apart from that everything at the bookshop was okay.

'So,' Luc said as he finished fastening a tarpaulin over the plants in the back of his truck, 'perhaps we should get these to my place, it won't take long. And I can bring the glass panes back when I return.'

'Oh, yes, you go,' Isabel said perhaps a bit too enthusiastically, 'don't hang around here, we can manage, and don't hurry, there's no rush. Take as long as you need. I don't have plans for lunch or dinner for that matter.'

I gave her another hard look behind Luc's back and she

responded with a sweet smile and some subtle, flapping hand gestures, encouraging me to go. What on earth was she playing at? This was getting embarrassing.

'Stop it,' I mouthed at her.

'Go on,' she mouthed back.

I was just baring my teeth at her in a snarl and making a slightly threatening gesture of my own when Luc turned and saw me.

'Are you okay?' he said.

I composed myself. 'Absolutely, I'm fine. Absolutely fine.'

Behind him I could see Isabel putting one hand over her mouth to stifle her laughter.

There had been no sign of the author-on-a-deadline-Bill from one of the *gîtes,* but just before we left, Marcus and Cathy appeared from their front door, took one look at the weather, and waved at us before going back indoors.

'I hope they have enough food and wine to keep their strength up,' Isabel said, 'perhaps I'll pop over later with a cake. Make sure they are okay.'

'You are horribly nosey; did you know that?' I said.

Isabel grinned. 'I'm a sucker for young love, or love of any sort really.'

'I hope you don't include me in that,' I muttered.

'No,' she said, wiping the mud off her hands, 'don't be silly.'

Love. No, I, of course, didn't need that at all. But what did I need? Companionship? Friendship? Someone to talk to?

I'd spent many long evenings on my own in the last few years. Not sure what I should be doing, still restricted by my old routines, which didn't really have much meaning any more and then perhaps resenting the times, like Christmas when things were out of my control.

There was no doubt about it, I was getting set in my ways, and if I didn't do something about it, I would miss out on whatever life still had to offer me.

* * *

We drove down the drive at a sedate pace a few minutes later and at the end Luc turned left instead of right towards the town.

'Thank you for this,' I said, 'it's very kind of you.'

'It's fine,' he replied. 'After all, as I said, I am local and maybe I have been keeping to myself too much. Perhaps sometimes I need more than my own company.'

'Me too,' I admitted, 'in fact, I'm not sure I even enjoy my own company half the time. But it's easier that way, I think.'

He didn't look at me, he was busy negotiating the lane, which was strewn with small branches. He seemed to be keeping to the middle of the road.

'Let's hope there's no one coming the other way,' I said, and he grinned.

I'm sure we were both remembering our first meeting.

'The road is not good,' he said, 'you can tell a local person round here, they always drive in the middle to avoid the potholes at the edges.'

We turned into his gateway, and up to his house. The skip had gone this time, and the place looked much better, less of a building site and more of a home.

The greenhouse was tucked away behind a high, stone wall in his garden, obviously new, the aluminium struts shining in the winter sunshine that was starting to come out as the last of the clouds blew away.

'I'm no gardener,' he said, 'but I'm willing to try now I have the time. The house is nearly finished, I need things to occupy me.'

'Gardening will certainly do that,' I said, 'there is always something to do.'

'You like it?' he said.

'I have a very ordinary garden,' I said, 'mostly lawn with some flower beds. I suppose it's quite boring really. But my ex-husband didn't like...'

I stopped. What had I been about to say?

Stephen hadn't liked disorder, clutter, muddle, or weeds in the garden, and he especially didn't like going out there to do anything about it. But throughout our marriage he had been very critical if I didn't. No, not critical exactly, more disappointed.

We got out of the car, Luc started to untie the rope which kept the tarpaulin down and I stood watching him, my mind elsewhere.

I should have said something to Stephen. At the time, and not just let his behaviour dictate mine. I'd had a mind and will of my own once, hadn't I?

And for a moment I imagined it. Telling him to rake up the autumn leaves. Suggesting he should weed the path or deadhead the roses. Or mow the lawn. But he had always been busy with something else, strangely I couldn't remember what that might have been. He'd been retired, fairly fit, but if I thought about it, most of his time had been spent in his study, reading obscure books about the Napoleonic wars or the state of the British economy. He had scoffed if he saw me reading one of the romance books I'd enjoyed, so I'd started to do even that in secret.

I'd only cooked the meals he liked, only worn the outfits of which he had approved. I hadn't even put out all my Christmas decorations for years. Why had I done those things? Was it because of his disapproval, so the house always needed to be tidy, the damn worktops clear? Was that why we hadn't had the grandchildren over very often? Because he didn't like the noise or the disruption to his ordered life? I felt the stirrings of anger for a moment, that he had gradually, over the years, restricted me, perhaps preferring me to concentrate on him rather than our wider family? On what few friends I had. I wondered if he was still doing that with Gillian. I hoped she wasn't putting up with it as I had.

Life here might be less ordered, but it was a darn sight more fun than I was used to.

As Luc coiled the rope up around his elbow, he turned to smile at me.

'I don't think these have come to any harm,' he said, 'our rescue mission will be a success, you'll see.'

A rescue mission. Yes, perhaps that was what I had needed, too, to find out how to meet people, how to make new friends, how to be myself and not just Stephen's reject.

It was one thing to be alone out of choice, and quite a different matter to be alone because I didn't know how not to be.

* * *

It didn't take us long to unload all Isabel's plants and seedlings from his truck. The shiny new shelves in the greenhouse were soon filled with the trays and pots. It was pleasant in there, out of the last of the wind, with the sun shining more strongly then, warming up the air. Perhaps that was what I needed, a personal greenhouse to encourage me towards the light and warm me again.

I watched him surreptitiously out of the corner of my eye. He was tall, handsome, intelligent, and somehow – what was it? – sad. Perhaps like me he was lonely? Men were famously unable to articulate their emotions, at least that was what I understood. They didn't have the equivalent of girly evenings when they could confess their feelings of inadequacy over a glass of wine, of dissatisfaction with their relationships or their appearance. No one ever asked a man if he was beach-ready or worried about wrinkles. But presumably they still had private doubts and fears. How did men cope?

And, thinking about it, when did I last have the opportunity for a girly evening? When had I ever spoken frankly with friends about my marriage, the lack of intimacy, of spontaneity? Of actually being silly and having fun. I couldn't remember.

'There,' he said at last, dusting the soil off his hands, 'all safely tucked up in their new home. I could do with a drink of water, what about you? What would you like?'

I followed him outside and watched as he slid the metal bolt closed. The last of the clouds had gone now, and the sun overhead was heating up the afternoon. The sky was bright, washed blue and there were birds singing in the hedges. And I realised, very suddenly, that I was happy. And as long as I didn't break any laws or upset anyone, I really could choose what I wanted. I could do what I liked. For too long I had been indecisive, and unsure and hesitant. I wasn't even in my own country. If I made a fool of myself, no one would know.

So, what would I like? I closed my eyes and thought about it. This was the moment I had imagined, that I had waited for, when I would voice my wishes and not just dither about with the normal: *oh, I don't mind, it's up to you.*

'I'd like you to take me into town and find a bar with a lovely view, and I'd like us to sit by the window and have a glass of wine. And perhaps a *croque monsieur*, one which is very hot with thick ham inside and a smear of mustard and with strings of melted cheese when I bite into it. And ideally there would be a red checked tablecloth, and a wicker basket of bread on the table.'

'That sounds an excellent idea. I know exactly the place,' he said, and he smiled at me, and I smiled back.

Goodness me, well that wasn't too hard at all.

After we had packed his spare panes of greenhouse glass into sacks in the back of the truck, we didn't go into the town, instead we went deeper into the countryside, which was looking green and washed after the rain. The sky was clear and bright, and on the narrow road there were puddles and water running down the edges. Earth banks on one side, and thick woodland on the other. Road signs to villages with unpronounceable names. Occasionally we passed a stone farmhouse, a horsebox left in a layby. Once or twice, we passed majestic houses, one with iron gates and sweeping lawns where there were two boys playing football. It felt very rural and French, even the light was different here; it couldn't have been England.

'That's a lovely place,' I said as we passed another one.

'I'm guessing a weekend retreat for some Parisian industrialist,' Luc said, 'where he can drop in with his helicopter and host lavish, champagne parties for his friends.'

'How marvellous, I wish he'd invite me too,' I said.

'Do you?'

I laughed. 'No, not really. I'm happy doing what I'm doing at the moment.'

'Me too,' he said.

I was happy, and so was he.

How amazing, and we hadn't really done anything particularly difficult. Just spent some time together, moved a few plants, even had a few laughs. But the big difference was that I had been relaxed, not worried, not fretting about doing the wrong thing or saying something daft. For the first time in years, I didn't feel that awful, clenched knot in my stomach, waiting for criticism or sighing disapproval.

He drove more slowly, almost stopping so that I could have a better look. That house had turrets and towers and a sign on the gate:

Attention au Chien.

Beware of the dog, accompanied by a picture of a slavering Alsatian. Underneath it stood a white, miniature poodle with a blue collar, staring through the bars.

'He might be fiercer than he looks,' Luc said.

'An attack poodle,' I agreed, and he laughed.

I flicked him a glance. Wondering how I had come to this place, sitting in this truck with a man I hardly knew, but feeling unexpectedly comfortable in his company. And we were going out for lunch together, people seeing us might think we were an actual couple. Couples did that all the time, didn't they? But I hadn't, not for several years.

We reached a small town where he pulled the truck into the side of the road and we got out.

'I can't provide you with wonderful views, but I can vouch for the food,' he said.

Inside was a low beamed room, quite small but wonderfully scented with garlic and herbs and woodsmoke from the open fire. And yes, there were couples sitting at tables, some of them chatting, others concentrating on their food and hardly speaking. We found a table next to a window, with a view over the garden and beyond that fields, which had been ploughed into orderly lines.

'You prefer red wine I think, you like Bordeaux?' he said, and I nodded rather touched that he had remembered.

He went to the bar returning with two glasses of wine and two menus.

'By all means take a look, but I know they do a very fine *croque monsieur*. And you did say that's what you wanted.'

'Perfect,' I said.

And it was. Although that lunch was so simple and some might say, unexciting, it was exactly what I had wanted. And as I sat there picking the strings of gruyère cheese off my face, the fledgeling feeling of happiness inside me increased.

'This is marvellous, such a treat,' I said.

He looked a little puzzled. 'It's just a modest meal, nothing out of the ordinary.'

'It is to me,' I said.

How could I tell him that asking for something simple and getting it was something I wasn't really used to. Stephen would have said it was just posh Welsh rarebit and not worth the price. That as we were eating in a French restaurant, I would have been better off with *steak frites*, or duck *à l'orange*. And then he would probably have ordered for me, and fool that I was, I would have let him.

'I wonder if the shepherd's hut has arrived,' I said after a few minutes, 'I can't wait to see it. I'd really love to have one.'

'And what appeals to you about it?'

'Oh, I don't know, just the thought of a small, private space like that, where everything is close to hand. Somewhere that doesn't need a lot of work, or stuff. Where I can put the things that really matter to me, rather than clutter that I have collected. I've been trying to get rid of things in the last few years since my marriage ended. I've realised I have too much, too many things, that no one will want after I am gone. So, to get rid of things now is good, I'm sparing someone else a task.'

He took a sip of wine and shook his head. 'You are very young to be thinking of that.'

I laughed at that, and he held up one hand.

'No, don't laugh as though you don't believe me, you are young. You may live for another twenty or thirty years. Shouldn't you be enjoying your life on your own terms, not worrying about making things easy for other people?'

Yes, perhaps I should. I sat up a bit straighter in my chair.

'You're right, I do that a lot,' I said, 'I worry about other people and what they will think of me. It's just the way I am.'

'I didn't used to think like that,' he said, 'but now I do. Something happened which made me change.'

Aha, for the first time he was talking about himself, what had made him decide to be so isolated for so long in a sleepy little corner of France.

'And what was that?' I asked, amazed at my own boldness.

He hesitated.

'Many years ago, I was lecturing in a university – English history as you know, and I met Sabrine. She was a research student. Oh, this was perhaps fifteen years ago, up until then I had not made the opportunity for finding a wife, but with her it felt right. Eventually we married, we were very happy, we had a little apartment in the middle of town near a park where we could walk and talk. She had her studies, and I had mine. She cooked, for me and for our friends. We made all sorts of plans for the future. Where we would travel, perhaps it wasn't too late to have a family, she was some years younger than me, but then two years later she died. A car accident, icy roads just outside Lyons, no one else involved.'

I gasped. 'I'm so sorry.'

'People were kind but eventually I couldn't bear the sadness, or the sympathy. People thinking I could be mended, it just reminded me of what I had lost. So, I made my work into my life again. Until the time came when I could not continue, because I was being encouraged to retire. Money, it all came down to money, and I was expensive to employ at a time when budgets were being reduced. And then I realised that without my work, without Sabrine, I actually had nothing. Oh yes, I had a home, my books, a few good friends but nothing that defined me, as a person. It was like putting my head over the top of the trench where I had been hiding. And finding that everyone had gone, that I was alone. But then I had made my choices, and I had to live with them.'

'You said you have a brother,' I said, 'other family members?'

'Yes, and they were kind and supportive, but people have their own lives to lead, a family tree branches out over the years, and the shade underneath can be very dark. I am not looking for sympathy, I assure you. I am just trying to answer your question. Sometimes I think I was a coward. I didn't take chances, opportunities that might have changed me.'

'No, I think you are being unfair to yourself. Life is difficult. We deal with it in our own way.'

'I, like you, also worried too much about what other people would think,' he said.

I laughed. 'Aren't we a silly pair? Have you met *other people*? Some of them are awful.'

He laughed, too, raised his wine glass towards me and we chinked them together in a toast.

'Here is to the future,' he said, 'doing things because we want to, because we can.'

I liked the sound of that.

We were there for a long time, just chatting and enjoying watching other people come and go. It was not the sort of location that would have been mentioned in any good food guides or tourist brochures, but it was a pleasant place, calming and restful.

Our waitress was a middle-aged woman in a pink overall, who didn't seem bothered that we were spending a long time over our simple meal. Occasionally she went back to the kitchen, returning with someone's main course or dessert. Once or twice, she asked if we needed anything, some *tarte tatin* perhaps or a *crème brulée*, and we said no, but in the end we had coffee which came with a *madeleine* in the saucer.

'Right,' Luc said at last, 'I suppose we had better get back and hand over the glass panes, otherwise your sister will be worried about you.'

'I doubt it,' I said, 'we both know she's been pushing me to spend time with you ever since I met you.'

'And,' he said, 'most importantly, I still haven't taken you to find some spectacles to replace the ones you slammed in your car door.'

I spluttered with laughter. 'I was so cross, wasn't I? And so embarrassed. I'm sorry I shouted at you.'

'*Tout va bien*,' he said, with a grin.

And suddenly, it felt that yes, everything was okay.

Despite my previous concerns about spending time on my own with him and getting to know him. Even the fact that I definitely found him attractive, it had all been so ridiculously easy.

Was this a good thing? But then did change always have to be hard? Couldn't it sometimes happen almost unnoticed?

21

Luc drove me back to Potato Farm, and the early evening shadows lengthened across the fields and hedgerows. He pulled to a stop outside the kitchen door, and almost immediately, Isabel opened it and Marcel and Antoine shot out, sniffing eagerly at the wheels of his car.

'Everything okay?' she said, darting looks between us.

'Fine,' I said, 'we went and had lunch somewhere after we had finished with the plants.'

'Where did you go?'

I turned to Luc, and he mentioned one of the villages with the unpronounceable names and Isabel nodded.

'Has the shepherd's hut arrived?' I asked.

She nodded. 'Come and see it, it's so sweet, I almost want to move in there myself. I mean, it needs sorting out and prettying up – you can be in charge of that – and bed linen and towels of course, but it's like a little playhouse. When we have done that, I must take some pictures to put up on my website.'

'I'll put the spare glass in the greenhouse and then leave you to it,' Luc said.

'You don't have to go,' Isabel said.

'I still have some painting to finish; I really want to get it all done before my things arrive. I've had them in storage, and now I think I want to get them back, so I can do some sorting out of the things that matter to me.' He threw me a look. 'Today has made me feel I should be organising myself at last.'

'Well,' Isabel said, as we watched the taillights of his truck disappear up the lane, 'what was all that about? What did you say to him.'

'Oh, nothing much.'

'Liar, liar, *pantalon en feu!*'

I laughed. 'We just had a chat about what mattered to us, how it was easy just to hang on to things that we didn't need.'

'And did you find out anything about him? His past?'

'A few things, but I am loath to tell you because then the whole town will know.'

'You are mean!'

We went back into the kitchen and the dogs flopped into their bed under the kitchen table, not interested in me any longer.

Luc and his past. What had I learned.

He'd known heartbreak, and loneliness, just as I had. He'd decided to do something about it, and I knew how much courage that took. I too was starting to hope that life had more to offer me than patiently waiting for something to happen. I was beginning to think about my life in a different way: I wasn't going to be satisfied with being at the edge of other people's lives, I wanted to be at the centre of my own.

'Let's just say that he is a really nice man, who perhaps, like me, has had a few setbacks, but is realising that there is still life out there to be lived.'

Isabel clasped her hands under her chin in delight. 'I knew it! I knew you two would hit it off. I'm never wrong.'

'Isabel, we didn't hit anything off. We just moved your seedlings and had lunch. And you have been wrong many times. You thought David Cassidy waved to you in the audience when we went to that concert, and that he was going to ask you backstage and then he would fall in love with you, and you would get married. Now then, show me this shepherd's hut.'

'So, you're really not going to give me all the juicy details?'

'There aren't any, and if there were I wouldn't tell you because you would tell Felix and then Eugénie and then everyone within a fifty-mile radius would know.'

'How very dare you! I wouldn't. And anyway, I'm your sister, it doesn't count if you told me. Do you know, Charles came to collect Eugénie in his car just after you left. He said he wanted to take her to Venice for her birthday, but I wasn't to tell anyone. Can you imagine that pair walking around Venice and getting lost?'

'I think you've just proved my point,' I said, grinning.

* * *

Over the next couple of days while Pierre repaired the greenhouse, Isabel and I fussed about in the *brocante* barn, restocking as things were sold, and Felix reported that the damaged window in the bookshop had been replaced.

And so, with all these problems sorted out, we turned our attention to the shepherd's hut. It had been connected up to the water and the drainage, and we wanted to make it look gorgeous. Isabel would just have put clean sheets and towels in there with perhaps a few decorative items. I had other ideas.

Fired up with the success of the newly renovated *gîtes*, I suggested that we theme the hut on flowers, pastel colours to match the pale green exterior and some of the beautiful porcelain crockery she had collected in the *brocante*. Even the tea towels I picked out were vintage in pale shades of blue and pink.

'It's not very masculine,' she said at one point, 'it looks like a she-shed. The sort of place where a writer would come to finish off their sweeping romance novel.'

'Then advertise it like that,' I said, 'writers are always looking for somewhere peaceful and gorgeous to write. And when they aren't doing that, they are taking pictures to put on Instagram. You must have seen them? #ruralpeace #inspiration. I read an article about a woman who writes medical romances, very successfully. She said she was inspired by always starting off her books in a treehouse in the Lake District.'

'What's that got to do with doctors and nurses?'

'Nothing, but it was the location that she mentioned. And after that, apparently they were inundated with bookings because of her. Perhaps you should put something up on social media, to let people know what you have to offer?'

'Well, okay,' Isabel said doubtfully, watching me arrange a lace-edged cloth into a wicker bread basket. 'I guess you could be right. I've done a bit of Facebook advertising before, but I'm not sure it made much difference.'

'Instagram? TikTok? That sort of thing?'

'No, not really, it never crosses my mind. Perhaps we could give it a go? Your idea about putting vintage things in the *gîtes* seems to be working. Cathy from *gîte* number one has already said she would like to buy the cups and saucers to take home. I don't know what to charge her.'

'That's great. And let's get those two *gîtes* some proper names too.'

'Why? I've always called then number one and number two – ah, I see what you mean. What do you suggest?'

'Something French and romantic. *Clair de Lune*, perhaps and *La Vie en Rose*.'

'Oooh, that sounds nice, and I could replace the teacups she wants to buy with those pink lustre ware ones, to carry on the theme. And there are some sheets embroidered at the top with pink thread. I don't think they've ever been used. I could put those in there.'

'Excellent ideas,' I said, 'And we could get one of your boys to paint some cute nameplates for the doors.'

'Sylveste, he's the artistic one,' Isabel said, 'although his girl-friend Margot is an art teacher, she does a nice sideline painting empty wine bottles to sell in the craft market, she might be the one to ask.'

'Even better,' I said, feeling very pleased.

'Well, the greenhouse is repaired, all the new putty has set, and we have cleaned the shelves in there. All I need now is my plants back,' Isabel said with a meaningful look.

'You mean you want me to go and get them?' I said.

'Exactly.'

I rolled my eyes at her in mock exasperation, but secretly, I rather liked the prospect.

Driving over to Luc's house the following day, I felt a silly buzz of anticipation, I was looking forward to seeing him again. I was wearing some new jeans because I still hadn't managed to get the concrete smudges out of the old ones, and a rather cute, checked shirt, in a nod to being a capable, workman type. I had scraped my hair back into a high ponytail and had bought a new, red sweater from the market, which said it was genuine *blended* 5 per cent cashmere. I didn't think it would pass the Vanessa test, and it was made in a country I'd never heard of, but it was a terrific bargain. I tied it around my neck in a way I thought was French and attractive and I'd even put on some make up and a slick of lipstick. And on top of all that effort, I'd brought a small gift to thank Luc for his help.

Perhaps I was overthinking this? It wasn't as though I was hoping for this to be a romantic meeting, was I? After all, we hadn't really spent much time alone in each other's company, but he did seem to like talking to me. And I liked talking to him. It was pleasant to be able to chat to someone who didn't already have an opinion of me, or my past or what I was doing now. Perhaps we would chat easily with each other, as we had that day when we had gone out to lunch, and he might say some nice things to me. What sort of nice things, I wasn't sure. Maybe he would pay me a compliment.

When I thought back, Stephen had seldom paid me any compliments and had always had a firm opinion about everything. Sometimes it felt as though he wanted to share them with me on every subject in order to persuade me that he was right. I think that was a man thing. Mansplaining.

I think a lot of men were like that, I remembered a man in our quiz team telling me the right way to make a Christmas cake, when I had been making them successfully for years. And Stephen, who had probably never cooked a meal in his life, once stood behind me and told me I was chopping the onions wrong. He didn't exactly tell me not to make such a fuss when I was in labour with Sara and swearing, but he came pretty close to it.

Luc wasn't like that. He just listened and laughed in the right places, which hadn't always been my experience. It was really refreshing. Was that really enough to make me like him? Just because he didn't argue? Was that a negative reason to like someone? Thinking about it, Isabel and Felix argued all the time, and they seemed happy.

As I got to his house, I slowed down, negotiating all the ruts and potholes in the lane, until at last I arrived. But it looked as though he wasn't there. The space where he usually parked his red truck was empty and I felt ridiculously disappointed. I should have rung him or texted him first, Isabel knew his number, after all.

I knocked on the front door twice, but there was no answer. And then I peered through the window, where everything looked distinctly tidy and unoccupied.

I stood for a moment, enjoying for a moment the tranquillity of the place, the sun warm on my face, the air crisp and clear. I took in a few deep breaths and coughed. I'd always been a city dweller, maybe I wasn't used to clean air. But perhaps I could begin to understand why he had moved here.

Oh well, down to work. I could move a few trays of plants just as well as the next person. I'd even put the seats down in the back of my car ready to fit everything in.

I went around to the greenhouse and slid back the bolt. It all looked very lush and healthy in there. Even in the last few days the plants had done well. Isabel would be pleased, and I was glad to feel I was helping when she had been so kind to me.

I started with some of the trays of seedlings, balancing one on each hand and took them to the car, where, of course, I had forgotten to open the boot or the car doors. So then I had to put everything down again, and mess about, moving the shopping bags and jump leads out of the way. And the compressor and the bottle of tyre gunk, which I would need if I ever had a flat tyre. I'd only ever investigated it once, and never managed to get all the tubes and cables back into the handy carry case. And whether I had the ability to use such a thing in an emergency was another matter. Perhaps I should watch a YouTube video when I got the chance. And weren't Isabel and I supposed to be making a video for social media? Perhaps I should give that some thought too.

The next bit was fairly easy, four more trips with little pots and one hanging basket. All that remained were the bigger plants. I realised that I should have done this in exactly the reverse order, put the big ones in first and fit the smaller trays around them. So, of course, then I had to take everything out yet again.

After the first one I started to think that this had been a bad idea. I'm fairly strong but lifting an earthenware pot filled with compost and a reasonably sized azalea wasn't easy, so I rolled it and dragged it to the car accompanied by a lot of grunting noises and complaints. How I was going to get it up and into the boot was anyone's guess. Why were cars designed like that? Why was there a foot high lip into the boot? Wouldn't it make sense to just have it flat, or even have some mechanism to raise things of this sort like they have on the back of removal vans?

Then I went back for another one that was even bigger. By the time I got it to the car I was regretting what I was doing even more, but I was determined not to give up. Eventually I pulled all five of the pots into position, perhaps if I had a little rest I would regain some upper body strength, enough to haul them up.

I sat down on the ground, with my back against the car wheel, and wiped my sweating face with a tissue. I was probably as red as my sweater with the effort of all this.

After a few minutes, my heart rate and my breathing had gone back to normal, and I decided to try again. What had Isabel said, you never know how strong you are until there was no option? And as there was no sign of any strong-looking person around to help me, there wasn't an option.

'Right,' I said, addressing the azalea, 'you're a pot, I'm a strong capable woman.'

I put both arms around the top and heaved the pot up and, spilling damp compost all over myself and the boot of my car, but I got it in. Triumph! Success!

The second one was bigger, and I gave a mighty heave and the sort of *gaaaaahhhh* noise that an Olympic weightlifter might have made. This time it didn't work. I lost my footing, my knees buckled, and I fell over backwards, tipping the pot, a lot of the compost and the plant, which I think was a rhododendron, all over myself.

I lay there stunned for a moment, pushing my hair out of my eyes, it seemed the ponytail wasn't working, and then got up, spitting out dirt, brushing myself down, and using words that my children and grandchildren would have been surprised I knew.

I untied the sweater from around my neck where it had morphed into some sort of garotte, then I scooped up the soil and the battered plant and put them back into the pot. Interesting thought, perhaps I should empty the pots first? Put them into the car and then put the plants back in?

No, I was sure that wouldn't be a very good plan, and then all Isabel's plants would die, and all this would have been for nothing.

I had another sit down, wishing I had brought something to drink. A bottle of water perhaps. Maybe there was a tap somewhere, he probably had some sort of outside water supply. I wandered around the house again, and yes, there was a neatly coiled yellow hosepipe connected up to a brass tap. Perhaps I could scoop some water up into my hands. But my hands were filthy. Perhaps not. I rinsed my hands off under the water flow, which was spluttering and slow, the water pressure round here was always unpredictable, and then dried them by rubbing them down the legs of my new jeans.

Round the back of the house, I could see through the windows into the kitchen, which again, was tidy and clean. On the worktop there was a kettle, and I looked longingly at it and thought about how close I was to tea bags and a clean mug. There might even be chilled water in the big fridge, or little, glass bottles of *Pellegrino Limone*, which I loved.

I gave a sad little whimper and thought how thirsty I was yet again. And my back was hurting, too, I thought it quite possible I had pulled a muscle or perhaps it was worse than that and I had slipped a disc. I imagined myself in traction in hospital with the nuns Eugénie had mentioned, gliding around my bed, sneering at me and telling me how foolish I had been.

I sat down on the step outside the back door with a wince of pain, and realised there was nothing for it, I would have to squirt some water into my mouth from the hosepipe. The pressure wasn't very good; I was sure it would be okay.

I lifted the hosepipe with its fancy, multi-spray attachment to my mouth and pressed the lever. There were a couple of pathetic splutters of water. Perhaps there was a kink somewhere in the neatly coiled hose. I gave an impatient tug and tried again. Of course, this time a fierce jet of water shot out and hit me in the face, making me rock backwards and fall, screaming, off the step onto the ground.

'What on earth are you doing now?' said a worried voice.

I looked up from my prone position on the grass. I'd managed to lock the hose and the water continued to pour out all over me. I was soaking wet, filthy dirty, my hair was all over my face and I felt more foolish than I had in my life.

'Hello, Luc,' I said, trying to wrestle the hosepipe away from my legs and sound as though this was an everyday occurrence and not one of the most embarrassing moments I had ever experienced, 'I thought I'd pop over.'

'To do what? Drown yourself?' he said, turning the tap off.

He held out a hand to help me.

When I was younger, I used to be able to spring up unaided, now I needed someone to haul me up like a sack of potatoes and when at last I stood upright, my back felt very painful indeed. I tried to look unconcerned and not wince with pain as the water dripped off my hair and down my face. I'd put mascara on that morning, too; I bet I looked a sight.

'I'm guessing you came to get Isabel's plants back?' he said.

'That was the idea,' I said, not sure whether to laugh or cry. 'But I couldn't lift them into my boot.'

He tutted a bit. 'Are you okay? Not injured? Why didn't you ask me? I would have brought them back.'

Who knows? For a moment I asked myself the same question, and then realised it was because over the last few years I had become used to sorting this type of thing out on my own. Had I wanted to seem capable or resourceful? Not expecting some man to come to my assistance. Well, that didn't end well.

'And what were you doing with the hosepipe?' he added.

'I was hot and thirsty,' I said, rather sulkily.

At that point he roared with laughter and despite myself I could feel the corners of my mouth twitching, and then I laughed, too, although I was having to hold onto the doorknob, and little stabs of pain were radiating down one leg. Even so, as we stood there laughing together in the sunshine, it was the best feeling in the world. He wasn't laughing at me; he was laughing with me.

'Oh dear,' he said after a moment, 'I think you have hurt yourself.'

'My back,' I said, 'I think I've done something silly.'

He unlocked the back door and helped me inside, where I made a trail of muddy foot marks on the clean stone floor, and then he sat me down on one of the kitchen chairs and went to put the kettle on.

'A cup of tea, I think,' he said.

If he had offered me a bottle of Veuve Cliquot, it wouldn't have sounded any better.

'Yes, please,' I said, 'and I've brought you a present, but it's on the front seat of my car, if you want to go and get it. I don't think my back is up to anything much at the moment.'

He came back with my gift of *Mère Poulard* biscuits in the cute tin with the swirly writing and put them on the table.

'You mean these? That's very kind,' he said.

'Well, you did say you'd run out,' I said, wincing as I tried to get comfortable.

'That's so thoughtful, thank you. Do you need *un antidouleur* – a painkiller? Or perhaps something to rub on your back? Some liniment?' he made little motions with his hands as though he was massaging an arthritic horse.

Oh my word, this really was one of the least romantic situations I had ever been in, and on top of that as my clothes dried I think I was beginning to smell rather rustic.

I sat and drank my tea and ate three of *Mère Poulard* biscuits, which really were rather good, while Luc moved all the plants into the back of his truck in about ten minutes. He came back into the kitchen and drank his tea.

'All done,' he said, 'how are you feeling?'

'Fine,' I said, moving to check that I did.

And, of course, I didn't. My back was jolly painful and the pains radiating down my leg were worse.

'I think I'd better take you home,' he said, 'I don't think you should be driving, do you?'

'No, probably not,' I said, feeling a complete fool.

I rubbed my hands over my face and felt dried mud meaning I probably looked terrible too.

22

I'd never realised that something as simple as walking to the car and getting in could be so difficult.

And, of course, it wasn't an ordinary car, where possibly I could have slipped down into the seat, it was a truck, where I needed to haul myself up what felt like an impossible distance. And I couldn't walk without wincing either. So, in the end, I borrowed a spade to lean on as a makeshift walking stick, the handle padded out with my lovely red sweater – so elegant – and Luc supported me on the other side while I hobbled around like some decrepit old tramp. And then he helped me get up into the passenger seat, as though he was loading ballast.

At last, between the two of us I got there, and he swung my legs round so that he could close the door. But then, before he did, he gave me a look that was filled somehow with both humour and sympathy.

'You poor thing, and you were just trying to do something kind,' he said and he leaned forward and kissed me.

I thought it quite possible I was going to explode with the shock.

Then he closed the door and went to get into the driver's seat.

'Okay?' he said, looking over at me.

'Mmm, yes, absolutely,' I said, my voice a bit croaky.

Inside my heart was thudding at unexpected and ridiculous levels. It was the first time any man had kissed me for years. I started thinking about how long it had been, and then stopped myself, because it really didn't matter any more.

He drove back, very slowly, avoiding all the worst potholes and divots in the road, because every time we hit one, I would yelp with pain, and he would apologise.

'Promise me you won't do this sort of thing again,' he said. 'Next time, ask me to help.'

Next time… I didn't think there would be a next time. Would there? I wasn't planning on lugging plant pots or heavy furniture or coal sacks any time soon.

I'd been in France for weeks now; I guessed I should really be thinking about going home. I was only allowed to stay until the beginning of April. Surely this was not the time to develop a crush? Or if not that, then an unrealistic attraction?

There were probably a lot of middle-aged women in the area, who would have formed an orderly queue if they thought Luc was out in public at last. The line from *Dirty Harry* was going around my brain; a man's got to know his limitations. Or in my case, a woman.

* * *

Back at Potato Farm, Isabel was outside, pegging out some washing and trying to keep Marcel and Antoine from dragging it off the line again, she turned and waved as the truck pulled up.

'Everything okay?' she said cheerfully.

'We have a slight injury,' Luc said as he came to open my door and help me down again.

I stood with my knees bent trying not to crouch too much.

'I think I've pulled a muscle,' I said.

There was a lot of fuss and exclamations from my sister at that point, and between them they helped me shuffle into the kitchen where I sat gratefully on a chair. Eugénie was already there, sitting in state at the other end of the table with her usual espresso.

'You idiot,' Isabel said, dithering around me, not quite sure what to do, 'what on earth have you been doing? Where's your car? And why are you so muddy and damp?'

'Don't ask,' I muttered.

'And, to be honest, you don't smell too good either,' Isabel said.

'Wet clothes are bad for the soul, and for the lungs,' Eugénie said, putting her cup down, 'you always seem to be wet; I have noticed this. Is this something English people like to do?'

'No, it's not,' I said wincing as I tried to get comfortable.

Eugénie's interest peaked. 'And you have pulled a muscle? What were you doing? Back problems have plagued me all my life. You can ask me anything. It was the potatoes at first when I was younger. Hours spent in the fields, you young people have no idea what hard work can be. I was underneath a doctor for weeks. Months. Crying with the pain, unable to lift a spoon. But you're not as bad as I was, I can tell.'

'I'll be fine,' I said, 'just a tweak.'

'Even so, you will need an operation, I know all about this. I expect you will be in a plaster cast from your neck to your knees, if there is no paralysis. I had a friend with back problems, by the time she was eighty-three she was in a wheelchair. Perhaps the good doctor here can advise you? His prescription tea worked a miracle with me. Eight whole hours I slept, it took me two days, but it is better than I am used to.'

'I think just some simple painkillers and rest,' Luc said, 'and no one is to upset you.'

'Then I will pray to Saint Gemma Galgani, who is the patron saint of back injuries,' Eugénie said kindly, 'and I will mention it to the priest when I see him. He is a great prayer, much better than the new curate. Père Phillippe knows what he is doing. Well, after fifty years, he should.'

'I'd appreciate it,' I said.

'But tell me what happened,' Isabel said.

Luc made a move towards the door.

'I will unload your plants and put them in the greenhouse,' he said, 'and then I will leave you to it. Perhaps a good book to read, in a comfortable chair. And no lifting heavy objects in future.'

He gave me a twinkling smile and just for a moment rested one hand on my shoulder.

Like some silly teenager, I imagined I could feel that slight pressure for a long time afterwards.

* * *

I spent the next half hour going over the morning's events and was rewarded by sympathetic and enthusiastic wincing and tutting from Eugénie, and dire warnings not to be so stupid in future from Isabel.

After a while I decided I really did need to go to my room and change into some clean, dry clothes, only to realise that I wasn't going to be able to get up two flights of stairs in less than an hour.

'No problem at all,' Isabel said, 'I said I needed someone to test out the shepherd's hut, so we will put you in there while you recover. There's everything you need in there, and I will bring clothes and toiletries down from your bedroom for you. It's the perfect solution.'

In a day that had been filled with disappointment, failure and pain, this sounded like a fantastic idea, and so Isabel helped me limp out to the shepherd's hut, where I sat in a chair that was exactly right. Not too low so that getting out of it would be a problem, and not too soft, so that my sore back had some support.

'I'll go and get your things. Stay there,' she said.

'I don't really have much option,' I replied, and she laughed.

'I'll bring your laptop out too so you can check if the broadband speed is okay.'

Eugénie came and looked inside and sniffed her disapproval.

'I would not like to be *abandonée* in pain and suffering in a shed,' she said, 'although my parents knew someone who had to live in a barn when their house was bombed in the war. No heating, no running water, nothing. The only good thing was the Allied soldiers. The British brought food parcels and the Americans brought chocolate and nylon stockings. So not all bad, I suppose. Their daughter, Giselle, married one of them and went to live in Oklahoma. I watched that film several times, but I didn't see her at all.'

'Here we are,' Isabel said cheerfully, her arms filled with some of my belongings, 'let me have your muddy things when you are ready, and I'll wash them. *Mamie*, when I was upstairs I saw the postal van outside your house, are you expecting anything?'

'Vitamins, toilet rolls and *bandages de soutien*,' Eugénie said, buttoning up her coat with excited fingers, 'I buy them off *l'internet*.'

I raised a questioning eyebrow at Isabel.

'Support bandages,' she murmured.

I changed into some clean clothes with a lot of wincing and complaining, and then settled myself into the chair again. Looking around, I was pleased with what I saw. The hut was small but well designed and looked very attractive with all the things Isabel and I had put into it. The kitchen was just a small fridge, an electric hob and tiny oven. There was a sink, and a bathroom with a loo and a shower, which had been put into the space with considerable ingenuity. It was perfect.

Isabel left me with my laptop, a cafetière of coffee, biscuits, some painkillers and a hot water bottle to rest in the small of my back, and all things considered, I didn't feel too bad.

But what was I going to do with myself, once the novelty of doing nothing in particular wore off? A couple of cars arrived at the *brocante* barn, and I could hear Isabel's chatter and laughter in the distance. I wondered if she was selling anything, and wished I could be there with her to help. But perhaps I could help in a different way.

I opened up my laptop and started typing.

* * *

Isabel popped in to see me every few minutes at first, and then realising that actually nothing much was happening, and two paracetamol hadn't instantly cured me, left me to it. So I spent a reasonably enjoyable afternoon on my laptop doing some research. At the back of my mind there had been a niggling thought that she was selling some of her treasures for far less than they were worth, and it didn't take me long to find out I was right.

'Look at this,' I said when she came in with my dinner on a tray. The aroma of the beef casserole was wonderful, but I had information for her that was equally as tasty.

'That iron cat door stop, that you used to prop open the linen cupboard. I noticed it had a maker's mark on it; Hubley. Which means it could be valuable. How much are you selling it for?'

'Five euros.'

'Then put an eight in front of that. Trust me, it's worth a lot more than five,' I said. I turned the screen towards her to show her one that was identical and had sold in Paris for one hundred and fifty euros. 'And that one had some slight damage.'

'You're joking?'

'And the enamel petrol signs. What price have you put on those?'

Isabel shrugged. 'Twenty euros. But I know those are really old because they used to be in the garage in town. Where Louis' father worked. You can see the shotgun marks on them from when Louis used them as a target.'

'Then they are genuinely old, not just modern reproductions. I'd suggest you put two in front of that. There are some here that sold only recently for five hundred dollars.'

Isabel looked absolutely gobsmacked for a moment.

'Some of them are rusty, and the enamel is damaged.'

'That goes to reflect how old they are. The *Train Blu* sign is incredibly rare, and worth about five hundred euros. You can't possibly sell it for twenty. And the blue glass ashtray, that's vintage from the *SS France*. The biggest ocean-going liner until the Queen Mary 2 was built.'

'One euro?' Isabel said hopefully.

'Twenty, if not more,' I replied.

'Flipping heck,' Isabel said rather shocked.

'And you remember that odd, sort of oblong piece of lace?'

'The one that came in the house clearance?'

'It's called a *fichu*, hand-made lace and its worth at least a hundred euros, maybe more. I'm just about to look at the prices online for embroidered French linen sheets. Those ones with the monograms that don't look as though they have ever been used. I think you're going to be surprised,' I said, 'no wonder people are paying to ship them back home. They are really valuable.'

'I had no idea,' Isabel said, 'I suppose I should have looked. But when people just throw these things out, how am I to know?'

'Leave it to me,' I said, 'I've got the time to do the research.'

'That's a bit boring, isn't it? Wouldn't you prefer a good book?'

I laughed and then winced as my back gave a warning twinge.

'Actually, it's not. And I'm finding out so much about French history. It's easy to go down rabbit holes of research, like Bill said about cyanide.'

'Ooh, that reminds me, I'm going to pop in and see if he's killed anyone yet. Well, if you're sure? Now then, eat your dinner before it gets cold. Darn it – I've forgotten the bread. I'll be back in a jiffy.'

'I can do without,' I said, but she had already gone to fetch it.

I had a few mouthfuls, and it was delicious. With a rich, slightly smoky taste that could only have come from the addition of a lot of red wine. I'd watched Isabel cooking quite a few times since I'd been here, and most of her recipes seemed to need a good slosh of wine at some point.

I heard her footsteps returning on the newly laid gravel path.

'I am going to start using more wine in my cooking when I go home,' I called, and spooned in another mouthful.

'I hope that will not be too soon,' Luc replied.

I swallowed hard with the shock of seeing him.

'I've come to bring you your bread,' he said, 'you know no meal in France is complete without it.'

He put his mobile phone and a little wicker basket down on the table in front of me and sat down in the other chair.

'How are you feeling?'

'Not too bad,' I said, 'still a bit sore and stiff. I don't think I will be going out dancing any time soon.'

'That is a pity, you must tell me when you are up to it,

although as I cannot dance at all well, we might give the whole thing a miss.'

I laughed. 'That would probably be a good idea.'

Luc looked away, and then examined his wristwatch, polishing the glass with his thumb. He seemed nervous, unsure of himself.

'But I suppose we could just go out to dinner one evening, when you are feeling better? I mean, if you liked the idea, and you weren't busy. You might not want to, and I would understand perfectly if you didn't.'

I looked across the table at him rather astonished. Was he actually trying, in his reticent way, to ask me out? And what should I say? Yes, please? Don't worry about it? Where are we going and what should I wear? I had nothing which could be described as evening wear in my suitcases.

Honestly, what on earth was the matter with me?

I was behaving like some giddy schoolgirl, not a strong, confident woman who had no interest in men or their invitations to dinner.

Although, of course, we might go to some glorious place by the river and the evening would be warm, the air sultry, and there might even be a little pipistrelle bat swooping about in the sky. (I like bats. They eat a whole shedload of mosquitos, which mean there are fewer around to bite me.) And there would be a candle in a wine bottle on the table, and we would have a simple meal of unparalleled flavour. Perhaps there would be a young chef, on his way to Michelin glory, who would come to ask us if everything was okay, and we would nod and smile and...

'Yes, okay. I'd like that,' I said at last, realising that my imagination had got the better of me and he was still waiting for my answer.

'Really? That's very good,' he said, smiling, obviously relieved, 'so you can't go home any time soon. Some of the best places are opening up now, ready for the new season's visitors. I will give it some thought. Now, please, eat your food, it will be getting cold.'

The trouble was, eating in front of him when he was just sitting there, was unbelievably embarrassing. Knowing me I would spill something down myself or drop my cutlery on the floor.

'I just wanted to find out if you were being well looked after,' he said, 'I felt terrible that you had hurt yourself, when I should have been there to help you.'

'You didn't know I was just going to drop in,' I said, taking a tiny, manageable spoonful of the casserole, 'I should have rung first. But I didn't have your number, and Isabel was busy.'

I took his mobile phone off the table and then I rang my own number.

'There, now you do have my number,' I said, 'and I have yours.'

'Yes, so I do,' he said.

I couldn't believe what I had just done and by the look on his face nor could he.

'Right then, I'd better go and leave you to your meal in peace. Nothing worse than someone watching you eat, is there?'

'No, you're right,' I said, rather relieved and surprised that he understood.

He stopped in the doorway. 'Would you like me to call in and see you again? Just to make sure you are all right, and you don't need anything?'

'Yes, that would be great,' I said.

'You're sure?'

'Yes, absolutely.'

He sounded startled, though why he should be, was anyone's guess. It was rather disarming.

Then my spoon wobbled, and I dropped a particularly juicy chunk of beef on my shirt.

'Oh, for heaven's sake! And I was being so careful.'

He laughed and closed the door behind him, and I sat chewing thoughtfully on my bread and wondered what I was going to do next.

23

When I had finished my meal, I started doing some research into a cameo brooch I had found in the box of oddments Isabel had bought. 'Honestly, it's just junk,' she'd said, 'you're wasting your time.'

The cameo was about an inch long and carved with a man's head on it. Which as I understood from my basic research was unusual, as most were of women. And he seemed to have a lot of grapes and foliage on his head. Perhaps it was a portrait of Bacchus? Anyway, I felt sure it was worth more than the ten euro price tag Isabel had put on it, even if the simple clasp at the back was bent out of shape. The pad of my thumb fitted neatly into the concave back of it, proving it probably was a shell and not just plastic. Perhaps I should take it to someone who knew more than I did and find out.

The rest of the box was full of pretty but probably valueless items. A few single earrings, a couple of silver brooches, several paste necklaces in lurid colours. I had the sudden wish that I had a jeweller's eyeglass, so I could look more closely at things and perhaps, like the experts on the television programs, look up and say things like, *well, this is an interesting piece. Has it been in your family long?*

Generally, the owner then says it was bought at a car boot sale for fifty pence, and then they burst into tears when they are told it is, in fact, a rare example of Fabergé, those glass stones are, in fact, baguette cut diamonds and worth more than their house.

Hmm, perhaps I was allowing myself to get a bit carried away with my new interest.

The door opened.

'I've come to get your dinner tray. I see he's gone. What did he say?' Isabel said, her face alight with interest.

'What did who say?' I replied airily, trying to be irritating.

'Luc, of course. Did you have a nice chat? He wanted to know how you were.'

'Yes, he asked if I would like to go out to dinner with him, when my back is better.'

'Fabulous,' Isabel breathed, clasping her hands together.

'I don't know why you are getting so excited,' I said, slightly annoyed with myself because that was exactly what I had been doing after all.

'Because it is exciting,' she said, picking up my tray and standing with an expression of rapture on her face, 'perhaps you will have a romantic dinner somewhere really swanky, and he will hold your hand under the table and pay you lots of compliments. And then you will blush girlishly and—'

I interrupted. 'Isabel, I'm sixty-three, I don't do anything girlishly.'

'—then he will walk you home in the moonlight—'

'Up a rutted lane filled with potholes, and I will twist my ankle and he will have to call an ambulance because I will have eaten my bodyweight in bread and desserts, and he won't be able to lift me. Or perhaps he could use your wheelbarrow.'

Isabel gave me an exasperated look. 'You're so prosaic, you're no fun any more. And you're very un-romantic.'

'You can thank Stephen for that,' I said, 'there wasn't much romance to be had as a rule. And after thirty-plus years of marriage it was hardly surprising.'

'Nonsense,' Isabel said, 'Stephen was an idiot. Felix is still terribly romantic. He says I am the most beautiful woman in France. Mind you, that is generally when I have made him Beef Wellington, which is his favourite meal. Or potatoes *au gratin*, which I won't let him have very often because it's just cream and cheese. And we have been together longer than you two were.'

'Yes, but in general. I mean ordinarily. I mean, are you still in love?'

Isabel frowned at the idea.

'Of course. I wouldn't put up with his snoring, or his inability to hang his clothes up, or his completely chaotic attitude towards putting his paperwork in order if I didn't. The number of times I have had to take bank statements out of the vegetable rack, you wouldn't believe it. And in the summer he would happily live in the same pair of shorts for days if I didn't take them away to be washed.'

'Stephen used to change his shirt twice a day sometimes,' I said.

'And Felix is colour blind. He once bought a shirt from a market stall, thinking it was green, and it was red. Which he paired with some blue trousers that were orange. The boys were in hysterics, and said he just needed some green shoes to look like a set of traffic lights.'

I laughed. 'Poor Felix.'

'That man knows when he's on to a good thing, believe me. I tell him often enough. Now do you want some cheese? I haven't bothered with a dessert and Felix is sulking. He may come out later and tell you how badly I treat him.'

'Why did you fall in love with him?'

Isabel thought about this for a moment. 'We had been going out for a couple of weeks, and he was trying to impress me. We were at the beach, near Bordeaux. And he had an ice cream, which he absolutely loves, and a seagull swooped down and stole the whole thing. And his face was such a picture, and then he started laughing, and right then, I knew he was the man for me. There was this marvellous, tingly feeling in the pit of my stomach. Daft, isn't it? Why, when did you fall in love with Stephen?'

I tried to remember, a moment when I had felt like that, and I couldn't.

'I don't know,' I said, 'I suppose there was a moment like that, but I can't remember it.'

Stephen had proposed one evening after we had been to his parents' house for dinner. I had wondered a few days later if perhaps he had asked their opinion on my suitability first. It wouldn't have surprised me. His father was fairly monosyllabic because he thought this made him seem interesting, when, in fact, he had little to say about anything, and his mother was a languid hypochondriac who made Eugénie look like a fitness trainer. It was almost impossible to imagine them summoning up enough enthusiasm to produce Stephen. Still, I had evidently passed the test, and he proposed at the traffic lights outside a supermarket. No one would have described it as a romantic moment.

'That's sad,' Isabel said, 'by the way, do you know you have a huge gravy stain on your shirt? I bet that didn't impress Luc.'

'He just laughed,' I said.

'Well, I'll go and get you some coffee and some painkillers and I have some marvellous brie, which is almost running off the plate, so you can have that too. Unless Felix has finished it off, which wouldn't surprise me one bit. He's such a pig.'

I was surprisingly comfortable that night, once I had hauled myself into the bed that had been tucked up against one corner of the shepherd's hut. I didn't usually like that arrangement because in the past I would always have to sleep next to the wall and then clamber over Stephen if I needed the loo in the middle of the night as I often did, but as I was on my own, it didn't matter. The sheets were beautifully smooth and soft, the pillows comfortable and as Isabel had proudly told me, the hut had fantastic insulation, so I certainly wasn't cold.

I'd had emails from Sara and John that evening, both reassuring me that they were okay.

Sara's divorce was proceeding to plan, the paperwork had been lodged with the court, and Marty had even had the girls for a weekend, sending them back with a lot of make up they didn't need and some overpriced trainers that didn't fit properly.

In Manhattan, John meanwhile was busy and had got very 'aggy' with someone, but he was also 'creaming a lot of cake', by which I think he meant he'd been annoyed but he was also making money. I had a short message from Vanessa, too, telling me all about Jasmine's role in the forthcoming school play where, as the only English student in the class, she was going to play George III. Meanwhile Bunny was trying to develop an American accent, despite all Vanessa's attempts to stop her, and was asking if she needed a therapist because all her friends had them.

It seemed everyone was coping perfectly fine, and for that I was grateful. It was an important lesson to me, they were adults, and my granddaughters were growing up fast, they might need the occasional bit of support or advice in future, but none of them needed the level of fussing and martyrdom I had been doling out. They were perfectly capable of sorting out their own lives and clearing up their own dirty dishes, metaphorical or otherwise.

So where did that leave me in future, I wondered, as I lay in bed, listening to the peace and quiet. If I wasn't needed to sort out their daily, domestic dramas, pick up after them and pander to their childhood fancies, how was I going to spend my time?

It was a rather exciting thought. It meant that I could do whatever I wanted. Perhaps coming here had been good for all of us. For me as well as for them. And I'd been able to help Isabel and Felix too.

I looked around the shadowy room. What would it be like to have a smaller space like this to look after, clean and decorate? Surely it would be cheaper and easier for me. Perhaps I should think about selling my house, it was too big for my needs anyway, and to keep it on just for the two or three occasions a year when all the family wanted to visit was ridiculous. And so was the garden.

I had already begun to see that I didn't have the physical strength or energy to maintain it, mow it, weed it and worry about it and that was for the grandchildren to have somewhere to play, hardly ever for my own benefit. And they were getting a bit old for hide and seek, and two of them were in America anyway.

I wasn't someone who liked to sit out in the garden on my own, and the weather was so unpredictable too. Putting chair cushions out and taking them back in again when it rained wasn't my idea of fun.

Many times, I had been alone in the house, having cleaned everything, tidied everything and rearranged every cupboard and drawer, and realised I had nothing to do, and I probably hadn't spoken to anyone but the postman for two days. Was I prepared to spend the rest of my life waiting for something to happen? For someone, anyone, to pull me out into the world? No, I wasn't.

I could think about travelling more, even though the prospect of doing it alone had been so daunting in the past. I had managed okay on this trip. Mostly. I'd even found a couple of sites on the internet that specialised in holidays for solo travellers. (Not singles; I knew there was an important distinction.)

If that was the case, where would I like to go? What did I like doing? I needn't consider anyone other than myself. This was groundbreaking stuff and very exciting.

I liked trying different foods, I'd always liked the idea of a painting holiday, or a guided tour around the chateaux of the Loire valley. Perhaps I really would go to visit New York – it was perfectly possible. Or Yellowstone National Park before there was the huge volcanic eruption that had been predicted for so long.

Maybe I would go somewhere next Christmas where there was proper snow and lots of it? I had a delightful vision of myself sitting by a window overlooking a mountain range, where the air was thick with snowflakes, and people were wearing colourful, Nordic sweaters and drinking hot chocolate. No, what was it they had in *White Christmas*? *Hot buttered rum, light on the butter.* I didn't know what that tasted like, but I could give it a go.

And did Luc feature in any of my thoughts? Surely he shouldn't. Having realised that I was now free of so many responsibilities, I didn't want to deliberately go out looking for new ones.

What had Eugénie said? *I just like to be chased; I don't want to be caught.*

Thinking about this and trying to weigh up the possibilities of a delightful Greek island with a turquoise sea, white sand and a conveniently placed beach umbrella and bar, versus a cute fishing village in Mallorca where there was a small promenade of enticing restaurants, I fell asleep.

24

My back gradually improved over the next few days, but the weather deteriorated into days of rain and biting winds. Resting in my little hut, I occasionally felt it rock with a particularly high gust, but I felt quite snug and safe, and I realised it was the first time I had enjoyed my own company for quite some time.

Instead of distracting myself with housework and mundane tasks in the garden, I had the chance to think properly about what I was going to do next. I had been in France for weeks now, and I knew I couldn't stay forever, the ninety-day rule being what it was. Isabel, my children and my grandchildren had their own lives, and their own paths to follow. I needed to do the same.

I pulled out one of the notebooks I had brought with me – the one with the picture of Wonder Woman on the front. My word, Lynda Carter really did have a spectacular figure. It was one that Bunny and Jasmine had bought for me, and I opened it, smoothing out the first page with my hand.

I remembered the conversation we'd had with Felix about women and their notebooks, how we liked to keep them until the right moment arrived. Well, this felt like the right moment.

I found a pen and wrote:

Next

at the top of the page, and then I underlined it twice, because this was important.

1. Do things I like to do. Particularly when it comes to going to concerts and films I think I would enjoy.

2. Don't do things I don't want to do. Especially cleaning the windows. All my neighbours seem to use the same firm, which turns up with a van and a long brush on a stick and they seem perfectly happy with it.

3. Travel to places I want to see, not places other people think I should see. I do want to go to Italy, I've always wanted to see the Sistine Chapel, but Stephen said the wait to get in was hours. So, I will splash out and buy a Fast Track ticket and hang the expense.

4. Learn a new language. Spanish? Italian? Both? There are daytime courses at the local community centre. As well as pottery, yoga and lots of other things. Investigate?

5. Throw out every black garment I own. Especially that dress Stephen made me buy for our thirtieth wedding anniversary. The one with the yellow and white stripe. It makes me look like a Liquorice Allsort.

6. Buy more colourful things.

7. Change my car.

I thought about this one for a long time. I'd never bought a car on my own before, Stephen had always been in charge of that, although the only thing he knew how to do was put petrol in it. The last time we went to several showrooms, where all the cars looked the same to me and most were grey or silver and the only preference I had voiced was that I would like a red car, so I was easier to see and presumably easier for other people to avoid.

I ended up with a grey car with a grey interior, so effectively, I was the same colour as the road.

When I had asked if the car had conformed to the proposed Euro emission regulations, Stephen and the car salesman who was a spotty oik called Jazza, looked at me in astonishment, the way one would a dancing dog, and they had both laughed. Although I don't think Stephen would have known a Euro emission if one had whacked him on the back of the head with a shovel. Therefore...

8. Go to a garage where they don't sneer, chuckle to themselves, patronise or make me feel like a fool and will actually speak to me without looking over my shoulder for my husband. And buy a red car. A big one. One that I choose.

Luc drove a red truck, and I wondered if I could buy something like that. A car that stood out a bit, that showed some spirit. A car with a rugged name like *Thug* or *Juggernaut*. I'd always had a bit of a thing about them. Perhaps I could have one now?

9. Buy some new bed linen with flowers on and chuck out all the old stuff. I don't like polyester sheets, particularly cream ones, and if I get a new duvet, I want one that makes that satisfying crackly noise when I turn over.

10. New pillows. The old ones have been used and washed so many times they are like Weetabix.

11. Find my white trainers at the back of the wardrobe and wear them as a fashion statement. I think they look cool, Stephen said I wasn't going to play at Wimbledon any time soon, so why pretend I was.

12. Go to Wimbledon.

13. Throw out the plastic washing-up bowl. Isabel's right. It's disgusting.

14. Visit John in New York, and stay at a hotel, not with them. Go to a Broadway show. Leave halfway through if I don't like it.

15. Get a decent haircut. I look like my mother. And go every eight weeks, not every eight years.

'I've brought you a flask of coffee. What are you doing?' Isabel said from the doorway. It was still raining, and she was peering out from under the hood of her raincoat.

Behind her, Marcel and Antoine stood, tails wagging, doggy smiles on their faces, completely unbothered by the weather, just glad to be included in the way dogs often are.

'Making a bucket list,' I said, looking up and being mildly surprised to find I wasn't already out doing new and exciting things, but was still only thinking and planning to do so. I went back to my list before I could forget this feeling.

16. Do the things on this list, don't just think/talk about them.

'Oh, have you developed some terrible disease since last night?'

'No, but I do think I need to have some direction in future. I've been paddling around in the shallows for long enough. I'm sixty-three, how much longer do I have?'

'Oh, stop it, you're beginning to sound like Eugénie,' Isabel said. 'I've brought you a bit of cake, too, in a sandwich bag. And some more painkillers in case you've run out.'

'Thank you, cake would be lovely, what sort?'

'I made sponge cake and flapjacks, but I left the flapjacks in the oven too long and they are a bit dangerous. I didn't know if your teeth would cope with them.'

17. Make a dental appointment for a check-up – not been for five years.

'But I don't think I need the painkillers,' I said, 'I think I'm okay.'

'You'll never guess what just happened in the barn,' Isabel said excitedly, 'I would have come straight over to tell you but then a couple called in and they bought all the little milk bottles, for something they are organising. I think it was a play. But the big thing is I sold one of those old enamel signs for a hundred and ten euros. And Felix took that cameo over to Gaston's wife. Mathilde knows a lot about jewellery, not just how to turn brake blocks into earrings. She might have an opinion.'

'That's excellent,' I said, pulling myself to my feet and checking to see how uncomfortable I was. No, everything felt fine.

'I'd like to go out somewhere,' I said, 'I've been stuck in here for days. Do you need any help with the *gîtes*? Or the barn?'

'No, I don't! I'm under strict instructions to make you rest.'

'Who from?'

'Luc. He rang me up a few minutes ago asking how you were, and he asked if you would be up for going out for dinner on Saturday.'

'Why didn't he just ring me, he has my number?'

Isabel shrugged. 'I dunno, ask him. Perhaps he thought you might be asleep.'

18. Ring people up. Don't just text or send emails.

'I'll ring him,' I said.

And I did.

And he answered and he sounded genuinely happy to hear from me. We talked to each other and made arrangements and exchanged ideas. And when I ended the call, I felt unreasonably pleased. And independent.

* * *

The following day the weather had improved and although it was still quite chilly, at least the rain had stopped.

Against all advice, I spent the day helping Isabel clean up the *gîtes* ready for the next people, and I also sold the auricular theatre to a new local ex-pat who also took one of Felix's leaflets about his language classes.

'I never thought I'd sell that,' Isabel said, 'and she took some tea towels too. I wish we could get more people in though. Perhaps we should do that video you mentioned. By the way, what are you going to wear on Saturday?'

I looked down at my smart trousers and fairly new Breton

sweater, which I had bought in a shop back home, not realising I could have bought an authentic one for less in France.

'Something like this?' I said.

'Absolutely not!' Isabel said, 'you need something new. My guess is you'll be going to *Le Poulet Argenté,* which means the Silver Chicken. I've been there once, it was lovely, but very posh. You need a smart outfit and some proper shoes. Or they won't let you in.'

'Won't let who in where?' Eugénie said from the doorway.

'Joy has a date on Saturday with Luc, and she needs something chic.'

Eugénie's eyes lit up.

'I don't own a chic dress,' I said, 'I don't own chic anything.'

'But I know someone who does,' Eugénie said, 'she has cupboards full of clothes, a lot of them never worn. Most of them will be too small for you, everyone is so much bigger these days, but perhaps some of them might fit. If you suck your stomach in and don't eat too much. You must come with me, and we will find something.'

Perhaps unfairly, the possibility of this did not inspire me. Eugénie was always well turned out, and she never seemed to wear the same outfit twice, but I didn't want to wear the clothes of an eighty-four-year-old woman.

'I really don't think that's a good idea,' I said.

Eugénie's nostrils flared. 'You think because I am an old woman now that I might not know about anything other than my aches and pains? The many disappointments and setbacks? The years of struggle and suffering? The problems with ungrateful family and friends? How my life has been beset with danger and difficulty? And ill health that no one will take seriously. And Paulette the same. To you she is a woman who makes food, the best onion soup in Brittany, possibly in France. But she had a life before that. Oh yes, don't look so surprised.'

'Isabel said she was a model when she was younger.'

'That is not the half of it. Where do you think I get all my things from? Certainly not the shop in the town. I spent much of my life in rags, pitiful clothes. No longer. I will show you.'

'*Mamie*, you were never in rags,' Isabel protested.

'No, but I might have been,' Eugénie said, '*alors*, we are wasting time. Isabel can drive us to the town. Seeing as you still do not have your car. Perhaps Luc has sold it and pocketed the money.'

'He would never do that. But I can't leave the *brocante*, someone might come looking for something,' Isabel protested.

Eugénie flared her nostrils in disdain. 'Of course they won't, leave a notice, closed due to illness. This is much more important.'

* * *

We reached the Sports Bar just before three o'clock, when – as Eugénie had predicted – the lunch time trade was easing off.

Paulette was waiting behind the bar, alerted by Eugénie's earlier phone call, and her face lit up when she saw us.

'*Je suis vraimant enthousiaste* – I'm so excited,' she said, 'Come, come with me.'

Louis who had been polishing some wine glasses, rolled his eyes.

'*Je ne comprendrai jamais les femmes*,' he said.

'No, you don't understand women, that's half the problem,' Eugénie fired back.

We went into the back of the building and up a flight of stairs. Eugénie seemed surprisingly nimble for someone who seemed to have so many unnamed illnesses and weaknesses.

'*Et voilà!*' Paulette said, throwing open a door.

Inside, the room was small but filled with clothes racks. There were shelves with shoe boxes, handbags in linen bags, interesting looking suitcases with battered travel labels stuck on the outside.

'I kept everything I could when I was modelling,' Paulette said, 'sometimes instead of my fee, I would ask for the clothes I wore, or for them to sell them to me at a reduced price, and as some of them were tailored to fit me, they agreed. They wouldn't do that now, I am sure. But hardly ever the evening gowns, which were thousands. I saw some in a museum only recently, such tailoring, such stitches. And what is two hundred dollars compared with a Chanel original? Not that they would fit me now, but they are still beautiful. But there are some I acquired that might do; things I wore later.'

Eugénie parked herself on a chair and we looked through the racks of clothes in amazement. There were suits, dresses, sweaters, tailored slacks and even a couple of ball gowns done up in calico bags. No wonder Eugénie always looked so elegant if she had this treasure trove to choose from.

'So you worked for Chanel? I thought it was Dior?' Isabel said.

'I worked for everyone,' Paulette said, with huge laugh, 'I have not always been sixty. I went all over the world. I was tiny, like a bird in those days. I had glossy black hair down to my waist. And what a tiny waist! I used to dance down the runways, I was called *Martinet*. There was even a spread in *Vogue* of me, they called it *French Dressing*. Big shoulder pads, crazy days.'

Eugénie shook her head sadly. 'What happened, Paulette?'

'Good things. I fell in love, I got old and happy,' Paulette said, 'and I learned to cook.'

'Joy needs something to wear for dinner,' Eugénie said, bringing us all back to why we were there in the first place. 'Not much here will fit her, I feel sure, and clothes then were proper sizes, not what they are today.'

'Thanks for the vote of confidence, *Mamie*,' Isabel muttered.

'You can borrow anything you want to,' Paulette said, 'but they must be returned. *C'est ma pension*. My – what do you call it – my nest egg.'

She pulled a dark green dress off the rail. 'What about this? I wore that at Ascot, with a big white hat. I was divine. And this?' Next was a pink satin cocktail dress, lavishly covered in tape lace and sequins.

'No sleeves,' Eugénie said, shaking her head, 'a woman her age needs sleeves. Unless she has been a professional tennis player.'

'She's absolutely right,' I said.

'Then perhaps this?' Paulette said. She pulled out a royal blue silk velvet jacket and stroked it as lovingly as though it was a kitten. 'It will enhance your eyes. It is Chanel. I never wore it. It was too big. They had to take it in at the back with clothes pegs. Now it is too small. I waited for the right day and then that day never came. I just loved the colour.'

I took it and looked in the label in the neckline:

Chanel

I didn't think I'd ever touched a Chanel garment before, never mind worn one. I tried it on, over my T-shirt and jeans it fitted perfectly, looked sensational, and the silk lining was as soft as a cloud.

'And these might fit you. I bought them back in the eighties,' Paulette continued, handing me some slim, dark blue trousers.

I tried them on. They were a bit snug if I was honest. I stood up straighter and pulled in my stomach.

'You are not as fat as I thought,' Eugénie sniffed from her chair in the corner.

Phew, got away with it then.

'And this,' Paulette said handing over a white silk shirt with what looked like a pattern of tadpoles all over it.

After some hesitation, remembering the parlous state of my rather ancient bra, and looking around for somewhere to strip off, I gave up and hauled my T-shirt off.

An immediate barrage of tutting filled the room from both Paulette and Eugénie, who dramatically pretended to faint off the side of her chair and had to be caught by Isabel, who heaved her back upright.

'No, I cannot believe what I am seeing,' she croaked.

'What?' I said, looking down. Okay, it sort of fitted, and it was still what I thought of as my comfortable bra. It had once been beige, so perhaps they were overreacting?

'I will tell you a secret that all French women know, that my mother told me,' Paulette said, '*Si une femme porte quelque chose de beau sous se vêtements, elle s'envoie un message très puissant.*'

'If a woman wears something beautiful under her clothes, she sends a powerful message to herself,' Eugénie interrupted, pointing at my bra, 'and *that* is not powerful, not *formidable*, that is not even slightly persuasive. There is no place in your wardrobe for... that!'

'But I like it,' I said, rather feebly, 'it's one of my favourites.'

They both laughed.

Paulette dabbed at her eyes with a handkerchief. 'You English! It's an old bra, not a beloved toy!'

'But no one is going to see it,' I said.

I cast a despairing look at Isabel, who just shrugged and pulled aside the neck of her shirt to show me the strap of a scarlet and very lacy bra. Her eyes sparkled with something like mischief.

'You must go to Zaza in the next town,' Paulette said very firmly, '*c'est impératif,* and tell her I sent you. She will give you *une réduction* – a discount.'

25

We went to Zaza.

Despite my feeble protestations that it wasn't necessary, I was overruled by all three of them. It wasn't as though I was planning to show my underwear to anyone.

Tant pis, was the answer. Tough, you're going anyway.

Zaza was a redoubtable woman in a rigid black dress who looked as though she had been corseted by armourers. She didn't speak much English at all, but what she couldn't say she more than made up for with hand gestures and eye rolling. And so, colours and styles were offered, some of them quite frightening to my untutored eye, straps were lifted, and things tightened until I felt like a horse being put into its harness.

Isabel sat outside the curtains for a while, flicking through magazines on a comfortable armchair, and then started wandering around the little shop, looking through the rails and muttering things like: *oh yes, I have this one, and this one. I like the look of that, perhaps Felix would be frightened, on the other hand he might think all his birthdays had come at once.*

Evidently my sister didn't have such a cavalier attitude towards these things as I did.

After an exhausting couple of hours, we left the shop with a carrier bag containing things which Zaza had approved, and despite the discount, probably cost more than I had spent on underwear in ten years. She also took away my old favourite chain store bra with a *moué* of distaste as though she wished she had tongs, presumably to consign it to the dustbin. So my hopes about keeping it and maybe wearing it a bit longer were dashed.

'Right then, you are sorted, apart from your hair and your shoes,' Isabel said.

'Leave me alone, haven't I suffered enough?' I said.

'Stop moaning, I have some you can borrow, kitten heels, pale champagne colour, go with anything.'

'When do you wear kitten heels?' I said, rather astonished. All I had seen my sister in up to then was walking boots and very casual clothes, sometimes decorated with mud and dog hair.

'You'd be surprised what I get up to,' she said with a wink.

I didn't ask. Perhaps I should.

* * *

On Friday I spent the morning helping Isabel out in the *brocante* barn and we had a very successful time. It was strange how things that had remained unsold when they were ridiculously cheap, suddenly sold when the price increased. Perhaps it was a psychological thing, that second-hand things selling for a few euros weren't worth having and were disregarded as junk, but the same items at five times the price were vintage and therefore desirable.

This set me thinking about the parallel between that and my own sense of self-worth. If I didn't value myself, why should anyone else?

Stephen would have been speechless if he had known what I had spent on three new bras and six pairs of co-ordinated knickers (which I was told in no uncertain terms should always match).

And then I realised that over the last few days, Stephen had been far from my mind and that I had stopped worrying about how he might have reacted if he had seen me. This could only be a good thing. It was as though his dominating presence, which had been sitting on my shoulder for so long, had been gradually fading like an old photograph, and now it felt like it had gone.

I hadn't forgotten him, of course, I hadn't. But now, although I couldn't quite vocalise it properly, life felt different. Something that Paulette had said resonated with me.

That beautiful jacket.

I never wore it. It was too big. Now it is too small. I waited for the right day and then that day never came.

Surely this applied to most things in life. I wasn't going to do as so many people did, wait for the right moment. Keep new things for best. Plan that trip of a lifetime for some vague time in the future. From now on I was going to wear those clothes, that underwear, that smile, because tomorrow might just be too late.

Early on Saturday morning, Isabel was wandering around fretting about the lack of customers and wondering if we should reduce the prices on things.

'Hardly anyone knows we are here,' she complained, kicking at one of the watering cans disconsolately, 'it wouldn't matter if we did have Fabergé eggs or Princess Diana Beanie Babies.'

'Let's do the video,' I said, 'and put it on social media. Telling everyone what a lot of fabulous things you have here. And perhaps mention the *gîtes* and the shepherd's hut at the same time.'

'Okay,' she said, sounding anything but enthusiastic, 'what do we have to do?'

'You can just walk around pointing at things and I'll film you on your phone.'

'I'm not doing it on my own!' she said, horrified, 'I wouldn't have the nerve. You have to do it too. And what would we say anyway?'

'Let's work it out, we can always have the words written on bits of cardboard. Lots of people do that. Bob Hope was famous for it.'

Isabel grinned, warming to the idea. 'Let's have a practice.'

I tugged a bit at the edge of my new bra, which while supportive was very different from what I was used to, and we went into the barn. I took Isabel's phone and started filming.

'Go on then,' I hissed.

Isabel looked blank. 'What shall I say?'

Never wanting to be left out of anything, Marcel and Antoine loped in and sat at her feet. Marcel scratched one ear and Antoine yawned.

I pressed the record button and started speaking.

'Here we are in my beautiful *brocante* barn, which as you can see if filled with—'

I sent her an enquiring look and she took up the thread.

'A lot of old junk, and some good bits that are probably worth a fortune, but I am too stupid to know.'

'We don't say stupid,' I said, automatically.

'Okay, I am just a simple woman with no qualifications in antiques, and no idea if this—' she picked up a cup and saucer, '— is *Sèvres Fontainbleau* or Ikea.'

She then posed like a magician's assistant in front of a display of farm machinery, and I started giggling.

'I have no idea what this is, but it's very old and I have two of them. So if you wanted a matching pair of whatever they are, come along to my *brocante* barn at *Ferme de Pommes de Terre*. We are open most days, and if we aren't, it means we are closed.'

She took the phone from me. 'You have a go.'

I picked up a bundle of embroidered sheets and held them against my cheek.

'Sleep like a queen in these vintage, embroidered sheets. Not Marie Antoinette of course, that didn't end well. Or amuse and delight your friends with these—' I picked up a couple of wonky pottery bowls, '—*objet d'art* which look like Meissen but were, in fact, made by my nephew for an art project about twenty years ago.'

Getting into the spirit of the thing Isabel picked up one of the tablecloths and swirled it around her shoulders like a cape.

'Vintage tablecloths, we have several, each more beautiful than the last.'

At this exciting development Marcel leapt up and sank his teeth into the trailing end of it, dragging Isabel off balance. She fell over into the display of watering cans, and she landed with an outraged *'ow'* and a shriek. Antoine joined in, leaping over her to have a tussle with Marcel, which ended up with him sitting on my sister's head.

I howled with laughter and then stopped filming and went to help her up.

'That flipping hurt you daft dogs,' she shouted, rubbing her hip.

'It was very funny though,' I said, trying to stop laughing.

'It's not supposed to be funny, I'm trying to sell stuff,' she said.

'Right, let's try again,' I said, putting the watering cans back into a row. I started filming again. 'Sell me that painting, the one of the old bloke on the horse.'

Isabel made a dismissive noise. 'No one's going to buy that, I've had it for five years. He looks like an axe murderer out on bail.'

'Escaping on his horse, people like paintings of horses, and there's a dog.'

'If you look closely, that dog has five legs,' Isabel said, 'the artist forgot to paint one out.'

'Or perhaps the dog did have five legs? Let's try outside where the light is better,' I said.

We lugged the painting outside between us where the sun was shining and Isabel's washing was blowing in the wind, like an advertisement for fabric conditioner. She propped the painting up on an upturned wheelbarrow and I realised I hadn't turned the recording off, and I was still filming. I wondered briefly if it was possible to edit such things. Isabel was obviously getting into her stride now.

'This is a significant piece from the— ooh, nineteenth century and it could be a picture of a very important man. You can tell that because he has a big horse with a very snorty nose, and a dog—'

'With five legs,' I added.

'Five-legged dogs were much sought after and very rare,' Isabel agreed, 'and hard to catch. This is an ideal decorator's piece, in the original gilt and what's it called – ormolu frame that would add sophistication and charm to any room.'

'And is it reasonably priced?' I prompted.

'It is indeed. Only one— two hundred euros. Including the string at the back, which is original, nineteenth century rope.'

I started laughing again and Isabel made some more 'displaying' gestures with her hands, which was all the encouragement Marcel needed. He leapt at the painting, knocking it sideways and Isabel grabbed at it, falling over the wheelbarrow with a scream. I prodded at a few buttons on the phone and only managed to flip it around and start filming myself.

'Oh, for heaven's sake,' I said. And then I stopped filming.

'I don't think we are very good at this,' she said, pulling herself to her feet.

'It's only our first attempt,' I said, 'let's try one more. What about all those salt and pepper sets. The novelty ones in the wooden box.'

'Well, okay, but this time you can do the talking and I'll film you,' she said.

The house clearance Isabel had been to had evidently been from a house where the owner had like collecting knick-knacks. Amongst these were about five cruet sets in frankly odd and slightly rude designs. We fetched them all and laid them out on the kitchen table, after first putting an embroidered cloth down, carefully positioned to hide the fang marks that Antoine had left on one corner.

Marcel crept into the kitchen with us and rested his snout on the end of the table.

'Go on then,' Isabel said, 'sell me those.'

'These are some of the most collectable items,' I said, rather unconvincingly, 'people come from far and wide to see our wonderful selection of novelties.'

'Rare novelties,' Isabel interrupted.

'Rare, some might say extraordinary novelties, which are very popular with... people. Collectors.'

My mind went blank for a moment, and I looked at Isabel with a fixed grin wondering what to say next.

'And I know the gnome is your favourite,' she prompted me, 'go on.'

I responded with an agonised stare. The gnome cruet set was one of the ugliest. A gnome bending over, each removable, ceramic buttock having been made into a salt and pepper shaker. I picked it up and balanced it in the palm of my hand.

'Who could resist this charming item? You will probably never see another like it.'

'If you're lucky,' Isabel murmured.

'These are highly collectable and very rare. So hurry to the *brocante* barn at *Ferme de Pommes de Terre* and complete your collection with this— um— unbelievably— really eye-catching piece.'

At that point I started laughing again and the ceramic buttock labelled salt, fell off and rolled onto the table and straight into Marcel's smiling jaws.

'Marcel! Put that buttock down!'

There then followed several undignified moments as I scrabbled around trying to retrieve it, accompanied by a lot of hysterical laughter from Isabel. Eventually I won the tussle and put it safely back into position. Marcel, having enjoyed the game gave an enthusiastic woof.

'Perhaps we should wash it before we sell it?' Isabel said.

26

Having decided we probably weren't that good at making satisfactory social media videos, we gave up.

That afternoon I had a shower in my tiny bathroom, where just as in the house, the water was hot but not particularly fast flowing. Then for the first time in months, I sat in my dressing gown and did my make-up and then my nails, painting them defiantly red whereas before I might have just stuck to a nondescript pearly pink.

Isabel came in with a box containing her shoes, which were indeed pale champagne coloured with a kitten heel and were still in pristine condition. It was hard to imagine my sister wearing such things, let alone keeping them in the box. When she had been growing up her shoes were things that lay at the bottom of the wardrobe in a heap, or more often, decorating the stairs in a way that had caused more than one accident over the years.

'I'm so excited,' she said, 'I can't wait to see you all dressed up with somewhere to go.'

'Stop it, please,' I said, 'it's just dinner, nothing more than that. You're making me nervous with all your assumptions.'

'I haven't made any,' she fired back, 'it's all in your mind, not mine. By the way, when did you last go on a date, do remind me?'

'Oh, shut up,' I said, 'this isn't a date.'

'Course it isn't.'

Well of course it was, and that made me even more nervous. What if I made a fool of myself, or got drunk, or behaved badly, or spilled food down myself as I was perfectly capable of doing. What if he didn't like me after all? What if...

'Right then, I'll just put your hair up,' she said, 'it will look as though you've made an effort.'

'I think my clothes will show that,' I said.

An hour, several hairpins and most of a can of hairspray later, I was ready. Isabel had managed to put my hair up into what I think is called a messy bun, which wasn't just me using an elastic band and a quick run through with a brush, but apparently quite a complicated thing.

I looked at my reflection and was relieved. I looked okay.

'You look gorgeous,' Isabel said, 'now come on, time to get dressed. And you'd better have that new underwear on, or I will tell Eugénie.'

I put on the trousers and the shirt, wishing they weren't quite such a good fit. Perhaps I was just used to my clothes being too baggy. Was that a sign of my age? That I had made friends with stretchy fabric, elasticated waists and layers to cover up my figure?

'These trousers are tighter than I remember,' I said, 'okay on the hips but a bit tight round the middle. Perhaps women then had smaller waists?'

'What? Tighter than your jogging bottoms? That's a good thing. It means they fit you,' Isabel said.

I slipped on the beautiful jacket and stroked the fabric.

'It is gorgeous, isn't it?' I said at last.

'You're gorgeous,' Isabel replied, 'you always were. You just forgot, that's all.'

I looked at myself in the mirror on the wardrobe door and yes, I did look rather good. Perhaps this was going to be okay after all.

* * *

At seven thirty exactly, Luc arrived. He had evidently given his truck a wash and even cleaned the empty canvas bags, bits of stone and gravel out of the back. That more than anything made me feel rather sentimental. I had made an effort but so had he. And he looked very smart in a dark suit and white shirt. He even had cufflinks on.

'You look wonderful,' he said as he saw me, '*très elegante.*'

'Thank you,' I said, fidgeting in my borrowed shoes, which were slightly too tight.

'Shall we go?'

I got up into the truck as gracefully as I could, remembering the last time when he had hauled me up, me squeaking and complaining with my sore back.

We went to *Le Poulet Argenté,* as Isabel had predicted. An unremarkable stone building set back from the road behind a gravelled car park, which was almost full of swanky looking cars.

'I hope you are hungry,' Luc said as we parked, 'the food here is wonderful.'

'Very,' I lied.

In fact, I wasn't at all. I hadn't had much to eat since my breakfast croissant because I'd been too nervous, and also the thought of the borrowed trousers possibly cutting into me had been on my mind. How they would cope with this meal was anyone's guess.

Inside we were welcomed by a stout chap who introduced himself as Arnaud. He was wearing a black shirt and black trousers, had obviously spent a lot of time and money on hair products and flapped his hands about a lot. He was rather sweet and reminded me of an enthusiastic seal.

Our table was by the window with a view over the car park, but was elegantly set with a white cloth, gleaming silver cutlery and four different wine glasses.

As we sat down Arnaud lit the candle in the middle of the table, and then fussed about with our dinner napkins like a magician. The menu was short and, of course, all in French.

Moments later Arnaud brought us a bottle of chilled water and some *amuse-bouche* on little porcelain spoons. It was a little sliver of smoked salmon on top of a tiny blini, plus a swirl of cream, a few grains of caviar and a tiny frond of dill. It was exquisite and my *bouche* was very amused indeed.

'The terrine here with black truffle oil is excellent. And I recommend the *sole meunière* if you like fish,' Luc said, 'it was supposed to be a favourite of Louis XIV.'

I'd seen Julia Child's videos in the past, and I knew what that meant. Fish cooked in a lot of butter. Sounded brilliant to me.

'That would be wonderful,' I said.

I watched him across the table from me for a moment, he looked as appetising as anything that could possibly be on the menu, and how amazing that he had wanted to bring me here.

I gave a little sigh of pleasure and went back to the menu, wishing I had put my reading glasses into my bag, and angled it back and forth trying to read the swirly font. It could have said anything. At this rate I would be ordering something I didn't like.

'I'll have the sole,' I said at last.

'And some wine?'

'Always,' I said, more confidently that time, 'what goes well with it do you think?'

'Perhaps a Sancerre or a white Burgundy?'

'Ideal,' I said, 'I like either.'

'And I am going to have the steak for the main course. What about you?'

Main course? I didn't know we were going to have that too. *Amuse-bouche*, starter, fish and then steak, not to mention the possibility of a dessert, which was often my favourite part of the meal. In fact, in the past, I had been known to have a starter and a dessert and do without a main course. I was going to have to be rolled out of there at that rate.

I gave a confident smile and put the unreadable menu down.

'Splendid. Me too.'

We ordered and Arnaud went off to find wine, a white napkin, ice and an ice bucket, which he brought back to the table and did a lot of fussing about with the cork.

'You taste it,' Luc said, 'see what you think.'

My ability to taste wine was non-existent other than to say it was very wine-y, but I did my best, swirling it around the glass and giving an appreciative sniff and a sip.

'Lovely,' I said, trying to think of some things to say that I had heard, 'grassy, with a hint of green.'

Arnaud went off satisfied and Luc's eyes twinkled at me across the table.

'I might be French but I'm not a snob about it. It tastes like wine to me too,' he said, and I grinned.

The starter came, a minute portion of terrine garnished with three drops of truffle oil, some pea shoots, one sliver of red pepper and one thin slice of melba toast. I gave a mental sigh of relief. If these were the portion sizes, perhaps I would be okay. And it was delicious, in fact, I could have eaten a big slab of it.

Actually, back home I could remember scooping pâté out of the packet in front of the television with some ordinary toast, but of course that was not the way things were done here. I picked daintily at my food, savouring every tiny bite, taking little sips of water and remembering to sit up straight, not hunch over my plate as though it was a school dinner.

We talked about his house, how he had been busy rearranging his furniture and belongings now that they had arrived from the storage unit.

'I am enjoying the process, but I would appreciate your advice, if you were free to come over one day. You need to pick up your car anyway,' he said.

'Of course,' I said, 'I'd promise not to make everything too – what did Felix call it – *l'air girly.*'

He laughed. 'I don't mind, it's a long time since my home had any feminine influence.'

'That's a shame,' I said.

He was about to reply when Arnaud appeared and cleared away our plates, checking very respectfully that everything had been to our satisfaction.

And then he brought the *sole meunière*, which was nestled comfortably in its own butter bath and was accompanied by three miniature new potatoes and three green beans in a china dish on the side.

I looked around at all the other diners, who were evidently having a pleasant evening too. No one was making a fuss or grumbling, no one was looking at their watch or complaining that the beans or the potatoes were the wrong shape. I bit back a smile at the thought of the speed eating and general dissatisfaction that had accompanied the meals in my house over Christmas. Wow, that seemed a very long time ago.

'This is possibly the best thing I have ever eaten,' I said after a few mouthfuls.

He smiled. 'You can see why the King liked it.'

As the meal progressed, the sole was followed by a tiny fillet steak that was the most melting I had ever tasted, again swimming in sizzling hot butter, plus five identical, hand-cut and probably much-loved chips in a metal pot. It was scrumptious, and I discovered that eating small amounts of food very slowly and thoughtfully, meant I felt fuller than if I had eaten larger amounts very rapidly; how odd.

I told him about my family, the town where I lived, how I spent my time. He told me about his life, what he had done since his wife had died, how he wished they'd had children. I could tell he was lonely, but then so was I. I don't think I'd really realised that. It seemed a bond was forming between us, one I hadn't expected.

'And what have you been doing today?' Luc asked.

I had a mental flashback to the five-legged dog, saving the ceramic buttock from the Marcel and Isabel falling over the wheelbarrow and grinned at the memory. I don't think I had laughed so much for ages. There was fun to be had, and sometimes in the most unexpected places.

'Something fun by the looks of it,' he said.

I chuckled. 'Isabel and I were trying to make videos for social media. Let's just say it didn't quite go as planned.'

Then there was the prospect of cheese before dessert, which was how the French preferred things. A tiny, equally unreadable menu was brought to us with a flourish, and again I squinted at it, wondering what these cheeses were.

What I really needed was a menu with pictures. Like in the Wimpy Bars I had frequented as a kid. You knew where you were then; a Brown Derby was in your face – a doughnut, ice cream and chocolate sauce. And the light from the candle on the table was romantic and probably flattering, but it didn't make life any easier. What should I do? Of course, the perfect get out of jail free card. I tucked the menu into my pocket.

'I'm just off to...'

... The Ladies, although I didn't say that I just tried to look mysterious.

Once in the lady's cloakroom, the light was better and there was a young woman in there, in a blue wraparound dress.

I hadn't actually needed the loo, but of course once in there I realised I probably should. Always take the opportunity.

When I came back, after wrestling a bit with the button on my trousers, she was still there, wiping the tap with a tissue and then examining her lipstick in the mirror.

'Can you help me? *Aidez-moi*?' I said, whipping out the menu from the pocket of my jacket.

'*C'est une menu*,' she said, looking confused.

'Yes, I know.'

There was a nice-looking but low chair in one corner, upholstered in *Toile de jouy* fabric. It might be pleasant to have a few minutes sit down, and the chairs in the restaurant were quite high and hard.

I flopped down into the chair. There was immediately a terrible, rending noise and I looked in horror at my companion. Perhaps it had been a mistake to wear vintage— no *forty-year-old trousers* and sit down in them without due care.

Oh God.

I sprang up and wheeled around a couple of times, trying unsuccessfully to see what damage I had done. I don't know what I was thinking. Who has ever seen their own rear view without a mirror?

Further examination revealed that yes, the forty-year-old stitches in the back seam of my lovely trousers had given up, and there was a huge hole that could never go unnoticed without remedial action.

The young woman and I looked at each other in horror and then she raised her eyebrows.

'*Oh, mon Dieu!*'

And then she made some clucking noises and put her fingertips over her lips. Whether in sympathy or to stop herself from laughing I wasn't sure.

'Have you got a needle and thread?' I asked.

She looked at me blankly and I scoured my remedial knowledge of French to think of another way of saying it.

'*Réparer...* repairing?'

She shook her head.

'*Adhésif?*'

And how exactly did I plan on gluing my trousers back together? And if I did what would stop them sticking to my knickers? I could almost see myself being carted off to the local hospital to have the whole lot removed by a giggling nurse with some surgical spirit.

'Ah!' she said, her face brightening.

She made a hand gesture telling me to stay where I was and opened her capacious handbag. She rummaged around in the depths of it, bringing out her purse, a small umbrella, a phone, several letters, a brush, a toy car and a colouring book and crayons.

'*Épingles de sûreté,*' she said proudly.

Oh, good grief. Two massive safety pins. I hadn't seen things like that since the children were in terry nappies.

'*Merci,*' I said weakly and took my trousers off.

Her face lit up.

'*Quelle jolie culotte!*'

What pretty knickers.

Oh *God*.

I went back into the loo and did what I could to pin my trousers together. When I came out the young woman had gone. I took a look at myself in the mirror and smoothed down my hair.

After all my playing about with trousers and safety pins, bits of it were coming down from the messy bun, so I just looked messy, and of course, being plastered in hairspray the strands were sticking out in all directions. And how long had I been in here anyway? Luc would think I'd had an accident. It didn't bear thinking about.

* * *

As I returned to my seat, he stood up very respectfully. Apart from throwing me a worried glance, he didn't ask where I had been for so long, and wisely, I didn't offer any information. I decided to let it go into the *'mystery that is woman'* category.

I sat down very carefully, knowing that there was a possibility that one of the safety pins could open up and stab me in the nether regions. I composed myself, folding my hands on the table and trying to look relaxed.

Then Arnaud wheeled out the cheese board on a trolley. There was a fabulous selection of course, because the French do cheese better than anyone.

Following on from my disaster in the Ladies and the split trousers episode, I tried to moderate my usual greed, and just had a small piece of brie and some roquefort, which was my absolute favourite. Luc had something wrapped in leaves. I had no idea what it was.

'Banon. Goat's cheese wrapped in chestnut leaves that have been soaked in brandy.'

'Hmm, I don't like anything goaty,' I said.

'Try it,' he said, holding out a fragment of cracker with a little bit of cheese on the top, 'you might like it.'

He popped it into my mouth and watched as I chewed. It was a very suggestive, almost erotic thing to do, and just then despite everything – my tight trousers, my pinching shoes, the need for two giant safety pins to hold my trousers together and the fact that the particular cheese was not to my taste – we didn't seem able to take our eyes off each other.

'I still don't like it,' I said, my voice a bit croaky.

'More for me then,' he replied.

For a moment it was as though the whole room was holding its breath, although obviously that wasn't the case. I realised I was.

27

We finished off with *crème brulée*, which was silky smooth, had a wonderful caramelised crispy top, and tasted like heaven. By then I had surreptitiously undone the top button of my trousers and hidden the fact by blousing the top of my tadpole patterned shirt over it.

'Would you like a *digestif*?' Luc asked as Arnaud took our dishes away.

'Nothing more for me, thank you,' I said.

It was on the tip of my tongue to say I was as stuffed as a sofa, which was something Sara had always said as a child, but wisely, I didn't.

'That was a wonderful meal.'

'It was good, wasn't it?' he agreed with a smile, 'I brought my brother and his wife here some years ago, I was afraid it might not have been as good as I remembered, but it was even better. And the company was excellent.'

Another of those looks passed between us and for a moment I was confused.

I was so out of practice with this sort of occasion. Was he

sending me subtle signals? Was I unknowingly doing the same? What happened next? I couldn't remember.

I shuffled around a bit, hoping the safety pins were staying closed.

* * *

Luc paid the bill and we returned to his truck. By then, a lot of the other cars had gone and the car park was nearly empty. It was nearly ten thirty, there was an obliging full moon to illuminate the path, and he offered me his arm as we made our way over an uneven patch of ground. I linked my arm through his, liking the way it felt. Sort of protective and masculine without being strange.

It made me realise how little physical contact I had on a day-to-day basis with anyone. The only people I kissed or embraced was my family on their occasional visits. People my age didn't go in for a lot of hugging the way that young people did. I don't remember anyone throwing their arms around each other and crying hysterically when we passed our O levels or got into university. Perhaps that was a shame.

There could be something pleasant and reassuring about the touch of another human; even so, I didn't think I was going to start embracing the postman or my neighbours when I saw them. So, that was an interesting thought. When did people get to the point when touch did become a comfortable thing?

It seemed it was that evening.

When we got to the truck, he opened the door for me and when I stepped forwards, he put his arms around me, and there in the moonlit car park we had what could only be described as a good old snog.

As we stood there, some of the fancy cars began to leave,

passing us with the occasional toot of their horns, but that didn't seem to bother either of us.

I was consumed with so many emotions. Surprise, pleasure and underneath everything something I recognised as relief.

I was not past it; I was still someone who was kissed, I was not someone who was important solely because of the place I occupied in someone else's life. I was me. I was still a part of the world. I was seen.

'Wow,' I said, when at last I came up for air, 'wow.'

He laughed. 'I have been wanting to do that for a very long time.'

'Why?'

Oh yes, that was a clever question, beg for compliments why don't you.

'Because you are beautiful, funny, clever.'

I actually bit the inside of my cheek to stop myself from disagreeing with him.

'Because something about you made me want to find out more about you, to understand why you are sometimes so serious, when behind your eyes there is a vibrant, exciting woman.'

I sighed and took these words deep into my heart. I didn't think I had been vibrant or exciting for ages.

'Thank you,' I said at last, 'you don't know how great that makes me feel.'

'I want to know more about you,' he said, kissing the tip of my nose.

'Me too,' I said.

I realised that had been a slightly confusing reply. Did I mean I wanted to know more about me, too, or more about him. Or actually, perhaps it was both.

'And now, I'll take you home,' he said.

'Thank you. I was hoping you would. I've no idea where we are.'

He laughed and helped me up into the truck, both hands on my waist, which I liked but also made me a bit startled, knowing that the button of my trousers was still undone, and the rest of my modesty was only protected by two safety pins.

When he was in the driver's seat, I sat looking at him and put my hands either side of his face, looking at him for a good, long while. Memorising his features, so that I could remember this moment. He looked back at me, his brown eyes clear and honest.

Yes, he was attractive, yes he was good company, but more than that I felt he was a friend. I hadn't been looking for a fling or love or anything like it when I came to France, but perhaps I had found something better.

* * *

The trip back was quite a quiet one. Perhaps he, like me, was thinking about things. We had kissed each other very enthusiastically. The question about whether each found the other appealing had been answered. But what next?

I still had no idea.

I suppose I investigated various possibilities during that trip. Would we go back to his house? Would he invite me in for a nightcap? If he did, would I agree or not? And if I did, what did that imply?

Would it mean that in the morning I would have to do the drive of shame, taking my car back to Potato Farm in the early hours, worrying that Isabel might hear me, the dogs would bark, Eugénie would spot me? I already knew that nothing stayed under the radar in this place. It would be all over the town in no time.

I looked down at my wedding ring and twisted it on my finger.

Interesting point to consider: why was I still wearing that? Till death do us part, that was what we had both said. But in the end, we had been parted by an estate agent and two firms of solicitors.

Up until that moment I hadn't even thought about it. Eugénie had said with some heat that she was still married to Bastien, even though she had been widowed decades ago. I too had been married for so long, and my life had developed strict boundaries as a result. How did the possibility of another relationship – if that's what it was – fit into my life? Did I even want to go there?

I suddenly remembered my Wonder Woman notebook, and the list of things I had written in it. All about doing things, seeing places, accepting new challenges and opportunities. I hadn't even considered another relationship, and yet possibly, unless I was reading too much into it, there was one on offer.

Perhaps it was the late hour, maybe it was the wine, but my brain was spinning with tiredness. I would do what Scarlett O'Hara always did in *Gone with the Wind* and think about it tomorrow.

I began to recognise the road, signposts and houses as we came closer to the town, and then it seemed he had made the decision for me, and he turned off into the driveway of Potato Farm. Part of me was relieved, part of me wasn't.

Perhaps I had been up for some romantic nonsense, some skilful French seduction. Him whispering things in my ear, me trying not to say something foolish, wondering if he had a spare toothbrush, would he notice that if and when my trousers dropped to the floor there would be a metallic clonk from the safety pins?

I laughed out loud then because the whole thing was so unexpected, so ridiculous that it was funny. He turned to look at me, his face illuminated by the dashboard lights.

'Okay?'

'Absolutely,' I said.

He stopped the car and took my hand, raising it to his lips and kissing the back of it. Well, that was a definite first. No man had ever done that.

'Goodnight, *chèrie*,' he said, and I felt a daft thrill.

So, I was *chèrie* now, was I? Another first.

I leaned over and kissed his cheek.

'Goodnight.'

'I'll see you soon?'

A question, not a statement, which I liked because it showed he wasn't assuming anything.

'*À bientôt*,' I said, feeling very chic and cosmopolitan.

The taillights from his truck hadn't disappeared from the end of the drive before Isabel was banging on the door of the shepherd's hut.

I opened it; she was in her pyjamas and dressing gown with a wool throw from the sofa over her shoulders. Behind her I could see Marcel and Antoine looking just as inquisitive as my sister.

'Well?' she said.

'Bit nosey, aren't you?' I said.

'Yes,' she replied, 'let me in, it's freezing out here.'

She came in, nudging the dogs to wait outside, and sat down facing me, her eyes bright with interest.

'We had a lovely meal,' I said, 'you and Felix really should go there. I had terrine to start with and the *sole meunière*...'

Isabel tutted her frustration. 'I don't care if you had beans on toast. How did it go?'

'Very well,' I said, 'it was a lovely evening, we talked non-stop, I like him.'

'So why are you here? And not over there making passionate love amongst the paint pots and dust sheets?'

I laughed, feeling quite light-headed at the idea. 'Give me a chance!'

'What I mean is, you know, was there a connection? Did you fancy each other?'

'Yes and yes,' I said, 'and we had a lovely snog in the car park before he drove me back, and he called me *chèrie* and kissed my hand.'

Isabel clasped her hands over her heart and sighed with pleasure.

'How marvellous! I couldn't be more pleased. And? Anything else?'

'No, that's about it,' I said.

'Are you going to see him again?'

'I expect so. Now go away and let me go to bed.'

Isabel stood up and pulled her blanket around herself more tightly.

'Excellent. Right then, I will leave you to it. But I will be asking more questions in the morning.'

'Don't tell Eugénie,' I shouted after her, and she laughed, and then nearly fell over Antoine.

I lay in my comfortable bed that night thinking how lucky I really was. I had my health, my family even if they had their faults. But I had flaws, too, quite serious ones if I was honest. I had been so busy pleasing people, clearing up after them, keeping Stephen happy instead of both of us, and consequently not actually being involved in my own life. After I had retired, I had come to regard my family as my job.

I had never been the sort of mother who boasted she was her children's 'best friend', but could I have encouraged Sara to confide in me more about what her marriage was really like, so she didn't have to numb the pain with alcohol? And then perhaps she wouldn't have been so hostile to Vanessa.

Why had John felt the need to keep his move to America secret from me until it was all sorted out? Did he think I would be annoyed that the pattern of my life was going to be affected by it?

I was proud of both my children. Had I ever told them? I thought I had but I wasn't sure.

A thought struck me at that point. Hang on. I was doing it again, making other people's happiness my responsibility.

I reached over, switched on the bedside light and picked up my Wonder Woman notebook, flicking though the pages of my list.

The last entry.

18. Ring people up. Don't just text or send emails.

I picked up my pen.

19. Stop taking the blame for everything. Stop being such a martyr. You can only live your own life.

20. As long as I don't break any laws or upset the horses, do things that make me feel better about myself. I am not just a sister, aunt, mother, grandmother and divorcee, I am me.

I put the notebook down and turned off the light.
And now there was Luc.
What would they say if they knew about him?

You'll never guess, the funniest thing happened when I was in France. I met this man...

So, was Luc going to be 21 on my list? *Have another man in my life who will need to be explained/introduced to your children and grandchildren.*

Did that really matter?

I had been so lonely, and at the same time I hadn't coped well with company. Christmas had been a perfect example of that.

And then I turned the light on again and took off my wedding ring and put it in the bottom of my handbag.

I lay down in the darkness and felt the place on my finger where the ring had been for so long. My finger was free, and so was I.

28

The following morning, I was woken at about eight thirty by the sun shining through a gap in the curtains. I pulled them back properly so I could see the view, made myself a cup of tea and went back to bed.

It was a beautiful day out there, and I felt very happy, with my situation at that moment, about life in general. So, what did I want to do with the day?

Isabel would perhaps need my help in the *brocante* barn. Maybe Felix could do with a hand in the bookshop? No, it was Sunday, wasn't it, so the shop would be closed.

Yes, but what did *I* want to do?

My train of thought was interrupted by the sight of Marcel's head, complete with wide, doggy grin appearing at the window and then disappearing again. Several times in quick succession. He was evidently outside, leaping up and down in an attempt to see me. Which meant Isabel was out there too.

A moment later she knocked on the door.

'Are you decent?'

I opened it, and she sat in the doorway blocking Antoine and Marcel from getting in.

'Just came to see how you were this morning,' she said. 'Sleep well?'

'Excellent thanks.'

'Not restless? No funny dreams?'

'None at all.'

'Good, hurry up and get dressed, it's cold out here, and then come over for coffee and croissants.'

I consulted my personal preferences and decided *yes, that would be an excellent idea.* I closed my eyes and imagined it. A big, creamy, aromatic, glorious *bol* of coffee, I could almost imagine the steam swirling around my face, the buttery richness of the crackling croissant as I bit into it. The sharp sweetness of the apricot conserve. Good heavens where did that come from?

I shook myself back into the real world and did a quick rifle through my clothes and pulled out a black T-shirt, a rather bobbly black cardigan and some very unflattering black leggings and put them all into a bin liner. After all, how could I criticise my sister for needlessly hanging onto things when I did the same thing.

Then I pulled on some jeans, a blue shirt and a pink sweater, which I had always loved, but seldom wore because it had been quite expensive.

The first problem was my outfit from the previous evening, and the damage I had done to the trousers. I took a look. Actually, it wasn't too bad, I had probably massively overreacted. All they needed was dry cleaning and a few stitches, the fabric was undamaged, what a relief.

Then I went over to Isabel's kitchen which was filled with the heavenly smell of freshly brewed coffee and proper French croissants in all their buttery, shiny glory.

Sitting in her usual place at the end of the table was Eugénie, of course. She had obviously been raiding Paulette's wardrobe again and was dressed in some very stylish striped trousers, a green jacket and a very cute maroon beret with a silver, bird shaped brooch pinned to the front. It reminded me of something. Had she ever been in the Parachute Regiment? It seemed unlikely but I thought it best not to ask.

'Ah,' she said as I came in, 'there you are. What have you been doing?'

'Just getting up. Nothing in particular,' I said, 'although I have been writing a bucket list.'

'Bucket list? What is this bucket list? You are going to make a list of all your buckets? How many do you have?'

Isabel explained. 'A list of all the things she wants to do before it's too late.'

'You are fortunate to have the time. For me, the buckets are all empty, so many dreams, so little time. And what do you want to do before your health gives out and you are left an invalid?'

'Things I enjoy,' I said accepting a *bol* of coffee from my sister. I paused for a moment, inhaling the wonderful smell. 'Travel, do the things I want to do, buy more colourful clothes, like you. That's a wonderful colour, a beautiful green. You are an inspiration.'

Eugénie preened a little. 'Old women are easily missed and overlooked.'

'Not you, *Mamie*,' Isabel said.

Eugénie was not one to be distracted. 'And I understand you had dinner with the doctor last night?'

I gave Isabel one of my best, hard looks.

'I didn't say a word about it,' she said.

'I heard from Arnaud. He is an old friend. He said you were *absorbée* – engrossed.'

'Oh, I don't think so,' I said, dreading what was to come next.

'He said you were *absorbée* in the car park,' she said with a knowing drawl, 'for quite some time.'

'Mmm, is one of those croissants for me?' I said, hoping to change the subject and trying not to laugh.

Not a chance. I began to look at the back door, wondering if I could somehow get out of this cross examination with my dignity intact.

'And is there much damage to the trousers Paulette lent you? My friend's daughter, Sophie, met with you in the ladies' room, she said there was some incident.'

Ah, the young woman in the blue dress with the safety pins.

'What damage?' Isabel said, looking puzzled.

Honestly, did this town spend every moment of everyday on the phone to each other?

'A minor problem, in fact, I need to go and return the lovely things Paulette leant me, and I think I will go now,' I said.

'But first, tell us about Jean-Luc,' Eugénie said, grasping my wrist. She felt surprisingly strong for a woman her age, I certainly wouldn't have liked to come up against her in an arm-wrestling challenge.

'We had a lovely evening and a delicious meal,' I said, 'and then I came home.'

'And what is this man to you?'

'A friend,' I said, 'and that's all. Like you and your friend, Charles.'

Eugénie looked a bit misty-eyed for a moment.

'Charles is *amoureux de moi*, I told you. Men and women cannot be friends.'

'Oh, I think they can,' Isabel said.

Eugénie held up a commanding hand. 'The sex gets in the way.'

'*Mamie*! Really!'

'Oh, I am right, as I am with all things. When you get to my age, you may know everything too. Men always think of sex. Bastien was the same, there is nothing wrong with it.' She rested her elbows on the table and looked dreamily into the far distance. 'Some days when we were first married we hardly planted any potatoes at all or dug them up for that matter. But then I was irresistible. He said I had the most beautiful legs in France, and heaven knows he spent enough time looking at them. He particularly liked my knees. He said I had the knees of a goddess.'

'I think I'd better go,' I said.

'I'll drop you off,' Isabel murmured, 'so you can pick up your car.'

* * *

I put my borrowed clothes into their protective bags and laid them carefully across the back seat of Isabel's car, and then we set off. I needed to go into town, ask about a dry cleaning and repair service and then see Paulette, but instead we drove to Luc's house.

As we pulled up outside his house, I spotted him. He was dressed in his workman's blue overalls, scrubbing away with a wire brush at what looked like a stone font.

He looked up when he saw me and waved.

'*Bonjour!* How are you both this morning?' he called.

Isabel wound down her window and shouted across. 'I'm not staying I'm just dropping Joy off so she can get her car. And I'll take your things back to Paulette and explain what happened. See you later.'

We watched her go, her car bumping off back down the lane, and then I went over to him, wondering what I was going to say.

'That was a lovely evening,' he said, dropping the wire brush on the ground and unfastening the top two buttons of his boiler suit.

I nodded; my gaze fixed on the small glimpse of his chest. Which was tanned. Perhaps when he was alone he sunbathed topless. Or even naked. Good heavens.

'I hope you enjoyed it too?' he added.

He undid another button. Was this deliberate? Was he flirting?

I nodded again, my throat tight with nerves. Think of the bucket list: I was going to do things I wanted to, not what people thought I should.

'Look,' I said, the words suddenly spilling out, 'where are you going with this?'

He looked at the old font, confused.

'I thought I might put it in the middle of the garden, perhaps planted up with something. You might be able to advise me. It could be converted into a fountain, but I wasn't sure if that was a good idea.'

I closed my eyes partly in frustration, and also because it was easier not to look at him. He was looking very attractive that morning, despite, or perhaps because of, the fact that he was a bit sweaty, dishevelled and doing something physical. I'd always found that a bit of a turn on, which is why I'd always had a soft spot for the rather rugged man in the house renovation programs who seemed able to paint a room in five minutes and construct a wardrobe at the same time.

'I didn't mean that,' I said at last, 'I meant where are you going with me?'

He shrugged. 'You could come inside and have a cup of tea? I wouldn't mind a break.'

'I mean us. Where are we going – no don't answer that. I know you will say we are going into the kitchen. I mean after last night. What are we doing?'

'Ah, last night, yes.' He looked down at his feet, 'That was a surprise, wasn't it? I hope you were not offended?'

'No, not at all,' I said, 'but I want to know—'

What should I say? What your intentions are? I would sound like Eugénie.

What are you expecting of me? No, this involved both of us. I might have expectations too.

What are we going to do next?

Are we going to take this any further?

I took a deep breath.

'I've been on my own for four years.' I rubbed the place where my wedding ring had been. I could still feel a tiny groove there. 'I am used to living on my own, not doing much that is different. I'll admit I have been stuck in a rut, and coming here has made me – *you* have made me – realise that there is more that I could be doing. I'm tired of doing everything for other people, for taking the blame when things go wrong, for making excuses for other people. I want some life for me.'

He nodded. 'I agree, I feel the same way.'

'Oh. Okay. I hadn't thought that there would be— that I could — that— that you would— I mean Stephen didn't—'

My voice faded as I struggled to find the right words.

His expression relaxed as he probably realised what I was trying to say.

'That I might find you attractive? Think about you when you weren't there?' He took a step towards me. 'Want to spend time with you? Find out more about you? Kiss you? Want perhaps more than just to kiss you?'

I suddenly understood. We were as bad as each other, hesitating and vacillating, being indecisive. One of us needed to take the first step and I wanted it to be me.

'Yes, those things.'

'But of course I do. I would have thought that was obvious. But now I see in you the same hesitation that is in me,' he said, 'the fear of failure, of rejection.'

How? How could a man like him have any doubts about himself? He was intelligent, kind, thoughtful, and handsome. No woman with a functioning brain cell would reject him. But then, of course, he hadn't exactly been *'out there'* any more than I had.

'Can we start off with coffee?' I asked.

'Of course, come in.'

* * *

And so we had coffee. We even ate a couple of biscuits, and then we looked at each other, over the table. One of us had to say something, and again, it was going to be me.

'I've come to pick up my car,' I said at last.

'I know, it's been quite safe,' he replied.

I finished the last of my biscuit. Under other circumstances I would have had another, because they really were quite delicious, but...

'Show me the rest of the house?' I said, 'I'd love to see what you've done.'

'I hope you like it,' he said, and he stood up and held out a hand to me.

I took it. I didn't need to, it wasn't as though I needed his help, but this was different. It was one of those moments.

'I will,' I said, 'I know I will.'

Another look passed between us, and I think both of us were aware of what I was saying. What we were doing. At least I hoped so otherwise I was going to look a complete fool.

We went upstairs together, our shoes echoing on the wooden

steps, and I followed him, my free hand trailing on the smooth painted surface of the bannisters.

I followed him into the rooms, one after the other, and he explained his plans. This would be a guest room, look at the lovely view, perhaps this one would be a study. There was a tiny box room where he had stored his suitcases, and a battered leather briefcase he had used when he was working. The bathroom was beautiful, with shining tiles and a big shower cubicle.

Some of the rooms were still empty, waiting for furniture and curtains and the sort of things that make up a home. He said he needed to buy a few items, maybe Isabel might have a nightstand or a cupboard.

I didn't want to think about Isabel, my family or anyone else at that moment. I didn't want to consider anybody but him. And me. The tension between us was almost palpable, sizzling through the air between us.

I had never felt anything like it before. A sort of sick, trembling insecurity, mixed with anticipation. Was I, at my age, allowed to feel like this? What would my family think if they could see me?

No, I didn't care.

At last, we reached his bedroom. There were white, wooden shutters at the window, which could be closed against the light. The walls had been painted pale blue; the carpet was slightly darker. There was a painting on the wall of a sparkling sea, framed by white voile curtains. The room felt fresh and clean, airy and filled with light.

The bed was honey-coloured wood and made up with white sheets and a soft, striped blanket. A wardrobe had been built into one of the alcoves around the chimney breast and there were shelves in the other one. I noticed a few books there, a glass vase, a leather writing case. There was a faint smell of lavender, perhaps from furniture polish and it made me feel suddenly wistful, thinking of him, doing that alone. Like me, making my place look immaculate but hardly ever sharing it with anyone who would appreciate it.

Being alone could have its benefits; being lonely didn't.

The air in the room was quiet and warm, and I suddenly remembered my new, glamorous underwear underneath my clothes with satisfaction.

Si une femme porte quelque chose de beau sous se vêtements, elle s'envoie un message très puissant.

If a woman wears something beautiful under her clothes, she sends a powerful message to herself.

I was indeed sending a message to myself. My new bra – pale pink and decorated with tiny ribbon roses – was probably powerful enough to start an international incident. It was the first time I had worn it. I hoped I had remembered to take all the labels off.

I walked across the room and closed the shutters on the view out over the river and Potato Farm in the distance, and then I turned to him and took a deep, brave breath.

'Luc—'

He came towards me and took me in his arms and kissed me.

He tasted of vanilla and warmth. And it wasn't like last night when there had been a sort of hunger, a crazy need for each other. This was tender and lovely and had nothing to do with the past – his or mine.

Contrary to what younger people thought, there was no age limit to attraction, to desire, to welcoming the sense of another person. The simple touch of a hand, a kind word, a gentle look. To feeling accepted and wanted.

At that moment we were just two people who properly saw each other as we were. We had been lonely for long enough. We were living in the same moment, brought together by chance, and I knew we both wanted something important to change.

* * *

It was the first time I had felt that way for a very long time.

I was appreciated. That was the simple truth of it, and I was appreciated for myself. I was not giving anything except me into the situation. There was no familiarity between us, no knowledge of what the other person liked or wanted or expected. We were new to each other. Everything was different from what it had been, it was a journey for both of us, and it was such fun. I hadn't expected that.

To be near to him, to respond and feel his responses was exciting and empowering. We were equals, we both had the same needs and hopes. There was an energising freshness to it all, memorable and in that moment not the same as it had been.

Perhaps it was the taste of him, the scent of his skin, his breath, my feelings. The place, the light, my awareness of him. It was a revelation to me in so many ways, each one more delicious than the last.

* * *

At last – not the five or ten minutes I had been used to, but something definitely more than that in every sense – we lay side by side in his big bed, the sunlight filtering through the shutters. Afternoon delight, I think it was called.

The rest of the world was doing a hundred different things in a thousand different places, but we lay there, slightly breathless.

I couldn't help it, I laughed with the sheer happiness of being there, on that day in that place with him.

He looked over and grinned.

'You are wonderful,' he said.

'We are wonderful,' I replied, and I stretched out my arms above my head. I don't think I had ever felt so sensual, so alive, so aware as I was then.

In that moment, life was a perfect thing. Fleeting, unpredictable and sometimes, just occasionally and unexpectedly, blooming marvellous.

I hadn't put this on my bucket list, but perhaps I should have done. When I got home I would. Number twenty-two. Or was it twenty-one? And then I would cross it off. That counted, didn't it?

'Only one thing can make this even better,' he said at last. He kissed me and then got out of bed, 'stay there.'

I wasn't planning on going anywhere. I rolled over in the rumpled sheets and lay on my side, looking at the light coming through the shutters. And then I closed my eyes and smiled to myself.

It didn't matter what happened after this, I had made a choice for myself with which I was content.

I had almost dozed off when he returned, and he was carrying a bottle of champagne and two glasses.

'This feels like a celebration,' he said.

I was grinning so much that I could hardly speak.

He poured out a glass for me and passed it over.

'*C'est pour toi, ma belle dame.*'

This is for you, my beautiful lady.

Well, I never, Paulette had been right. That underwear had really worked.

* * *

And so, I went back to my shepherd's hut.

It was early the following morning, the air cold on my face as I walked to my car, Luc's arm around my shoulders. I could have stayed for longer. He asked if I wanted to, and he promised me crusty bread, cheeses and local ham, cut thick. He had a bowl of tiny, sweet tomatoes, a quiche from the market, not to mention the other, unspoken delights on offer. But I said no. I needed time to think, to go over everything and remember.

He kissed me as we reached my car.

'I would like to see you again?' he said, a question again, not a statement.

I smiled up at him. 'You will.'

He didn't pressure me, asking for dates or times, suggesting places we might go or things we might do, and that pleased me. I wanted to make my own choices and plans. And yes, maybe they would include him, because even then I knew it would be easy to fall in love with him, really love him as I had always wanted to love. As an equal. Not as a grateful, confused and uncertain woman. But maybe those decisions would be separate, because first I had to learn to appreciate myself, and realise that I was – as the advert says – worth it.

We stood for a moment in the dawn light, which was brightening as the sun rose, and he held me against him for a moment, my hands on his warm, wool coat, and whatever happened, I knew I would always remember this moment.

What was it Isabel had said?

It's time you started the next bit. The rest of your life.

* * *

When I got back, Isabel was waiting for me, almost hopping up and down in excitement. I turned the car engine off and took a deep breath, waiting for all the questions to begin. Even Marcel and Antoine were there, sitting at her feet with inquisitive expressions on their faces. I half expected Eugénie to appear too just to get the party started, but for once I wasn't the cause of all the excitement.

'You'll never guess!' Isabel said. 'We've got a virus!'

'Is that a reason to be pleased?' I said, rather confused.

'You know those videos I put up on social media last weekend? It's gone mad! Everyone has been looking at them.'

'I think you mean we've gone viral?'

'Since you left, I've had twenty-one customers. At one point I had to move my car to let people get in. And I've sold such a lot of stuff. There was a reporter from the local paper here, too, wondering what was going on. I've never known anything like it, and the phone has hardly stopped ringing.'

'Really? That's amazing. Hang on, you mean all those awful spoof things we did? I didn't think you were going to use them? We were supposed to be doing them again, weren't we? Proper, sensible ones.'

Isabel threw her arms around my neck with a joyful cry.

'Yes, but in the end, it seemed too much of an effort, and they were really funny when I looked at them again, so I just went for it. And it worked. We must do some more. At this rate I'm going to have nothing left to sell.'

I was absolutely astonished. 'That's marvellous!'

'And Mathilde phoned me up last night, about the cameo brooch. You were right! She asked a friend of hers in the museum to take a look at it and it's worth a small fortune. Apparently its really old and unusual. Her friend thinks I should put it into a specialist auction and I had it marked at five euros!' Isabel hugged me again. 'I'll be able to pay off the bank loan! And the electricity bill! You're brilliant!'

'Oh, Isabel, I'm so pleased!'

She released her grip on me. 'And by the way, where have you been and what have you been doing? Scrub that, I know where you've been, and by the smile on your face, I know what you've been doing!'

I laughed at that and linked my arm through here.

'Let's go inside and have some coffee,' I said, 'before Eugénie gets here.'

'I am here already,' said a voice behind me, and yes, there was Eugénie, chic in a vintage Burberry trench coat and matching hat, hurrying towards us, not wanting to be left out.

'Good morning,' I said, and she took my arm as we went towards the house.

'You have been to the doctor's house,' she said.

'He really isn't a doctor,' I replied.

Eugénie flapped a dismissive hand at me.

'Who cares? And I can tell you were not just discussing medical matters. What is he to you now?'

We got to the kitchen table and Eugénie took her usual place and removed her hat, patting down a few strands of her hair.

'He's a friend,' I said, 'a very good friend.'

Eugénie gave one of her classically French shrugs and pouted.

'I can see just how good from your expression. Ah well, *Il ne faut pas attendre d'être parfait pour commencer quelque chose de bien.*'

You don't have to wait to be perfect to start something good.

How true that was.

I felt a sudden burst of affection for her. She might be eighty-four, tetchy, plain speaking and a bit of a hypochondriac, but she was still firing on all cylinders, wanting to engage with the world, curious to find out everything. I had a lot to learn from her.

29

TODAY

I look back at the time that has passed, and sometimes I am amazed. That woman, the one who didn't know how to cope with life, who was anxious, insecure and worried, had been me.

I went back home on 1 April, crossing the channel in a very different frame of mind from the one I had felt all those weeks ago when I had arrived. So much had changed for me and for other people too.

Sara and the girls moved into their new place and last month I put my house on the market. I am going to find somewhere smaller and easier to deal with. Who knows I might buy a small place in France. Maybe a shepherd's hut at Potato Farm where I can go when I need to breathe in that clean, invigorating air and wake to birdsong and more likely, the dogs barking.

Sara was the first in the family to meet Luc and was prepared to be suspicious of him, but in the end, she was won over by his kindness and his charm. The way he cares for me.

Her divorce has been made final now. Marty and the secretary split up soon after their romantic Christmas break, and he did make some pathetic attempts to reconcile with Sara, but that time she spent alone with the girls made her see she was perfectly capable of running her own life after all, and more than that, she was enjoying doing so. I'm proud of her, and yes, I told her so.

Mia and Poppy seem to have adjusted to their new lifestyle of spending most of their time with Sara and occasionally being introduced to Marty's latest girlfriends, all of whom they find *cringe*, or occasionally *cheugy,* which means they try too hard. They came to stay with me for a week during the summer holidays when Sara went off with some friends for a spa break, and we had such fun.

John and Vanessa adore New York, and so do their girls. Luc and I went to visit them for Thanksgiving in November, and they seem to have adapted to life there perfectly. Far from acquiring a New York twang, both Jasmine and Bunny have developed clipped English accents, which apparently their friends and more importantly their friends' parents, find *'just adorable'.*

Isabel has continued making crazy videos of her *brocante* and attracts more customers than ever. As a result, her *gîtes* and the shepherd's hut are practically sold out for next year; she's thinking of expanding the place and now she has the money to do it.

Felix found that far from being a risk to his business, the English editions of books were incredibly popular, and half his shop is now stocked with them. He remained unconvinced about the notebooks but occasionally sells some.

Most surprisingly, Eugénie and Charles did go to Venice for her birthday, didn't get lost at all because Charles had an unexpected ability as a map reader, and when they got back she announced *'nous sommes fiancés'* as though it was always on the cards. She was wearing a socking great sapphire ring to prove it. Whether they will marry is another matter.

Isabel tells me Eugénie continues to lead Charles a merry dance, one minute affectionate, the next treating him like a naughty schoolboy. She told Isabel he may have to chase her a bit longer before she allows herself to be finally caught.

Luc and I did, as I had hoped become good friends, and who knows – maybe more than that. I know we love spending time together; he came to visit me a few weeks after I had left France. He said he wanted to see York and London again, but then he admitted he just missed me. So, in the end I went with him, and we spent such a lovely time, looking at castles and historic sites, where he knew so much about them already that he made them come alive for me.

And what did I do with my list? When I look back through it, I can see I've achieved a lot. I still have some to cross off, but I'm getting there:

1. Do things I like to do.

I've certainly done this! I've learned how to cook more exciting meals, stopped buying dreary clothes and going to bed to watch television at seven thirty!

2. Don't do things I don't want to do.

Apart from anything else, I did get a window cleaner and I'm very happy with him.

3. Travel to places I want to see.

I spent a week in Rome with Luc and yes, I did get a Fast Track ticket to see the Sistine Chapel and it was well worth it.

4. Learn a new language.

I'm learning Spanish. *Dondé es el gato?* Where is the cat? Probably in the barn, sleeping on top of the tractor.

5. Throw out every black garment I own.

Done.

6. Buy more colourful things.

Done.

7. Change my car.

Done, and 8 – it's red.

9. New bed linen.

10. New pillows.

Done.

11. Find my white trainers.

I'm wearing them. I have three pairs.

12. Go to Wimbledon.

I went and I had a great time.

13. Throw out the plastic washing-up bowl.

Done. Good job too.

14. Visit John in New York.

I did, and I did stay with them. My granddaughters were so pleased to see me, and we are getting to know each other much better. We even went out shopping together and they showed me the best diners. I never got to see a show on Broadway, perhaps next time.

15. Get a decent haircut.

Done. I lost about four inches of hair and ten years at the same time.

17. Make a dental appointment for a check-up.

Done. Not as bad as I thought.

18. Ring people.

Still not very good at this but I am a demon texter and I know all about emojis and gifs.

19. Stop taking the blame for everything.

This one's a hard habit to break but I'm getting there.

20. Do things that make me feel better about myself.

Yes, I know I am doing that. Maybe just small things occasionally, but I do them for me. And I recognise them for what they are. Even if it's just going out for coffee with a friend.

Luc...

As someone once said, love starts as a feeling, but continues as a choice. And funnily enough I find myself choosing Luc more and more as time goes by.

I have just arrived back in France to spend Christmas with him in his cottage and I'm looking forward to it immensely. I will not wear myself out trying to cater to everyone's needs, I will, just for a change, allow someone to look after me. And I will enjoy myself. And I will not try and lift heavy objects.

The most important thing is that now I am enjoying each day, and I am not afraid of the future.

I have made new friendships and rekindled old ones. I am busy and happy. I don't have to make life perfect for anyone.

As Eugénie said to me when she saw I was back.

'Petit à petit, l'oiseau fait son nid, des grandes choses peuvent être réalisées.'

Little by little, like the bird makes its nest, great things can be achieved.

ACKNOWLEDGEMENTS

As always thanks are due to so many people who helped me when I was writing this book.

To Jane, who has listened, commented and made many good suggestions.

To my agent, Broo Doherty, who has been so supportive and encouraging.

The whole team at Boldwood Books who have helped me so much. Especially Emily Ruston, Nia Beynon, Jenna Houston, Amanda Ridout, Ben Wilson and Niamh Wallace.

To the proof readers, copy editors and cover designers who always do such a tremendous job.

To the Boldies community who are always there to commiserate or cheer.

To Freya Webb who has helped enormously with her author marketing services.

To my family who are always so incredibly supportive and encouraging.

And of course to Brian, much loved, much missed.

ABOUT THE AUTHOR

Maddie Please is the author of bestselling joyous tales of older women. She has had a career as a dentist and now lives in rural Herefordshire where she enjoys box sets, red wine and Christmas.

Sign up to Maddie Please's mailing list for news, competitions and updates on future books.

Follow Maddie on social media here:

facebook.com/maddieplease

x.com/maddieplease1

instagram.com/maddieplease1

bookbub.com/authors/maddie-please

ALSO BY MADDIE PLEASE

BECOME A MEMBER OF

THE SHELF CARE CLUB

The home of Boldwood's book club reads.

Find uplifting reads, sunny escapes, cosy romances, family dramas and more!

Sign up to the newsletter
https://bit.ly/theshelfcareclub

Boldw☾☽d

Boldwood Books is an award-winning fiction publishing company seeking out the best stories from around the world.

Find out more at www.boldwoodbooks.com

Join our reader community for brilliant books, competitions and offers!

Follow us
@BoldwoodBooks
@TheBoldBookClub

Sign up to our weekly deals newsletter

https://bit.ly/BoldwoodBNewsletter

Printed in Great Britain
by Amazon

51862462R00174